PEACH BUTTER

PEACH BUTTER

POETRY, LOVE, AND THE MOST ULTIMATE
CLIMAXES OF SEXUAL PLEASURES--WITH A
LITTLE BITE AND A SWEET STING

CHERYLETTE DORIANE

Edited by
BRENT MILLER II

PEACH BUTTER

by Cherylette Doriane

Editor and Chief: Brent Miller II

Cover designed by MiblArt

Author photo by Ecurbproductions

ISBN-13: 978-1-7370664-0-8

Printed in the United States of America

Publisher: Doriane Dezine Publications

Authors Website: CheryletteDoriane.com

This book is dedicated to my **Creator** *(my Lord and Saviour) for giving me the gift of creativity, favor, and blessing me with the BEST family in the world.*

Dedicated to my **Mom** *(who will never read this book)*
Ma, if you do (which I strongly doubt) just skip the sex scenes

My two sons, ***which are my ROCKS***

*My brothers**, the ultimate SUPPORT SQUAD***

ACKNOWLEDGMENTS

Thank you Tannisha, sis you are BEAUTIFUL!

Thank you to the readers of my drafts, including the feedback and support you shared.

People who celebrated with me

Grateful for extended ears to hear my stories

All my family and friends that supported me throughout this journey

"people will forget what you said, people will forget what you did, but people will never forget how you made them feel"

— -Maya Angelou

TABLE OF CONTENTS

Chapter 1

PILLOW PASS

*B*ullet gets a standing ovation for being a smooth talker. He's clean-cut, loved, and well known. He and I met seven years ago at an amateur poetry night in my hometown, New Orleans. After he concludes his poem, he seizes the souls of many women. His voice is deep and mesmerizing as he speaks with confidence, authority, and arrogance. My attraction is instantaneous. My eyes track his every move until he locks eyes with mine. My character of aggression is peculiar yet soothing. I am determined to get to know this brother.

The poetry venue has a seductive setting. Dim lighting hits the stage, as the remaining background is dark with a hint of light from the bar. Poetry night is a treat whenever I have time to go. I had been preparing to take the stage many times in the past. Each time at the last minute, I would shy away before entering the platform. However, this particular night I give myself an ultimatum, now or never. I told anybody who would listen to come out and support while I read my poem. My dear friend Al wanted to go, but he is in the hospital. At a distance, my mother, father, and brother extend their encouragement. I have a sister too, but she could care less. Tonight I am pressured by my bestie, Dillard, not to cower away from reading my poem. Dillard, Lex, Bam, and Edgewood are my biggest supporters. I am standing at the bottom of the stage when Bullet finishes his poem.

My turn is to follow. I'm profoundly engaging in his words; I didn't even notice him looking right at me. I give a slight smile once we make eye contact. Thereafter, while people are standing and whistling, he concludes with a cunning expression. He walks down the stairs; gives me a short nod. My introduction is up as the microphone is adjusted. The room silences immediately. I examine my surroundings, then smile the minute I see my cheering squad front and center. My heart is pounding fast, but I soon get control and begin to speak.

"Greetings to my fellow sisters and brothers. My name is Indigo, but I go by the name Peach Butter. I would like to share a little part of me through my poem, called Pillow Pass. I hope you guys enjoy it.

PILLOW PASS
Scene: Lying across a rose petal bed of white roses
Aroma: Subtle soft scented cologne
Lighting: Distant flickering candlelight along with
    whistling wind as
raindrops are heard across the windowpane.

Pillow Pass is in desperate need
My feet respond from an air of touch
My body melts as one toe is kissed slowly, softly, and
    gingerly
One hand moves up that thigh as the other follows
    suit to the other
Kisses and licks of moisture until the belly button
    feels the heat of passion

Big strong hands to both inner thighs, no touch to
    that spot of explosion

Tease, tease, tease
Around to the side; but, no clit action
The moisture increases with anticipation of passion
Yes! The LIPS has met LIPS of desire
Long-stroke tongue...right-left... in-out... and all-
     around inside
As my body motions...up, down, and swerve around
Lick and love until the flood overflows with PEACH
     BUTTER

Oh...now there's more
Finger to join
As the wave of water gently moves in a rhythmic
     motion
Slow...up...down...up...down
So does that motion of that tongue to digit
One hand up to meet the point of my penciled
     areola
Rub until the sensation has peaked to the point of
     explosion
Uprising begins as he moves to kiss gingerly the
     nipples of my breast
Slowly he enters into my connective soul
As we mold the grid of our immortal essence
Slow, passionate, strokes...

'What?' Yeah...I'm here
No, I'm not sleep!
I was just quite because I had some deep thoughts
He continues to speak on the other end telling me
     about his girlfriend
As his voice utters words to me
I'm melting away with pure ecstasy
Does he not realize it's me?
I'm tired of listening and being the agreeable,
     supportive friend

But, this is the only way I'll be apart of him
So, I listen… I support…I stay the friend…
as I fantasize of one day having a **PILLOW PASS**."

AS I AM RECITING MY VERSE, I MAKE EYE CONTACT WITH onlookers. I perceive Bullet's attention is piqued. Occasionally I hear shouts of, "yes, yes, that's what I'm talking about, and uh-huh's." I motion my body with every erotic word spoken. I engage with my soul, becoming one with my lyrics and the energy. It feels good. Promptly after I finish, Dillard and the crew begin yelling and screaming. The crowd stands, claps, and shouts. Exiting down the stairs, I return to my table to continue enjoying the show. Brothers and sisters approach expressing their fondness of the poem.

Before the end of the evening, the bartender comes with a drink and a note. The message on the napkin reads, "This is from an aspiring future friend. I will fulfill your pillow pass desires if you become my friend." No signature or any hints of who it is. I catch Bullet looking my way and smirk at him. He then smiles back.

Dillard is watching my facial expressions then dives in with his two cents. "Well, heifer, who is it from?"

"Dillard, damned if I know, there is no signature." Before I can finish, Dillard jerks the napkin out of my hand, looks around, and catches Bullet still watching.

"You mean to tell me you don't know who this is from when he's staring at you the whole time? Girl, I'm too through with you."

Dillard gets out of his chair and beckons for the others to join him for a drink. "Leave her ass here so HE can get his thing or whatever going, we may be a distraction."

"Dillard, don't leave me here!" I snap.

"NO! Just stay here, Indigo, and see what happens. We will be right back in five minutes!" Dillard purses his lips and grins.

Before Dillard is ten steps away, here comes Bullet to the table. Lex and Dillard simultaneously look back and snicker.

When Bullet approaches, I get a whiff of his cologne that draws me closer.

Bullet leans over, "So, will you be my friend?"

Laughing inward, "It's always nice having a good friend. Of course, I would love for you to be my friend."

With the extra vacant surrounding seats, Bullet settles closely next to me. At this time, I can get a wholesome look at him. His eyes are light brown, appealing smile, mocha-colored skin, and his style is neat. His stare is hypnotizing. I catch myself feeling shy as he gazes. I bashfully look away, pretending to look at my half-filled glass of wine. Trying to keep my composure, I start fidgeting with my fingernails; another temporary solution.

Internally I coach myself to calm down. My palms are becoming sweaty. I hope Bullet doesn't notice my sudden onset of anxiety. I puzzle myself. I can't figure out why I'm so anxious around this man. I never had this problem before with any other guy. There's something about him. I like him, yet I don't even know him. I sense a connection. I want him to like me. Bullet is talking, but I don't remember what he is saying because I am so focused on trying to look calm and relaxed. When Bullet smiles or laughs, I do the same. Feels like I am in a trance while watching Bullet's lips move. Amazed that he's still sitting next to me, having some good laughs. This daze could last forever, but it broke when my friends returned back to the table.

Dillard addresses Bullet.

"Hello, I'm Dillard, this is Edgewood, and that's Lex. That was a very nice poem you recited on stage."

Dillard is very outspoken and theatrical. I describe him as my "extra" friend. With Dillard, there is always extra attitude, extra, extra, extra everything. He is a no-nonsense type of person. He takes charge and gets things happening. Upon entering any venue, Dillard captures attention. Dillard stands at six-feet two inches tall with slick blonde hair, hazel eyes, never seen in the public without custom-made attire from head to toe. Dillard gets his blonde hair from his mother. Dillard's mother is white, and his father is of black African descent. He definitely is flip yet funny, which attracts most people wanting to be in his company. Dillard and I have been friends since I could walk. Dillard breaks the hearts of countless love-seeking men, but as a friend, there is none better. I have learned to embrace Dillard's "extra" personality. All his extra attitude is done in love. Besides, his extra is what makes him Dillard.

Lex anchors her chair next to mine. All I can see from Lex is her white teeth lighting up the room. Lex is a mix of Puerto Rican and Filipino. She has shoulder-length puffed red twisted loose ringlets, petite frame, outgoing, goofy demeanor, and is effortlessly loved by everybody.

Lex introduces herself to Bullet, barely taking a breath, "Hello, I enjoyed your poem as well. I see you have joined our friend Indigo. What you guys talking about over here? I knew there was something there. I knew it the whole time after that note came to the table. That was you who sent it, right? I think you guys make a cute couple. Am I talking too much? What's your name again? Sorry if I keep going, but where is…"

"Lex, please give the man some space and sit your ass down." Interjects Dillard.

Lex defensively responds, "Damn, Dillard, I was just asking a few questions."

Dillard is communicating direct and frank with Lex, "Yes, we know how those few questions go. You will need to excuse miss Lex here; she's our special friend. As you can see, she's not shy at all."

Bullet smiling, then side eyes a look at me. I shrug my shoulders and smile back.

"My name is Bullet, and yes, did you say your name was Lex?"

"Yup, Lex is my name."

"Well, Lex, you are right. I was extremely attracted to this young lady next to me. Her poetry, smile, and dark coal eyes intrigued me. Wanting to get to know her, if she would allow me. Are you going to allow me to get to know you a tad bit better?"

All eyes are staring my way. Edgewood is very quiet and says nothing, only grins. Dillard has one eyebrow raised; I can read his whole demeanor. If he were to utter a word, he would probably say something along these lines, "you better jump on that man and claim what's yours" or something close to those terms. However, I'm sure it would be expressed a bit more vulgar. I feel Lex leaning all over me with that continued smile. My answer is thoughtless, "Yes, of course."

Bullet hugs my chair as if he has more to say til Bam walks up with two drinks.

Bam is Cuban with a lingering accent. Bam is a breast cancer survivor and claims she has a "fluid" sexual life. She loves men and women; we never know whom she's engaging with. She has large looped short curls. After her chemo five years ago, she always kept her hair short. Bam's name suits her well because her figure is like a large curvy hourglass. When Bam gets fired up, she starts to speak in her native language, which we all tend to ignore. But that's Bam. We see it coming when she starts to mumble to herself.

Bam surveys everyone's face before she starts to speak, "What's going on here? All I see is smirking. What did I miss? Oh, hello, Mr. Poet, man. I see you're getting well acquainted over here. I'm really out of the loop."

"Bam, why do you have two drinks? That's what took you so long? I was waiting for you, and you disappeared on me," cries Edgewood.

Edgewood is quiet among strangers, but once he warms up, he is the craziest and funniest. He and Bam are incredibly close friends, similar to the relationship Dillard and I share. Edgewood is the only one that occasionally entertains Bam's outburst. However, if Bam's irrational whining becomes too excessive, Edgewood even tunes her out. Edgewood reaches about six-feet, five inches, friendly, hand-some, yet not conceited. Edgewood is a white male with a heart of gold and a humbling spirit. Locs are beyond his shoulders, always kept neat and pulled back. He avoids commitment due to a past heartbreak. Therefore, he consistently parades a new Barbie doll when we get together.

Bam directs her response to Edgewood, "No mi amigo. I ran into an old friend in the restroom then I retrieved my drinks; thank you very much. For your information, I need two drinks because I plan on feeling good tonight. First of all, I'm not driving, and I plan on getting me some tonight. I like to feel real good when it's time for my nightly fix."

Dillard reacts, "You one scandalous hoe! You always talking about getting some! Nobody needs to hear all that right now."

"Well, Edgewood asked, and I delivered the answer. So nobody responded yet. What is all this cheesing about? Indigo, who's Mr. Poet man?"

Bullet counters promptly, "I can speak for myself. My name is Bullet. The smiles you see are just the beginning of what will be placed on Indigo's face once we really get to know each other."

"Uh-huh, you weren't expecting that one were you? You're not the only one that may be getting some," blurts Lex.

With a swift response, "Lex! Nobody said anything about me getting some from Bullet!"

Lex has a rapid response to my statement, "Maybe not tonight, but possibly in the near future. I mean NEAR. Indigo, face it. It's been a while for you. It may do you some good. I'm just saying."

Lex always says whatever in front of whomever.

"I can't be around none of y'all! Y'all just have no home training! I mean, this man doesn't need to hear about Indigo's lack of dick in her life. This man is trying to get to know Indigo. Shit! This is just too damn much in one encounter," asserts Dillard.

Bullet is finding this whole conversation amusing, laughing the entire time. I'm looking at each one of them in disbelief. I can't believe my sexual life is being discussed in front of this stranger. Bam places her hand over her mouth and widens her eyes my way. Dillard winks.

Edgewood nodding in agreement with the statement of "me needing to get some" and Lex continues to be all up under me practically leaning on my shoulder.

Thank goodness! The lights go dim again, right on time. Intermission is over and poetry continues to grasp our attention. Bullet remains sitting at the table with an occasional look my way.

At the end of the night, before I depart from my friends Dillard whispers, "Indi, do you feel okay alone with Bullet?"

"Yes, sure, I feel pretty safe alone with him," I reassure him.

He then hugs me goodnight and walks to his car with the others. Bullet and I are now alone. Bullet escorts me to my car. He explains that his job requires him to travel often, saying he will be leaving town in a few days but will return in two weeks. He asks if I am available for a night out in the city in a couple of weeks once he returns. I happily accept his offer for an upcoming date.

Chapter 2

CHARMS

*I*n the two weeks before the date, we speak on the phone almost daily. Bullet tells me his dreams, aspirations, and current position. The conversations flow smoothly. I felt content to open up about my life, goals, and aspirations as well.

Two weeks swiftly approaches for our first date. Bullet takes charge of the engagement. He calls early morning, instructing me to be ready by two p.m. because the day is jam-packed with adventure. I decide to meet him downtown for our first encounter.

"Let me know where you will be, and I'll meet you there."

"Meet me at the Seven-Eleven store on Carrollton near Xavier University. Then you can just follow me."

I am excited about our first date.

I get there first. I want to make sure I'm on time. Bullet pulls up in a black S-Class Coupe Mercedes, smiles, and then blows his horn.

Bullet calls my cell, "Sorry I was running a little behind schedule, so follow me to the parking garage. I'm so happy to see you. The place is not far. We will be there shortly."

"Sounds good, no worries. I'm following right behind. Nice to see you as well."

We pull into the garage and park alongside one another. Bullet is a gentleman and opens my car door, hugs me, and kisses my cheek.

He says he likes my dress and perfume, then clutches my hand, and off we go.

Bullet reserved front row tickets to a show at the Mahalia Jackson Theater of Performing Arts.

"See, I listened to you. You said you love the arts, you dance, and you also write. I wanted you to experience something you love."

"You did listen. I love this! I wanted to attend this particular show but hadn't booked anything, thank you."

He smiles and looks down at me. I couldn't hide my excitement.

The play was phenomenal.

When the play ended, it was still daylight outside. No sooner could I catch my breath before he whisked me away to phase two of our date.

Bullet grabs my hand and we then fetch a ride on the French Quarter Carriage Tour. I mutter, "remarkable" and sit close to him while the personal tour takes place.

I continue, "I've lived here all my life and never took a carriage tour before. It was a beautiful thing to have my first with you."

Bullet displays a broad smile, takes out some tickets, and waves them in the air. "One more thing before I want to end this special night with you."

I grabbed the tickets and read "Steamboat Jazz and Dinner Cruise for two."

"Is this for tonight?"

"Yes, it is Ms. Indigo. Are you hungry and ready for your late-night Dinner Cruise?"

"I certainly am, Mr. Bullet."

Cruising, jazz, and dinner is the icing on the cake. My first date with Bullet is astounding, permanently etched in my memory.

The night ends charmingly. Intimacy is shared, but not verbally or sexually. What did happen is an exchange of spiritual connections without any expectations. We stroll to the parking lot. Both of us click to open our cars at the same time. He walks me to my car and opens my door. I sit my purse in the seat because it is just awkward and in the way. While saying my goodbye, he pins me against my car, straddles over me, and kisses my forehead. I wrap my hands around his waist, with my eyes closed, to melt in the moment. In my mind, the stillness lasts forever.

He then backs away, grabs my hand, and says, "I feel you."

Astonishment must have been plastered all over my face. "You feel me?"

He looks at me again and repeats in slow motion with his finger pointing towards my chest, "I feel you."

Before I can respond, he chants the phrase once again. His right-hand grabs below my chin to level our eyes together. Eye-to-eye, without blinking, his mouth pronounces every syllable from his inner being, "I FEEL YOU." In my panties my Peach Butter moistens from the heat of his breath. At this very moment, I feel him too.

Chapter 3

SCAR

*W*hile lying flat on my back, I focus on the eggshell-colored painted ceiling. Still tired, eyes heavy, my head is foggy as I look at the closed blinds and draped curtains. What's apparent is a yellow fluorescent bright shine that muscles through the creases of the screens. The house's tranquility breaks with horns, moving engines, and the Saturday morning garbage truck that makes its presence with a loud clatter. Nestled warmly in bed, I peer at my rambled sheets lying across me.

Grabbing my head, I think, "Damn, this headache from last night is still killing me."

I continue to lie for a few more moments. Thoughts flood my head about everything I need to get done before seeing him tonight. I beam with visions of our possible future. Reminiscing on conversations with Bullet creates overwhelming excitement.

Recapping his smooth way of saying, "I complete his circle. I'm his Yin to his Yang."

The alarm startles me. I quickly mute out the sound. I ponder, "Just five more minutes then I'll get moving."

Time is moving fast. It's 9:45 a.m. and I'm still lying in bed. I reluctantly move as my eyes slowly focus. Thoughts are nonstop.

Last night's conversation with Bullet was intense with anticipation for the weekend. Bullet and I started to see each other immediately after our first encounter. Things moved lightning fast.

Bullet's philosophy is, "If it's right, there's no need to question time."

I never understood why he would always make that statement, but now, I know. And so far, we have been right from day one. My union with Bullet counts seven years today. In that period, we made the best out of a distant relationship due to both our frequent travels. Bullet had a couple of consecutive business trips, shy of two months. Work kept him so busy that we haven't seen each other in a while. Gathering myself together, rambled hair, I sit on side the bed, dangling my feet freely. Right away, I hear a beep acknowledging an incoming text. I grab my phone and see Bullet has sent an early morning greeting.

"Good AM, baby I can't wait to see you later. I can't get enough, my every thought is you. This day has been way overdue. Just the thought of seeing you, my heart skips a beat."

"Good morning love, I know I can't wait either." I text in return.

My feet barely kiss the carpet when the phone startles me. Still, in a stupor, I answer with a slight whisper. I see it's Bullet, so I sit back in bed. Affectionately I position my knees as a tepee, greet Bullet with delight, and proceed to give Bullet my full undivided attention. I love to listen to his voice, it's deep and soothing, especially early morning.

"Well good morning baby, I just responded to your early morning text."

"I know, Indigo, I can't get you off my mind. I want you to just listen to what I'm about to say. Although I said it last night, I want to repeat it. I've really missed 'us'. Seven weeks is way too long to go without being with you. I want you. I want us. I can't wait to feel you next to me. Shit, I can't wait to be inside you. I want, no, I need our connection to interlock. I love you, girl."

"Bullet, I miss 'us' as well. But now you listen to me. I'm yours whether in a mist of respite or on my everyday high on you. The things you do and say have made me this way. I embrace the warmth of your body in its motionless or better yet that; aerodynamic, radiate, smooth, free-flowing state. The sound of your voice, the tender touch of your hand, that iconic stare moistens my channel as a flowing river. My inner me can't get enough of that outer you. So yes, I'm yours in the morning, evening, or midnight hour. So with a warm welcome, please enter my channel to meet the sea. I aim to be all your fantasies. I love you too."

"Baby, you already are all my fantasies. I've always fantasized about having you to myself and now I do. Even though you invariably have been for me. Love you more, my darling...

And I can't wait to enjoy the flow of your sea."

"I must be in my feelings a bit this morning. It's the anticipation, voice, and genuine love that's been driving me crazy since last night. After I talked to you, all I can do is imagine our past moments and look forward to the new. I imagine lying on top of scented black sheets, with my arms stretched to hold and grasp across the covers while you create moisture that leaks down my thighs. Then the classic move makes my breath pause with every lick of your tongue. I love how you taste me. The pleasure you express and the movement of your thrust. This is just a few of my thoughts as I lust for the night we will share."

"Indigo baby, I can't wait for you to sit those plump lips on my face to let me taste your juices. I'm anxious to feel your inner pouch explode from the pleasures of my tongue parting your seas. I can't wait to feel your arms around my neck while I slowly enter inside of you and take slow constant strokes to make your juices flow all over me. That ass is mine."

"You know I love the things you do with that tongue. Then you throttle yourself in...so nice and slow to really get my juices flowing. My heart palpitates with just a mere thought of what's to cum; oops did I say that? I mean, come."

"Oooo baby, you have me aroused early this morning," states Bullet.

"Thank you, Bae. You always keep a smile on my face. Tonight will be extraordinary. I need this. I can go on and on telling you my thoughts and feelings, but I have a few things to get done this morning, then I'll be on my way."

"I'll be waiting. Call me Indi when you're en route."

"You know, I will. Bye, hun. I love you."

"I love you more."

Both phones disconnect. I get moving. Now Bullet is definitely on my mind even more intense. He travels quite a bit with his job. My dancing and writing keeps me on the go and often leaves us with limited access to each other. I can't believe I have the butterflies again. Every time after a long hiatus, he brings out that hidden high-school girl in me. It's been several weeks of dialogue, video chat, and texting. This morning exchange of words heightens the excitement just that much more. Today is the day I finally see him face to face.

When opening my top drawer, I see a piece of paper jammed on the side. Tugging to remove the wrinkled half-torn sheet of paper, I chuckle as I read. It is written thoughts I noted from our early dating stages seven years ago.

"TODAY"

Today we see each other. This time on different
    terms.
He exposed his feelings.
I've exposed mine--the first of longing days.

I'm excited yet relaxed. He's a comfort zone. I can be
    myself.
The conversation stimulates my mind. Our spirits
    connect. I feel peace.
There are laughs and joys. There are no
    expectations. Just good vibes.
This is newfound happiness. I like it...No I love it!

I feel he has some type of emotion, feeling, or
    curiosity too.

I love the slow interaction. It builds on a better
    foundation.
Quality & longevity takes effort. No rush. I want
    clarity.
Time will reveal.
Past decisions were my own—this time,
I want to take a back seat and allow the puzzle to be
    put together smoothly.

Patience...
What does he think? How is he feeling? Does fear
    have a firm grip on him?
Does he even want a relationship? What does he
    seek?
I don't know---I only have a few unclear clues.
What do I want, desire, or seek from him?
Essential factors: loyalty, communication, & time.

The question: What will happen between us? Is there
    a future?
Are we able to fulfill each other's desires or wants?
The answer: I hope we are.
But if not...I'm grateful for the convo & spiritual
    connection.
I would simply continue to be a conversational lush
and feed him my Sunshine.
Either way: it's all happiness and joy
However it goes....
Time will reveal---it always does

I GIGGLE WHILE I STRAIGHTEN OUT THE VINTAGE POEM AND PUT
it away, remembering my feelings at that moment. I want to look my
best for Bullet on this busy day. The entire day is gloomy and gray
with on and off showers. My hair appointment takes the longest.

Three hours for wash, press, and style is crazy ridiculous. Usually, I skip the beautician on Saturdays and often schedule during the weekday, but today is special. Hanging with my girls Lex and Bam, make my day pass by fast. We go to the salon and have our nails, toes, and waxing. Everything is on point for my man tonight. The evening is quickly approaching. Separating from the girls, I go home to shower then head out to see Bullet after a seven-week absence.

The aroma of fresh rain floats in the air. The evening mist tenderly rests upon my skin as I scurry to my vehicle. The ignition is sluggish. Surroundings are in slow motion. My car is progressing forward as I experience an out of body floating sensation. My exhilaration and anticipation are high.

On my way to his house, my phone rings, "Hey baby, I'm home. Be careful because the fog is intense tonight. I can't wait to see you."

My comeback is gitty and childlike, "Yes, me too."

Thoughts are overlapping in my head. I start to talk to myself out loud, "Do I smell good? How is my hair? Is he nervous? Or is it just me? Why am I tripping?"

I counsel myself, "It has been quite some time, so Indigo take a deep breath and just breathe. Focus, and have a good time."

I listen to my own advice and take a deep breath, then continue. Raindrops slowly start to plummet down. After parking in Bullets driveway, no sooner as I get out the car with my umbrella, Bullet is in the doorway walking towards my car. Instead, he greets me with his umbrella along with a welcoming soft kiss to my lips.

"I have been waiting a long time for this moment. Your travels took a bit, so I started things already," states Bullet.

When entering the doorway, floor coverings showcase white rose petals, no lighting except the glow from the lit fireplace, and sweet scents from the flickering candles. Soft music is in the background. Shortly after that, the sound of rain starts bucketing down outside.

"This is the-"

Before the words drip out my mouth, a passionate kiss attaches to my lips. My purse crashes to the floor; the soothing effects of kisses are embracing. I wrap my arms around Bullet to cherish the moment further.

He abruptly pulls back and states, "Let's dance."

"Okay."

Bullet turns the music up so loud I feel the thumping in my chest. The music takes over my balance, movements, and rhythm of my feet. Eyes closed and shoes off; this is tangible. Butterflies have vanished, and calming comfort feelings settle. Dancing takes me on a natural high. Bullet knows what I love. Our evening bond consumes us with hor's d' oeuvres, wine, conversation, laughs, and welcomed lip caresses that pry itself when words can only be half-spoken.

A few hours past before Bullet tells me to close my eyes, grabs one hand to guide me to the bedroom gingerly.

"Open your eyes."

A candlelit bedroom adorned with two-dozen long stem yellow roses to each side of the nightstand and sprinkles of chocolate kisses, rose petals on the covers, and sexy red-laced lingerie draped across the bed. He slowly starts to undress me.

Bullet whispers, "I want to see you with this on tonight. I'll step out of the room for a minute so you can get a little more comfortable."

I quickly oblige to his request. "I'll do just what you ask. I'll signal for your entrance when I'm ready."

Bullet eyes brighten. The corners of his mouth curved slightly upward as he walks out of the room, closing the door. The lingerie is barely a few pieces of thread sewn together; nonetheless, I loved it. The top half has circles of holes with no overlaying for the breast. The rear has even less coverage with only a mere line. The string of clothing is what he likes, not to mention it fits me like a glove. As he desires, every curve is exhibited perfectly for his pleasure. Tonight will be exceptional. Before calling Bullet to the room, I position myself in his favorite pose. Kneeling on his king-sized bed with ass up and shoulders down, I summon for his entrance. I lean my head down to have a birds-eye view of his facial expression. As he walks in, I notice the astonishment. An excitement triggered when he sees me. He is only wearing boxers that quickly drop to the ground, greeting me in flesh, touching me skin-to-skin from behind.

"Babieee, you know I love this! You look SOOO good!" Bullet proclaims.

"I told you I'd be all your fantasies tonight," responding seductively.

He proceeds to rub my back and spread my cheeks to greet all that's exposed with his tongue to cherry.

"All is open and available for your pleasure," I whisper.

Lick by lick creates moans of gratification. At a snail's pace, Bullet grinds his body next to mine and enters from the rear. I hear him speak but can't understand due to the squeals he's causing.

"You missed daddy?" I finally make out.

Words are still far from formulating as the gratifying moaning is again departing with a groan. Bullet's back and forth movements rock my body uncontrollably.

"Yes…yes… yes…" Finally, I exhale.

The night of extreme positions, howls, and rubs continues until both our bodies fall into inertia and sleep. A few hours later, at four a.m. I feel the morning tap from behind. Emotions of love, giggles, excitement, and spontaneity knocks and unexpectedly enters. Late night music remains audible from earlier moments of the night. Sleep slumber was dearer to me until the lust of warm hands acknowledges my body with comfort. The still of the night is sensual. Every being of me is enjoying the shared moments of heat with Bullet. Continuation of the love we shared from earlier retakes place. On my side, he rolls me to my back. His hand reaches to feel where moisture quickly comes back to life. The wet sound of liquid love is on beat as his finger moves in and out of my canal. I spread open much more as the morning rub wakens me to yearn for added delights. I roll over, climb on top, and reverse the ride to expose and receive all of him inside of me. Up and down movements, slushes, and his finger slightly rubbing inside my ass create climaxes for both. The morning tap is so satisfying that it has me pursuing more. I can't get enough. My body missed these thrills and indulgences.

I see his silhouette lying next to me as I gesture to move a bit closer. I feel one of his arms stretching. My inner being lights up with joy to drive in nearer for just a fragment more.

"What are you doing?" I inquire.

Still perplexed, "Are you pushing me away?!"

He turns to his side and avoids looking in my direction. The arm stretch isn't a motion of lust or desire; instead, it's a dismissal. He turns his back.

"Sorry, baby, but I need to wait for a minute. I'm not ready."

Annoyed and shocked, "May I at least have a kiss and hold you?"

Bullet nonchalantly responds, "No, not right now."

No kiss, no touch. Have I misunderstood tonight's sexual yearnings? I come to my senses and my heart starts to pound. I'm being rejected, unwanted, and, wait is this the man I thought was the one who would wear the crown? I lie silently in disbelief, disappointment, shame, and pain.

At this point, I'm angry. I'm practically yelling. "Are you serious after what we just shared? I can't believe this shit!"

Bullet has no reply. He continues to lie on his side then closes his eyes to greet the earlier sleep we both had before the morning tap.

Disillusioned and angry, I continue to lie in silence. I turn to my side, lie on the edge, and begin to think. "What is this? The past had never presented this type of issue with us ever before."

My thoughts begin to ramble in rhythm. A reflection to myself before falling bay to the night fairy, hoping your kisses do not become scars. It's not possible! If I follow my thoughts, is this the conclusion of our love? A lie? Destruction? Can we live like this with rejection?

As my thoughts of anguish consistently run through my head, I eventually allow my body to fall prey to sleep. The morning after keeps reproducing the ruminations of the night before. The time for Bullet to leave is approaching soon in just a few more days. Our time is short and we have to make the most of every second. We have a ritual of riding the coast, enjoying the sand, and finding a quiet spot to focus on each other without interference from the outside world.

This weekend will be a bit different due to the rainstorm and the night before. We decided to take our usual two-hour ride on the coast. After that, our drive home will be our peaceful alone time. While riding the shore, I gaze at the reflection of the rise and fall of my chest, inhaling and exhaling of my breaths. Reflections from the window mirror display sadden eyes and a questionable image. I know it's me I'm looking at, but it's not the me I like to be. I feel a touch to my hand and a sense of eyes peering my way. He speaks with such sincerity and concern.

"Baby, are you okay?"

I muster a weak short, "Yes."

I give a half-smile and then look away. Distant green trees are endless in sight. The misty overshadow of fog and hints of dew are pleasantry to the eyes. I sit motionless with thoughts that I hope to dissolve and wash away. Something has happened. Something is missing. We, he, us as one has made a shift. Joy has closed her door to my heart when I look at him.

Rejected, unwanted, disappointment, pain-- rejected, unwanted disappointment, pain--rejected, unwanted, disappointment, pain keeps fluttering in my head.

Our relationship status is the first of many doubts I have about Bullet and myself. Funny how life throws a curve and knocks the wind out your sail. The high is slowly deflating. The silence is welcomed and clear that not much is to be said. The music from the radio brings mental calmness and harmony to the atmosphere.

Again deliberations in my head are ceaseless. We, he, us, one still remains an untold story. Do I have a choice of pleasure to soothe my pain? Will my scar of intimate rejection ever be healed again?

Sitting in the passenger seat with my eyes pierced out the window, my thoughts of rejection slowly shifts to feelings of neglect and heartbreak. I begin to think of my dear friend Al. Meditations on Al brings me some joy. Then I feel guilty. Al is in the hospital. I've recently neglected Al and need to see him soon. My mother is another factor that needs my attention. She is a wreck after the news about her sister. While having deep thoughts of all I need to deal with, I don't hear Bullet. His touch to my left thigh startles me and reconnects me to reality.

"What, huh, what did you say again?"

Bullet repeats himself, "So what do you think? You really didn't hear me, did you? What are you thinking? You look like you have a lot on your mind this morning."

My startled look remains pasted on my face as I gawk at Bullet and stay mute. I try to dissect what he is talking about.

Bullet echoes himself once again, "I said I'm happy you came to see me last night. I hope you enjoyed last night as much as I did. Once we finish riding the coastline, I want to show you something. I also want to apologize for last night's late-night 'thing'. I know you were a little upset, but I promise I will make it up to you."

I assemble another half-smile; however, I have nothing to say. I was not in the mood to discuss the reasoning for rejection. My concentration has already shifted.

My voice slightly louder than a whisper, "We can discuss it later. I've missed you. I was happy to see you last night after many lonely nights."

My thoughts quickly shift back to what I plan on doing in the next couple of days. Bullet is not one of those considerations. I want the ride to be over and need time to ponder the rejection that happened the night before. Possibly what I believed I had with Bullet has been just an illusion, or perhaps he is seeing someone else. Whatever the case, I can't focus on it right now. My next stop will be to visit Al in the rehab center and check on my mom since her sister's death.

The coastal ride is different; I don't enjoy the moment like the previous times. We talk while riding to and from the coast as we share breakfast. Alone time takes place mostly in the car due to all the damp areas on the beach. I feel a bit distant, but I am not sure if Bullet notices. Once we return to Bullet's house, I decide not to stay long. Bullet goes to the kitchen to prepare a meal. I can hear him shoveling the pots around. I immediately retrieve my belongings and say only a few words about our time together. Bullet tries to convince me to stay longer with no prevail. He finally backs off and accepts that I want to leave.

Before Bullet and I depart, he says, "I'm not going away for long, I'll be back in a few days for the funeral."

"Acceptable," I reply.

"Indigo, baby, please be safe. Call me when you get in."

"Yes, yes, of course, I always do."

"Indigo, something's on your mind. Are you going to talk to me about it?"

In a dry, indifferent tone, "No, Bae, maybe later, but I'm okay. Love you. You be safe too."

Bullet holds me with both arms stretched while he stares with concern for a second. Shortly after that, he pulls me in, hugs me tight, and whispers, "You know you have my heart, and I really love you."

"Yes, I know, Bullet."

Then I stop speaking for a moment to give him an intense stare. I proceed to talk.

"Bullet lately, maybe we need time to reflect on making sure this is what we both want."

"Indi, what do you mean?" Bullet inquires while remaining front and center in the doorway.

"I mean, I don't know. This past weekend was different for me, and possibly you need some reflection about us as well. All I'm saying Bullet, I have a lot on my mind and I-"

Bullet discernment of concern gradually shifts to an unfamiliar demeanor. Bullet eyes start to have a darting glossy glare. Anger is my initial thought until I see his forehead frown with a slight hint of confusion. Bullet grabs both my arms tightly, clinching me from departing.

"Indi, are you trying to tell me something I need to know?"

I rip my arms from his tight grip then he proceeds to grab my arms again. This time, his grasp is even more uncomfortable. When he catches me the second time, he simultaneously pulls me towards his body. The smoke alarms immediately begin to whistle. Food on the stove is starting to burn. The loud buzzing doesn't move Bullet one bit. I see thin clouds of smoke wavering. The resonances from the alarm seem to irritate Bullet.

Now we are face-to-face with less than an inch between us. This aggressive disposition is a side I've never seen displayed by Bullet. I observe the beads of sweat popping on Bullet's forehead as his eyes move uncontrollably from side-to-side with an unblinking scowl. The smoke from the stove is getting thicker. Bullet aggressively pulls my wrist, jerking me in the house. I am unable to escape his tight grip as he slams the door behind us.

Chapter 4

SUNBEAM

*S*tillness and silence. I start to feel my earlobes throbbing, my heart is racing, and I literally feel steam evaporating from my head. Bullet's clench slowly begins to loosen as he stares in my eyes. Unyielding, I stare directly back. While compressed against the wall, I'm grasping my purse so hard my hand is beginning to feel numb. The howling is nonstop from the smoke alarm.

Bullet continues to ignore the smoke detectors.

Face-to-face Bullet shouts, "Indi!"

I shove him away once he frees me from his clasp.

"Indi, I just need to talk to you! Please lets not end things ugly. This weekend has been a long-awaited time together."

Subdued and infuriated, I remain against the wall. Again Bullet starts to move in closer.

"Indi, I'm sorry I grabbed you like that. My reaction was not to let you go."

"Well, guess what? I'm going!"

Bullet tries to keep his composure. Finally, I observe his attention is slightly gearing toward the thickened smoke from the kitchen. I notice his attempt to remain calm is a challenge. His glare is frightening as his eyes are moving in an uncontrolled side-to-side motion.

Holding back his aggression, Bullet bends down to give me a peck. My lips remain unmoved. Elbowing him to the side, I swing the front door open.

"Indi, just wait!"

My rage prevents me from looking back. I leave cold, without any gesture of goodbye.

Once I arrive home, I have a mental debriefing. Allowing my pen to flow freely, I take my thoughts to paper.

I QUESTION
I'm drained and tired
Am I giving too much of myself and losing my true
    identity?

I question at times
Who have I become?

I question myself- why now do I empty myself and
    pour out diamonds, gold,
and fine incense yet it's not appreciated?
More and more is always demanded

I question myself-
have I become a figure of happiness or a shadow of
    disconnect?

I question myself- where, what, how, next, simply
    WHEN?
What was, thought to be, or is--am I connected?
Or simply still
Questioning myself

WRITTEN THOUGHTS ARE MY THERAPY. FOR A MOMENT, WHILE

writing, I experience liberation from life issues. After I finish, I figure enough thinking about Bullet. Tomorrow I have a different focus, which is Al.

The following morning brings me joy. I'm excited to get a chance to see Al, finally. This past weekend gave me time to reflect on what's significant in my life. Today is a perfect day for a visit; the sunshine refreshes me after my morning run.

I drive up to a brown stucco mini-mansion rehab center that only the wealthiest can afford. This is where Al momentarily resides throughout his rehab recuperation. The entrance is double-gated; a somewhat covert place. Everyone has to be buzzed in or possess a special card to enter. Al is one of the VIP residents, therefore I am privileged to retain the entrance card to the gateway. Initially approaching the building, it's not recognized as a rehab center. There are no evident signs or large billboards. The center is very renowned. After passing through security, the views consist of water-falls, manicured bushes, large oak trees, and a walking bridge over a large duck filled pond.

Stanley is the daily security officer that always salutes me with a nod and head tilt. He is a man of scarce words but retains a golden smile. Mr. Stanley is a vast fellow, towers about six-feet, give or take, at the tiniest three hundred pounds. His appearance is tickling. He always tucks his button-up white shirt in his neatly cuffed black khakis, although his belly is dying to escape free.

With his customary smile, Stanley looks my way. However, this visit, he steps out his cubbyhole, flagging his hand in the air as to wave or stop me. Thereafter, I smile and wave back. With one leg out the doorway, I hear Stanley shouting.

"Haven't been seeing you around lately, Ms. Indigo. You must've been busy with business."

While still in my car, I roll down my window. Coming to a slow, steady stop, I respond to Stanley with the same warmth.

"Yea, taking care of business. How have you been, Stan?"

"You know I've been in the hospital for a couple of days. They said I had a mini-stroke. My doctor said I have to lose some of this weight and give up the cigarettes."

"I didn't know Stan. I hope you are feeling better. You're looking terrific. You need to take care of yourself, so I can keep seeing your golden beam."

"You are absolutely right. I'm trying Indigo. I'm really trying hard. Well, I'm not going to hold you up any longer talking about my issues. Ole Al-ly Al will be happy to see you. Don't tell him I called him that because he hates when I do that, but that's my fella. He talks about you all the time. So, Indigo, you take care. It's nice seeing you."

"Likewise, Stan. Always a pleasure."

Pulling off from Stanley, I probe the area. Every time I pull up to the rehab, I recap the whole incident in my head. The night Al called me. For one, Al never calls me late at night unless it's business-related. The call came around one a.m. while I was sleeping. The calls were repetitive, back-to-back, which the unceasing vibration eventually aroused me. Al's voice was different. He told me to come over now because "something wasn't right." He wanted me to be there. He was declaring that calling 911 was not an option. Hospitalization would only take place if I were to bring him. The ride to Al's house was daunting that night. I had every imaginable worst-case scenario going through my head.

Al experienced heart issues that night I brought him to the hospital. The pain was so excruciating Al could not even walk. Three weeks after his hospital stay, he was immediately transferred to the place I'm entering now, The Corner Rehab Center. He is such a hard worker. Possibly he ran his body to the point of exhaustion. In hindsight, his body needs this rest and recovery.

Al always says, "Work, work, work, then wealth is on the way."

Al is a gentleman, maturely aged, mellow, observant guy that never makes much time for anything except for work. Al's parents died a few years ago, first his father then one short year later his mother. Al, a private Italian, is an only child, and his mother's best friend watches over him. Pretty much reserved, which is why his circle of friends is few and far between. He is a loner with many secrets, but Al is dear to my heart in countless ways. For the past twelve years, he and I have an undisputed unique bond. After the death of my aunt, I realized that people are fundamental. I need to make time for all my loved ones in my life, including Al.

It's been about two weeks since I've visited Al in rehab. Typically, I visit at least twice a week. Al has a ritual of calling me daily, although the convos are always brief, no longer than five minutes. It's astonishing how much can be said in a short amount of time. In the last couple of days, Al hasn't been calling. My attempts to reach him were unanswered. Texting is definitely out of the question because Al very seldom would read or, better yet, respond to a text. I had no doubt in my mind that Al was perhaps upset that I hadn't been to the rehab center in awhile. I had every intention of coming, but there was always something that deterred my visit. Of course, there is no valid excuse, especially if I told Al.

Al may be mad that I've neglected him for so long, but life is a bit outlandish with Bullet, my sister Sky, and dancing. I know that still doesn't justify my recent neglect.

As I enter further in The Corner Rehab Center, I observe residents sitting outside along with staff on their smoke breaks. I see familiar faces and wave my hand to acknowledge one of the senior staff members.

"Hey, Mr. Ralph."

"How you doing, Indigo? It's always a pleasure seeing you."

"Thank you, Mr. Ralph, everything's good, it's always a pleasure to see you as well. See you in a little bit."

I enter the front doors. As I walk the hallways, I notice plenty of desolate faces, shiny-wax floors, and the scent of metallic rubbing alcohol—loud chatter echoes from the nursing station. My gait is swift with eagerness and excitement to get a glare of Al's olive, smooth, flawless skin.

His eyes are always straight with worry or deep thoughts until I enter his presence. He calls me his Sunbeam of Life. Our relationship is quite eccentric. I arrive at a half-closed door that only has a small crack to peek in. I see his room number and name on the door, Room 811, Alfonsi Sabbatini. My gift of balloons and flowers is a plea for an apology for my past absence. The room is dark as I enter with a guarded manner.

"Good morninnngg my Al."

I get no response but a slight head tilt and an emotionless stare. Before he utters a word, I begin to explain.

"Al, I know you may be a bit livid about my desertion these few days, but I promise I will make every effort to avoid any continued habits."

Al just sits there. One, two, over five minutes of silence. His masculine, faded, vocal echoes, "I'm happy to see you, my Sunbeam. I've missed you. In time we will make up for lost moments."

Then a slight grin follows in suit. Al pushes his once weak body to one end of his bed and pats his left hand to motion for me to join and sit. I remove my shoes, grin, and join my Al to enjoy the silence and a warm hug as I lay on his chest for comfort.

"Al, you're my fortress in time of disparity and I promise to be here for you as the same."

"I know my Sunbeam. You're the reason I live. You don't have to explain. It's probably something I don't want to hear."

"No, Al I..it's not…"

"Shhhhh …it's okay, Sunbeam lets enjoy this moment."

Thoughts flood my head.

I can stay here forever. Al really loves me. How would I survive without him? Tomorrow is the funeral. How will my mother survive through this? Indigo let go and enjoy the moment with Al. No stress, all will be okay.

The good news today is discharge day. Al is now healthy, independent, and ready to get back to real life. After a moment of silence with Al, I disclose how the house is clean and prepared for his return.

Still, in the arms of Al with my head slightly lying on his chest, Al looks down at me.

"Are you going to stay with me the first night back, Sunbeam? I really would love for you to be there, if only for the first night to have your company in an empty house."

I remain mute. Al doesn't budge. "Well, I'm waiting for a response, Sunbeam. I haven't seen you for quite some time, and I need you now. You have your room, and I have mine, but I just need you there for the first night."

I express a small sigh of agreement.

"I know you need me, and, like I always say, I'll be here for you as you are always present for me. In a couple of days, there is the funeral. I will need to leave early to take care of family issues."

Al doesn't say anything at first, just nods.

"Yes, Sunbeam, I know, I know, I just need you there for tonight."

Before discharge, we both have a mutual understanding. Tonight will be the first of many to spend some time alone. It'll be like old times before the rehab stay.

Al and I leave together.

As onlookers peer at mansions and pass below giant oak trees, the St. Charles Streetcar sends off a coarse sound that echoes in the background. Al's home receives accolades for its beauty. His house is on St. Charles Avenue in the heart of the Garden District, known as a circa 1848 Historic Center Hall home. Al's home is nine thousand five hundred eight square feet with nine bedrooms and six full baths.

His place welcomes us both as we are approaching a precisely trimmed lawn, Al's face livens as he harmonics, "St. Charles Avenue. I'm finally back home."

Upon approaching the house, the black iron-surrounding gate glistens from the reflection of the sun. The home's front façade has a twelve-step central stair, deep front porch, and four large symmetrical round columns. Additionally, outside garnishing's has a multitude of windows and decorative pinned shutters.

Porch chimes, flickering large lantern lights, and a downwind aroma of sautéed onions, bell peppers, celery, garlic, and spices are the welcome mat to the front entrance. Prior to taking the first step, Momma Deah opens the door with a grin to her face, coupled with glee to her eye.

"Home sweet home lil' Bean. I bet yuh hungry and can't wait to get some good cookin'. I've tossed up a welcome home meal just fa yuh. Indigo, I have something for yuh too. I came early to have it done before y'all got here."

Momma Deah is a jovial, wholesome figured, short woman up in age, reaching approximately four-foot eleven, with a head full of gray shiny curly coils. Her gait shifts from side-to-side with a large bow in her legs. A smile stays plastered on her face. She keeps the house tidy and prepares meals for Al since the death of his mother. First, I assumed she was Al's aunt or close relative. However, Al disclosed how she has always been in the family. She was his mother's best friend. Al mother died the same month Momma Deah's husband died. Momma Deah has no children of her own; she's always called Al lil' Bean. After her husband and best friend's death, Momma Deah comes over to bring Al meals. Then she starts to clean Al's place because she says Al isn't tidy enough, although that's not true, just an excuse for her to come to his home often. Thereafter, regularly, Momma Deah continues her routine. She never stays long but does her job exceptionally well. I honestly believe Momma Deah enjoys seeing Al, cleaning, and cooking for him. She hums, sings, and dances as she cooks and cleans, never allowing or showing a gloomy spirit. I enjoy her presence. I can tell Al does as well, although he never admits to it.

I acknowledge Momma Deah, as does Al, and I carefully walk up the stairs, "I bet the meal you prepared is beyond delish Momma Deah. I can't wait to see what's in the kitchen."

Once at the top of the stairs, Momma Deah can't hold back her tears with a pasted smile. She wraps her chunky arms around Al's slender physique and holds him tightly. Al pats Momma Deah on her back while grimacing down at her.

"I'm so happy yuh home lil' Bean. Believe it or not, I miss that stony ole face. But I know how to bring on a smile. So go on nah. Get freshened up. Momma Deah needs to fatten yuh up some mo. Na, I can't stay, but there's some shrimp etouffee, big mixed green salad, and garlic bread. Desserts include bread puddin' and freshly made beignets just for yuh Indigo. There's some fresh-squeezed lemonade in there too. Lil' Bean I made enuf for the both of yuh for a few days. Y'all call me if yuh need me nah. I love yuh both."

"Thank you, Momma Deah. I appreciate all you do. I love you too," replies Al.

"Yes, love you, Momma Deah; you know how much I love beignets. Thank you very-very much!"

Momma Deah hugs me while her keys are dangling from one hand. She whispers in my ear, "Thank yuh Indigo for looking out for my lil' Bean. He's all I got."

I look down snicker and whisper, "Of course always."

Momma Deah dawns her head scarf around her head, places her purse across her bent arm, keys to the other, enters her car, and waves goodbye with a broad smile.

Upon entering the house, immediately there are Al paintings on the wall. Portraits of me are throughout the house. Decorations on the living room wall is a collection of carnival masks and photography of his still work. Far off in the kitchen, I see a peek of the golden puffed French beignets. The kitchen isn't the first stop in the house. Instead, we remain in the living room. Continuous audio of jazz is playing in the background. Al is an avid jazz listener. Among many of his talents, he is very gifted at playing the sax. Occasionally he serenades me and I dance for him.

Once in the house, I open the windows. My white flowing sundress showcases how blustery the outside air came rushing in. Wailing from the wind is soothing and tranquil. At this time, I turn up the jazz background music.

Seizing one of the masks off the end table, I leisurely place it over my eyes. Al loves when I wear the masks and dance for him. While wearing the half Venetian gold and white-feathered disguise, I slowly put both arms above my head then intentionally brush one arm at a time down one side of my face, while the other caress down my neck. Deliberate and teasingly, I begin unzipping part of my dress, allowing the wind to flow through my hair. I keep my eyes closed, and I dance to the harmony of the saxophone; my body sways becoming fluid with the beat.

I dance, he chuckles. I grab one hand so he can join. He nods "no," but I remain persistent.

Al stands, smiles then grabs around my waist as I wind side-to-side. I spin, remove the scarf wrapped around my hair and play with him to get in the rhythm. From behind squeezing my waist firmly yet tenderly, Al takes control of my hips, guiding and directing them at his leisure. The touch of his hands is soothing. My body falls victim to his demands. His body becomes closer and closer until we are one unit. Steady hands wrap around my waist-line. He then leans down to rest his head on my shoulder while moving to the melody of the background jazz. With one arm above my head wrapped around Al's head, we sway from left to right. As the music comes to an end, Al turns me to face him. Then he takes both of his hands, rubbing them simultaneously down my cheeks. His hands stop at the center of my chest. After a short pause, Al repositions his hands to my midriff once more.

Al looks in my eyes and whispers, "It's nice to be back home. You being here with me is an added bonus."

It seems like time is moving in slow motion. Al bends down and kisses my lips slowly and softly with a long pause. Thereafter, he pulls back and kisses my forehead while clinching me tightly in his arms. I return the snug hold. My head is firmly against his chest, I hear the beat of his heart, feel the warmth of his skin, and embrace every second we share.

The first night back home is fantastic with Al. Late night drinks are pleasant and refreshing. Especially after the ordeal I had the night before with Bullet. At the end of the night, Al is stretched on the sofa in a side sitting position. As I lay between his legs, we talk and laugh until I fall asleep in his arms.

The next morning I get ready for an early departure because I have so much to do. The sun is barely peeking over the horizon, morning dew freshly lying on parked cars. Al remains in a half-sleep slumber upon my rising. Al is holding me tightly. He and I were no longer on the sofa. I wake up in bed. I am in Al's bed. Both of us are naked skin-to-skin. I don't remember coming into bed. My memory was of us on the sofa. I lay in bed, look at Al, and try to decipher what happened.

I glide out of Al's arms to go and freshen up. I stare at myself in the bathroom mirror, questioning silently. "Did Al and I have sex?"

I reach down, touch between my legs to exam if any wetness is present. I feel intently to discover unknowns.

"I can't tell. Hell, I'm always hot in the morning. It's not that difficult to get my juices flowing. But was it from Al?"

I just decide to get myself together. Al has a little power over me that I have never been able to control entirely. I opt not to question what happened last night. I decide it's best. I don't know. Al will question some things if I inquire. I want to ask but have to keep face and avoid any display of upset.

Upon returning to Al, he remains across the bed in the same position. I smile because I'm happy he's back home. Al wakens completely; his eyes begin following my every move as I gather my things.

I return to him and sit in my original overnight spot, stating, "Al last night was beautiful. I'm happy we shared your first day back home together. I love you, Al. I need you here and healthy, so eat Momma Deah's goodies, and as she says 'to fatten you up.'" I giggle. He smirks.

Morning words of goodbye, "I love you, Sunbeam, and if not sooner, I will see you at the service in a couple of days."

The customary kiss to my lips from Al then follows. To my surprise, for the first time, my Peach Butter reacts from the kiss of Al's lips.

Chapter 5

LIT

*I*t's a brisk sunny day with leaves dancing in the street. The wind is singing and whistling. Trees shelter birds that are harmonizing angelic sounds of tweets. People are standing and chatting. I'm in a dazed state of mind remembering the day I received the call about the sudden death of my Aunt Star.

A seizure? When did she start having seizures? And why did it occur while she was driving?

My mother only had this one sister and they were very close. My mother is a strong, matter-of-fact type of person. She is a lady with many words of intellect and speaks to you only if she feels you are worthy of speaking to. Her tolerance for ignorance, stupidity, or what she thinks is a waste of time will never get a second look. Many consider my mother as proper or simply too bougie for common folks. Indeed, that is not the case. My mother was brought up poor and always wanted better for us. She was determined to get us educated and receive mentoring from the most proper intellectual people she encountered. Bayou is the youngest son, and Sky is the oldest daughter. The three of us have a great life, although each one of us is very different.

On the other hand, my father is a jokester and welcomes the whole neighborhood to join his parties. This usually doesn't fare too well with mother, but they have been together for forty-two years, and the love and happiness remain strong. My father set the standard for looking for a mate and what the expectations should be. That's what he always says anyway.

"What time is everybody getting here? I'm always being rushed, but no one takes account of my time too."

"Sky, please stop complaining, you know mother hates hearing the bickering all the time. Mother just lost her sister for goodness sake. We all have to be patient and get along just for today anyway," states Bayou.

The family starts to arrive as Dad is supporting Mom throughout this sad occasion. In my mind, I have trouble rationalizing how short my Aunt Star's life was.

I thought that this incident might finally bring our family closer together. Sky is always our troubled sibling, while Bayou keeps us all knit together by playing peacemaker.

Tears slowly drop down the cheeks of loved ones. The singing and sermon orchestrate beautifully. I'm determined to live a happy, carefree life. It all still seems surreal.

Sky practically stretches out during the funeral service. The female Ushers gather around Sky to fan her down; too many theatrics from Sky. I refuse to be a part of any of her shenanigans. Sky loves to be seen and absolutely lives for drama. My mother hates when she causes a scene. Bayou, of course, is over there catering to her regular acting out.

My best friend Dillard is sitting next to me, holding my hand for support. Occasionally Dillard taps my leg when he sees something dramatic or comical. Dillard has been my best friend since second grade. We have experienced many life ups and downs.

I lean over to Dillard and whisper, "Dillard, you know this is too much to witness from Sky over there."

Dillard purses both lips together, remains looking forward, then turns only his eyes my way to acknowledge the foolishness at the front corner of the church. Father looks back at me. I nod to assure him I'm okay, then my father rolls his eyes in the direction of Sky, to reference, "here we go again." Once the service is over, I embrace my mother tight for comfort. Al approaches and expresses his condolences, along with a warm embrace. He gives hugs and kisses to the family.

Thereafter, my eyes start to search for Bullet. I know he is here because he smiled at me from a distance during the service.

Everyone is outside mingling. Dillard has a captivating spirit. For some reason, people always gravitate to him.

"Dillard, you always look so nice. You should've been a designer. What kind of shoes-?"

I see Ms. Bertha talking to Dillard. I politely approach the two of them, "Excuse me, Ms. Bertha. I'm sorry to interrupt your conversation. Dillard, did you see Bullet?"

"Yea, he was talking to Sky over by the oak. Over there."

Dillard points in the far distance signaling where he saw Bullet. At the same time, he walks away from Ms. Bertha after he answers my question. He leaves Ms. Bertha and myself standing alone together.

I acknowledge Ms. Bertha before I begin to walk away, "Ms. Bertha, how you doing? I'm happy you came to the service."

"Baby, your Auntie Star was such a good person. I was so surprised to hear what happened. How's your mother doing? I said hi, but she must didn't see me because she just nodded her head and didn't say anything else. I wanted to ask her what Star husband Kyle did when all this happened. I know he must be devastated. These men out here move on quick tho. I saw him on the front row. I was trying to see if he was cry-"

"INDIGO, we need you over here to take a look at something!" Yelled Dillard from a distance.

At this point, Dillard had escaped Ms. Bertha and her gossipy conversation.

"Okay, I'm coming. Excuse me, Ms. Bertha. I need to go see what's going on over there."

"Well, come back so we can catch up. I'll be over here after I get something to chew on. You lookin' good in them heels Indigo. I remember when I was that size."

"Alright, Ms. Bertha, I'll talk to you later." I give Ms. Bertha a half-smile and walk away towards Dillard.

"Thank God, you rescued me from Ms. Bertha."

"I felt the same way when you walked up asking about Bullet. You know Ms. Bertha will talk you to death. Always talking about folks."

"Yea, I hate when she traps me. My mom can't stand Ms. Bertha with all that mess. I knew she wouldn't miss a funeral for nothing in the world, just so she can talk about everybody who is there and everybody who isn't."

"Now you were asking me about seeing Bullet. You know he has to be around here somewhere. I'm going inside to get something to eat because it's hot as hades out here. You coming inside?"

"No, I'm going to look around a little bit more. I'll come in a few. You know I'm leaving out of town early in the morning, right?"

"Oh yea, for Al, right?"

"Yes. Only you, Al, and my mother know I'm leaving out tonight."

Dillard responds, "Don't leave before letting me know you heading out. Oh, did you see Garrett em' in the back of the church?"

"No, I didn't see him."

"I talked to Garrett earlier, but he already left. It was a few people from work there. They all sat together in the back. Possibly, that may be the reason you didn't see them."

"That was nice, but I wished I had seen them. However, I did see the flowers that were sent from the office."

"Well, I'm going in Indigo before I melt. Don't be out here in this heat looking for no Bullet. If he not looking for you, then you know what I think about that. Shit, it's your Aunt that died. Don't be hunting down, no man."

"Okay …Ok…go inside! I don't need all this right now, Dillard."

"Whatever, Indi, you know where I'm at."

Dillard turns to go inside, before reaching the door he is stopped by my cousin Tye. Tye's mouth is moving fast and wide. He is talking so loud that the deaf in New York City can hear his conversation. I could tell Dillard wants to get inside. He has one hand on the door, but Tye is standing in front of the door blocking the way in. I see Dillard push Tye to the side but can't hear what he says. I laugh to myself because I know Dillard probably said something slick and flip to Tye. Dillard isn't going to let anything stand in his way of getting inside.

Bayou approaches me from behind with ice-cold water.

"Hey Sis, how you doing? You saw Mom took it pretty hard."

"Yes, I know. I'm happy Daddy is here."

"Are you coming to the house after all this stuff over?"

"No, I have a couple of things I need to get done for work, so I'm not coming. Why was Sky acting all crazy? She always embarrasses the family when she cuts up like that."

"Indi, you know how Sky is."

"But you cater to that behavior. Bayou, you need to stop giving her attention. That's the only reason she does stuff like that is for attention. She knows Mother does not play that."

"I did it because of the circumstance. Mom already pulled her to the side and said a couple of words to her out here."

"Bayou, how you know?"

"I was standing right next to her. Mom pinched her arm and dragged her to the side. I saw it, dad saw it, and even Bullet saw it."

"Bullet saw it?"

"How did he see it? Where was I?"

"I have no idea where you were. You probably were still inside talking to whomever. I escorted Sky outside because she was acting out so much. I wanted her to get some fresh air."

"Yea, Bayou, but that still doesn't explain how did Bullet get in the picture."

"Let me tell the story Indi before you ask questions. I was shocked when Mom did what she did, so I need to explain the full scenario."

I hiss, "I'm happy she got what was coming. I'm sorry I'm listening."

"So, Bullet came outside. He wasn't even coming in the direction by me and Sky. Sky called him over, but soon as she called Bullet,

Mom and Dad looked in our direction. You could see the fire in Mom's eyes as she approached us. There weren't too many people where Sky and I were standing. It was a perfect area for Mom to say whatever she wanted. Mom snatched Sky's arm so hard and twisted the smallest pinch of skin while Sky squealed in pain. Mom told her, "Shut up! Now let me tell you something this is my sister's funeral and you have made a mockery of our family. You flopping your big ass all over while Bayou trying to hold you up. Knowing so damn well that Bayou can't hold your big ass. I buried my sister, but I will not bury my son too because YOU killing him. I will bury you right now in front of all of these people if you do one more igno-rant commotion. My tolerance is low and I'm not for it today, Sky!"

I listen intently as Bayou is telling the story, "Bayou no! You know Sky and her weight is a sensitive issue. Mom never talks about her size and we are forbidden to say any negative words about her weight too."

Bayou continues, "That's what I'm saying. That goes to show how mad Mom was. All this was going on while Dad just stood there and didn't say one word. Sky was embarrassed while all the intensity was unfolding. Bullet was just looking as the ordeal occurred raw and uncut."

"What did you do?" I probed.

"I said absolutely nothing. Sky had "real" tears this time falling down her face. She didn't cause a scene. She simply stood there, turned red, and took it all in. Eventually, people started coming out, so Mom didn't say as much as she wanted. She whispered and told Sky, 'I'm not done with you.' Then walked off while people were coming to extend their condolences."

I feel an essence of relief hearing what Mom did.

"That's good for her. Mom needed to address that situation because it was ridiculous. So that's why I haven't seen Sky hanging around after the service?"

"Nope, you not going to see her around either. She was feeling hurt. After that ordeal, she asked Bullet could she talk to him. They went under the oak, and I walked off. Surprisingly, Bullet and Sky ended up leaving together. I don't know where, but not too long after the incident with Mom they were pulling off. Mom and Dad even saw them leave. Seeing that, Mom said something like, 'good, she's leaving. She's shamed me enough for today.' Dad mentioned Bullet asking, 'why was he in the car with Sky?' That was basically it. Bullet probably came back, but I know most definitely Sky is not coming back."

"Quick question Bayou. Whose car did they leave in because I don't see Bullet's or Sky's car?"

"They left in Sky's car."

Just call Bullet Indi. Sky was the one feeling some type of way. Bullet was probably trying to help heal her bruised emotions."

"Yes, of course, Bayou, I'm getting ready to head out soon. Give me a hug."

I embrace my brother, look down at my watch, and notice the time. I scout once more for Bullet, but my search is void. I decide to call Bullet, but his phone is going directly to voicemail. Time is getting away from me, so I have to make my departure. Walking back inside, I first spot Dillard and say my goodbyes. Thereafter, I see Mom.

"The service was beautiful, Mom. Love you."

"Indigo, call me once you settle in from tonight's travels and be safe. Love you too, dear."

I have to leave town immediately after the repast. I want to tell Bullet I will be taking care of business, but I cannot reach him. I even call Sky's phone, but it just rings. I leave her a message to call me, along with texting Bullet to do the same.

After the services, I go off to get ready for an urgent last-minute late-night business flight. The funeral distresses me. I deliberately begin reflecting on my life. I call, then text Bullet again, still no response after multiple attempts. I ponder why Bullet is not replying or calling back. Frustrated from the failed call attempts, now I don't want to hear from him. I just need my time.

My phone beeps. I thought it was Bullet responding to my text message; however, it is Al.

"Hello, my Indigo! I hope you doing well. Call me."

Al never text, and if he does, it's very brief. I phone Al, to my surprise, he ascertains my gloomy spirit. Instantly he states he has a surprise for me requesting that I be ready.

"Al, you know I'm leaving out of town tonight for you."

"Exactly, I know just that. I know you have a late-night flight, but I need you to be available, packed, and ready for departure at approximately six p.m."

"I love surprises, Al. I'll be ready."

Al never fails to amaze me. With all whites in display, he arrives in a limo with wine, flowers, and a dainty gold bracelet.

"Al, what are you doing? Why are you doing this?"

"Sunbeam, I know today has been a long day. I can hear the sadness in your voice. I sense you have more than just your Aunt's funeral on your mind, so I just want to put a smile on your face. We are just going to enjoy some wine. Your flowers will be watered while you are away and a golden bracelet to give a sparkle to your eye. These few hours are yours to talk, sing, or just be silent. Whatever you're choosing, I want to be here for you, Sunbeam."

I lean over to put my arms around Al and instantly am at ease. I sit on one end, take off my shoes and place my feet on Al as he massages them. While sipping wine, I begin to feel Al's hand gliding up my leg towards my upper thigh. His strokes are gentle. Al leans in to get in a better position. My once closed eyes open wide as I jump back to resist. The red wine that once cradled in my hand spills over onto Al's shirt and pants. Every minute thereafter, I become awkward. Suddenly my phone starts to ring. It is only my alarm. It startles Al. Al moves back into a gentlemen's position and stops the forward motion of his gliding touch.

"Al I don't know what you're doing but-"

Al interrupts me before I can finish my statement.

"Sunbeam, I know. I know."

"No, Al, you don't understand. Let me-"

Al cuts my speech short once again.

"Sunbeam, not now. Please later."

We both sat in silence. I begin to look out the window. My mouth becomes dry and I become frozen. Al reaches over to touch my hand.

"Indigo, don't change on me. I've missed you. Indigo come close to me. I shouldn't have."

"Al, I'm not upset. I have so much-"

"Indigo, say no more." Al pulls me into his arms, holding me securely in silence.

Chapter 6

BUSINESS

The advances Al makes doesn't have my attention for long. Al and I have an understanding for at least this small moment. I can't help but wonder what transpired on our first encounter when he returned from rehab. Afraid to ask, I quickly dismiss the thought. Momentarily drawn away, my mind programs on why I haven't heard from Bullet. Annoyed about his silence, I peered down at my phone and realized I did receive a text from Bullet. The time reflects 08:20 p.m. Needless to say, the funeral was over approximately seven hours prior to that time.

Internally blazing, my thoughts are flaming, "I texted his ass almost eight hours ago and he's JUST texting back."

After continuously analyzing the time of his text, he only adds fumes to the fire. More text messages are in my phone from Bullet. His back-to-back late messages accuse me of purposely avoiding his calls and text. I'm not in an up to par place to respond. His behavior is out of character and unwarranted. Already disgusted, I turn off my phone to shun out Bullet or anybody else. I have to be invisible a few days for business anyway.

Al notices my irritation as I read my text messages.

"Are you okay, Sunbeam? Whatever is disturbing you, don't

allow it to get you in an unhappy state of mind. Keep smiling and share your beam with the world."

"Thank you, my Al. Thank you for everything tonight. I needed this more than you can imagine. I get into London tomorrow morning, nine local-time. I'll keep you updated on everything that takes place with the Halo's while I'm there. Keep your fingers crossed for exceptionally great success. Love you, Al."

Al's action is neutral. Even after the earlier incident, Al never attempts to come on to me again during this encounter. Leaning over, I hug Al and do the usual peck on his lips. Al stays in the limo. The chauffeur assists getting me out of the car, fetching my luggage.

It's early. My flight departs at 10:50 p.m. it's almost 9:00 p.m. I waver through the airport struggling to keep positive thoughts of Bullet and Sky leaving together from today's funeral. Failed attempts of any remote good thing could come from Sky. I bring to mind how Sky is sneaky and not ever to be trusted. For some reason, Sky has always been a jealous sister towards me. I trust Bullet, but do I trust Sky? No, I don't trust Sky. Why did Sky want to talk to Bullet in the first place?

My phone is still off from my earlier frustration. Struggling to shut out Bullet, I turn my phone back on. Butchered thoughts are killing me with the possibilities of Sky's motives. Now he is not answering his calls again.

It's now 10:20 p.m. and time to board. I am an early boarder settling in first class. Upon entering the plane, the flight attendant appears young, kind-smile, and neatly dressed. A whiff of newness is the scent of the aircraft. The seats are flush, and the temperature is cold.

"Would you like a warm covering and pillow for your travels today?" said the young flight attendant in a British accent.

"That would be lovely, thank you very much, Amanda," as I read her nametag on her blue blouse.

I make one more attempt to speak with Bullet just before the plane finishes boarding. Bullet answers.

The conversation is brief, "Hey Indigo, I need to call you back in a few."

"Bullet. I have-"

Hastily Bullet interrupts, "I promise I'll call right back, give me a minute."

"Well, okay." I then say goodbye and hang up. I turn my phone to airplane mode. Soon after, take off is in motion.

On my long flight, I am able to get plenty of rest. I occasionally engage with the TV monitor to pass the time. The movies playing don't keep my interest for long. In between snacking, videos, and resting, I daydream about Bullet. To drown out any other surrounding noises, I put my headphones on a high volume. Each song I listen to, I can relate it to Bullet in some form or fashion. With my eyes closed, I envision I can feel Bullet. With a firm caress slowly, his hands glide down the arch of my back. The soft-touch then slithers down the curvature of my ass. His hand pauses on one cheek to slightly shift my panties to the side. With a peek of one finger, he slowly prowls for a caress of moisture from my ripe Peach Butter. His hand to my back and his kiss behind my ears, always makes me a victim to what Bullet seeks. I sense his desires as he senses mine. Fondling of his finger increases the wet steam from my vertical smile to produce more with every stroke. Bullet folds me to a forward bend to meet and greet my vacuum. His long stiff pistol hits the bulls-eye, causing a sudden cry of pleasure. I bend to rest my arms on the edge of the bed, as Bullet takes a firm grip to spread my back cheeks even further. The motion starts off slow with increasing speed. Sweat pours down his chest while my panties are soaked, skirt lifted, and slapping skin-to-skin is something I welcome. Harder and harder it comes. Then gradually, it slows. I rise, keeping my back pressed upon his chest. He remains inside me as I wrap one arm around his neck. Bullet hands move up to grasp both breasts tightly in his grips as he kisses my neck and nibbles my ear. The thrust from him never ceases as I welcome every movement in. One hand remains to my breast as the other hand moves down to tease my clitoris. The touch of my clit produces increased fluids. The moisture becomes audible. Love liquids drip down my leg.

Bullet backs into the wall, as I remain attached. Caressing, rolling in and out brings abundant gratification.

"Excuse me. Sorry miss, excuse me."

I feel a hand tapping my leg. I look up to see the flight attendant looking my way.

"Excuse me, miss."

I remove my headphones to hear what she's saying.

"I'm sorry to disturb you, miss, but I will need you to place your seatbelt back on. We are heading into some serious weather. I'm sorry, but all passengers need to be buckled in again."

"Oh okay. No problem I'll buckle in again."

The flight attendant is composed as she politely disturbs others who didn't hear the overhead announcement to buckle in. I was so into my thoughts about Bullet. I am kind of annoyed to stop my romanticized fantasies while my songs play loudly in my ear. Dreams of Bullet are endless. I keep my headphones off for a moment. I didn't recall seeing possible storms for my travels to London. Al and I are usually good at tracking what to expect when traveling afar. I guess since this is a last-minute business trip, I failed to look at the weather forecast before departing.

I peer over my seat to witness more travelers to become more alert as well. The passenger across from me starts to become anxious. I see her significant other, I assume it is her husband, attempting to calm her down.

Breathing shakily, she is reaching in her purse nervously, looking for something. "I can't find it! I can't find my nerve pill." I can hear her continue, "I knew I should never have gotten on this plane. I hate planes. What if it crashes, then what?"

Tears are continuously rolling down her cheeks. The husband tries with no avail to comfort his mate. He then starts to reach in the purse. I assume looking for the pill too. He looks like he may need a pill just as much as she does. Both of them seem to be falling apart, more her than him. He appears to feed off his mate's unnerving actions.

Sighing with an internal relief, "I'm happy I'm not sitting next to him or her. They both look a mess."

I look over at other passengers who seem not to be phased one bit. Those travelers are veteran flyers, such as myself. The flight continues to be smooth. There is no turmoil yet, although I'm sure soon it will be coming. Flight attendants rarely are that aggressive about wearing seatbelts in the middle of flying. It's up to passengers to pay attention to the seatbelt signal and simply oblige to its recommendation, but never have I had one tap my shoulder mid-flight. I figure I am in store for one hell of a rainstorm. I say a prayer and leave everything in the hands of God. I don't stress too much. After the flight attendants take their seats, we slowly start to enter directly into violent weather. My heart drops a few times with gusts of air pockets, one of the worst intense turbulence I've ever experienced! Even veteran travelers are awake with occasional screams. I wish now I had a "nerve pill" like my fellow travelers across from me. I remain calm and continue praying.

The pilot keeps all passengers well informed of weather updates. Calmness is soothing coming from the pilot's voice. He rest assures we will be out of the windy torrential downpour soon. Storms last approximately forty-five minutes. We are at the tail end of our flight, with only a few more hours remaining before landing. Once out of the raging rain and wind, I hear sighs of relief. Children stop crying. My fellow "nervous" passenger misses out on all the action. She and her husband slept through the entire storm. "That must have been a great 'nerve' pill. Next time I think I will bring some of that too." I had chuckled to myself.

Since we have a couple of more hours before landing, I decide to watch a movie. I figure there is no sense in going to sleep. I'm wired from all the lousy weather mayhem. I need a drink, but figure I will wait until later. Before the movie ends, the pilot welcomes passengers to London along with the current weather report.

I am ready to get off the plane finally. Now it's time for a significant business encounter. I have a few hours to gather myself and relax before meeting up with the Halo's. I have my Oyster Card in hand and ready for the day. The Halo's always express their disapproval of me using public transportation, but I hate the traffic in London. By all means, I attempt to avoid extra delays and I find public transport in London suits me fine. After dropping off my luggage, I phone mother to tell her I made it safely. Mother will spread the word to the rest of the family. I call Al as well. Lastly, I phone Dillard.

"Indigo be safe out there by yourself. I know, I know you feel like you're at home and all, but you're not at home, so be aware of your surroundings. Close deals and make it home soon."

"Dillard I'm always safe, thank you for caring. I'm getting ready to go to the London markets in a few."

"Indigo, you and markets. Please be careful, sis. You know I think those markets look a lil' shady. But I already know you going out there anyway. Call me later once you settle in. What time you meet up with the Halo's?"

"I meet with them today a two p.m. I have a few hours. I plan on going to the market for only a minute to look around because I need to come back to my room to prepare for the meeting."

"Indigo, listen to what you just said. You need to prepare for your meeting with the Halo's. Leave them damn markets alone and go later, or hell, not at all. Indigo just stay in your room, rest, prepare, execute your meeting like a beast then focus on pleasurable things later."

"Dillard, ughhh, you always use logic when it comes to business."

"Indi, trust me. Stay focused and hurry your lil' ass back home. Promise me, Indigo, you will focus then enjoy the market later."

"Alright Dillard! I will stay in, prepare, execute, and then pleasure."

"That's my girl! Good! Love you, sis. You will thank me after that deal closes. YOU AND AL, for that matter!"

"You so crazy, Dillard! Kisses...kisses... I'm thanking you now. That's why you my besty. Love you. I'll call you later."

I hang up with Dillard and realize his suggestion has better logic. I take out some work and start to prepare for business. After an hour passes, I try to keep focus on my presentation. I'm wiped out, as I review everything I realize everything is all together. I turn the music on and pour myself a long-awaited glass of wine. The turbulence, long flight, and missing Bullet warrants the alcohol intake. Besides, one glass of wine takes away an edge of stress. The music is pleasant. I sat in bed, close my eyes for a moment while leaning my head back on the pillow. I sip slow and steady, wanting to savor every bit of the satisfying berry mixture. I begin to daydream of memories with Bullet. I picture the night I danced for him.

Reminiscing, I relive the moment of placing a chair in the middle of the room while Bullet's eyes are covered with a blindfold. He smiles deviously, knowing something good is in store. The cozy space has a hint of light from the single wicked candle. The music is turned up. "No peeking," I remind him. I wear red baby doll lingerie with peek-a-boo panties. One hand at a time, I touch his inner thighs. I cradle my hands in place to dance to the music. I move my hands up until they are met with an erection. Slow-motion strokes to his erection begin in hopes for late-night house games. The rhythm of the music rocks my hips side-to-side. As I plant my derrière to roll from east-to-west on the mountain, I feel his hands begin to inch up my thighs.

"No, no, Bullet. Not yet. No hands, remember?" He chuckles.

Speaking softly, he mumbles, "Okay, but it's hard. I mean literally, everything is hard."

I have no response. Instead, I kneel to comfort his erection with the moisture of my tongue. Tongue to the tip, down the middle, cupping the sacks, then complete entrance. Bullet repeatedly moans, simultaneously grabbing my head and rubbing my hair. The rules of "no hands" are entirely out of the window. Bullet rocks back and forth in the chair, engaging with every lick and suck. I remove Bullets blindfold and he looks directly into my eyes. I straddle on top and begin to kiss his lips, slowly transitioning into deep lust; my heart flutters. Bullet's hands rub my back up and down, exposing each breast one at a time, then he begins to affectionately stroke each nipple, first the right then the left. My peek-a-boo panties make it easily obtainable for entry. The once tasty erection has now entered into my Peach Butter for effortless delight. He grabs me tightly as I embrace his neck firmly. My body movement mimics the waves of the sea. Rhythmic movements, strong embraces, and palpating heartbeats with a flicker of wax light intensifies every second. The candle fails to illuminate the entire room causing only hints of silhouette shadows.

Bullet comes to a stand while embracing me around his waist. To the bedroom, we go. I'm positioned in the bed on my back. He stares and smiles, "I love you."

"I love you." I respond in return.

Bullet leans down to kiss----

BEEP-BEEP-BEEP!!!

My alarm startles me out of my deepest thoughts. The reminder on my phone keeps making a beeping noise until I acknowledge it to shut it off. Today, every time I have pleasant memories of passion with Bullet, I keep getting interrupted. However, this time I am happy I'm disturbed. The meeting with the Halo's is critical. My wine is done, so I gather myself then freshen up once more. Soon I get a call from the Halo's assistant informing me that my driver is on his way to pick me up. This is the big moment and I'm ready, pausing to take a deep breath. After that, I wait patiently for my party to arrive.

Meeting the Halo's for the third time is fantastic! The meeting is exceptionally successful. I especially love the warmth that is shared by the Halo's. I figure Al will be pleased to hear good news. After the meeting, Al is the first person I call.

"Al the meeting was a huge success! Everything was executed perfectly. Mr. Halo himself said, 'express to Mr. Alfonsi Sabbatini we miss seeing him, but we love his replacement even better. Mr. Sabbatini is a great businessman and we love what he has to offer for this company's success. Tell Mr. Sabbatini to give me a call personally. I would love to speak with him. We look forward to a successful couple of years doing business together.' Al, that was his exact words. Mr. Halo loves you. The meeting was the best, needless to say."

Al is extremely pleased.

"Thank you, Sunbeam. I knew you could close out this deal. I truly appreciate you. I would have came, but since my recent hospital discharge, it left me in a compromising position."

"Al please, you don't have to explain anything to me. I'm here for you. I just wanted to share the great news. Please be sure you give Mr. Halo a call."

"Indigo, I will call him now. You come back tomorrow, right?"

"Yes, I'll be back tomorrow. In the meantime, I plan on going to the London market. Thereafter, I plan on coming in to rest and get ready for my early morning departure."

"I will see you soon, Indigo. Keep me informed when you get to the airport and land."

"I know the usual routine, Al. I always do."

"Have a good day, Indigo. Thank you again. Love you, Sunbeam."

"Love you too, Al."

Chapter 7

THE RETURN

I fall asleep with my phone on the bed. It's two a.m. when my phone vibrates, startling me with an incoming text. I try to focus on seeing who's texting, but instead, I leave the phone in my hand. I stretch my palm while holding my phone under the pillow to mute out any other sleep interruption. It is too early to focus. The juddering from the phone stuns me again at five a.m. In an early morning slumber, I silence the phone. Ten minutes later, I feel the pulsation again. This particular morning, dragging myself out of bed is a genuine struggle. I manage to wake up eventually. I just lay in bed, looking around. At this moment, I grasp that I am not at home.

"Wait, it's five a.m., I'm still in London! I have to get up to catch my plane!" I squeal to myself.

In a mad rush, I run to the bathroom to freshen up for the day. Even though I am still in the restroom, I receive a call in my room. I dash to answer.

"Hello!"

"Good morning Miss Savoy, this is Iona from the front desk, your driver has arrived to escort you to the airport. Do you need any assistance with your luggage?"

"Good morning Iona, certainly that would be a huge help thank you!"

"The Bell will be up immediately to gather your luggage."

"Okay, great, thank you, Iona!"

I hang up the phone then return to the bathroom to gather my things. I feel my forehead sweaty and underarms wet. I reset for a moment to fan myself. My belongings are all over the room.

"What was I thinking? Why didn't I pack last night?"

I hear a knock at my door. It is the Bell. I open with a panic smile.

"Good morning Miss Savoy. I'm here to collect your luggage," states the Bell in a British tone.

"Okay, great, give me one minute. I have a few more things."

"No problem Miss Savoy, take your time."

I finally gather all my things and allow the Bell to take them down. I survey the room one last time to ensure I have all my goods. I finally feel a sense of tranquility. Through the large hotel window, the outside looks gloomy. An older gentleman with a grin plastered across his face greets me.

"Good morning Miss. Have a good day."

I return the warmth with a partial smile.

"Thank you. You have a fabulous day as well."

My driver patiently awaits my approach. He is standing outside the car, looking in my direction. The driver is a few inches taller than me, reaching possibly five-feet four inches at max. He stands tall with his back straight and erect. The driver nods and smiles as he opens the back door.

While on the way to the airport, I finally noticed I have nine text messages, and four missed calls. My few calls came from Al, Bullet, Mom, and Dillard. With my mad rush this morning, I failed to turn my ringer back on, which caused me to miss each call.

I begin to read the text messages.

Mom: "Good morning, my dear, have a safe flight. I'm praying for safe travels. Love you. Text me before you take off in the air."

Dillard: "Hey Indi, I tried calling you to make sure you are awake. I know you sometimes oversleep, so make sure you call or just text me letting me know you are up and on your way back home."

Al: "Ciao Bella, I'm so proud of you. I will be waiting for your call."

I also had a group text from Mom, Dad, Bayou, and Sky. Mom started off the text messages.

Mom: "Hello, all my loved ones, today Indigo is traveling. Everybody say a prayer."

Dad: "Praying for safe travels, baby girl."

Bayou: "Hey, fam. Safe travels, Indi."

Mom: "Family is important. Love all of you."

Sky: "Be Safe."

The text messages bring me inner joy. I recognize my family and friends are a blessing. The last text I read is from Bullet. His call was missed earlier.

Bullet message reads, "Just lying here thinking about the last time I saw you at the funeral. We didn't have a chance to talk and I'm sorry that we have not communicated. You probably upset and not answering my calls on purpose. I just want you to know I love you, Indigo. This morning you weigh very heavy on my mind. You have me feeling some type of way this morning. I woke up very hot and bothered. I miss those moments of pure ecstasy. It's when the desire is reciprocated and the want is equally balanced between the two. I miss the taste of your lips. I miss the caress of your hand. I miss pushing those panties to the side to feel your overly ripe moistures exploding out of the deep and dark places (as you always say that Peach Butter) that only true love reaches. Because when I think of that place, there is nobody else I could think about. You are the only one who has ever explored the true territory of my love. I miss it when I first push into your deep and wet love canal—letting my canoe explore the raft of your open and waiting sea of love. I miss being one each time I pulled you in closer to try and get a little deeper into your heart. To taste your juices all around the end of my lips as I swipe my tongue around the edge of my own lips, making sure to catch every drop. To see that shaft go into that mouth. It's not just the act. It's that the act is done out of pure desire and love. Then at that moment, when I look at you, I feel it's so easy to love you because God mended our hearts together. That's why we explore places that no one has ever been able to discover."

After reading Bullet's extensive text, I marvel with heartfelt delight. Bullet and I are in sync. He is thinking and missing me just as much as I am missing him. His text is perfect. I eliminate any negative thoughts about the funeral regarding him and Sky. I make a decree to myself to enjoy my real yearnings, and best of all, enjoy this day.

Dark melancholy clouds are all around, yet I feel sunshine all over me. My steps have an extra pep because of all the early morning attention. I feel loved. Soon after reviewing all my text messages, I repeatedly read Bullet's text messages. As I am on my third go-round of reading Bullets text, I arrive at the airport. The driver removes my bags and refuses my tip.

"No, mam, I cannot accept any money from you. All expenses have been taken care of by the Halo's. As a matter of fact, upon your exit of the car, Mr. Halo requested I give you this package."

"Thank you," I reply as I stare down at the package. I take it and shuffle inside the airport for check-in.

Once I'm settled, I call Al along with responding to all my text messages except for Bullets. I want to answer with a well thought out response. Lastly, I say a prayer before boarding the plane. I phone Bullet, but no answer. It's already time for me to board.

The minute I get situated on my flight, I take my bag and unwrap the enclosed package. The package is in a Harrods shopping bag. Inside I find the Welcome bag from Dolce and Gabbana. The elegance of the bag mimics a vintage appearance, one of my favorites. Next to the bag is a box labeled "Charbonnel el Walker." The little box contains seven pieces of Dark Marc de Champagne Truffles. Lastly, in the bag, there is a Harrods Rose Gold Slim Diary. Inside I discover a note from Mr. Halo.

"Indigo again, it was a pleasure seeing you once more yesterday. Accept these parting gifts as a token of gratitude for the contribution you and Al bring to my company. The slim diary is to imply forthcoming dates for future meetings together with continued business. Warmest Regards, Luca Halo"

The gifts from Mr. Halo is a bonus to my already bright day. I place my goods under the seat. The window seat reflects the sun attempting to peek through the dark clouds. Before boarding, I manage to grab a familiar American meal. I want a hardy lunch rather than eating breakfast. Before taking my first bite, I relax in my seat. Remaining guests continue to board the plane as I look out the window, waiting for take off.

Before the door shuts, I decide to text Bullet for the first time since arriving in London.

"I sincerely want to thank you for making me feel like your one and only Queen. You express so much love. It's hard not to shine just with a mere thought of it. Thank you for making me feel beautiful, sexy, appreciated, wanted, adored, and the list can continue on and on. Thank you for keep bringing joy & love to my life. I love you."

My text has no response. At least I knew he did think of me at some point because of his morning text. Bullet still not talking or answering, possibly because of a few days I have not been in contact. Due to last-minute adjustments, I had to take a business trip for Al and meet one of his business associates, The Halo's. The meeting was late and unexpected. Unfortunately, I had to leave immediately after the funeral. This business closing was huge and was worth millions of dollars if Al acquired this contract deal. Due to Al's recent illness, traveling was ill-advised by his physician. I often travel for Al, but by far, this was the biggest. Everything had to be brought to the table. My presentation had to be perfect.

During my London meetings, I kept my phone off most of the time. I tried to contact Bullet, but no answer to explain I'll be unreachable for a few days due to business. I was alone, but it would be challenging to tell why I am out of the country for someone else's business interest, especially for Al. Bullet would fear the worse, although it was just all business. Mother, Dillard, and Al are the only three initially aware of my whereabouts until mother sent out the group text, including Dad and Sky.

When leveled in the air, there is a slight turbulence. I have Beats muting out announcements and surrounding noises. As the sun is beginning to rise, I see dramatic cotton clouds with a hint of orange-yellow palette color schemes to the left of me. While looking out of the cold double-plated plastic oval window, I hear the airplane motor vibrating over my headphones' sound. The grainy sound can't be avoided. I feel the jolting beneath my feet. Flickering plane lights are seen out my window as the color palette of orange-yellow hue fades slowly. My neighboring passenger is bright and bushy eyed, while she is looking at movies on her laptop. She pauses for a moment from her computer. Thereafter, she looks my way as I consume my morning meal.

Unable to maintain any silence, my neighbor states, "You're the first person I've ever seen have yogurt instead of Chick-fil-a fries with their meal."

I swallowed, then respond, "It's delicious. Have you ever tried their yogurt? Besides, since it's technically still early morning, the yogurt serves as a partial breakfast. At least that's the way I ratio-nalize my food choice this early in the morning."

"Trust me; I understand, no judgment from me. I eat whatever, whenever too. But I never had the yogurt from them. I like their fries, heck I love any fries."

We exchange friendly smiles as we both transition back into our gadgets and food. Again, I have deep thoughts about Bullet in the midst of me listening to music. I have missed talking to him. Bullet and Sky still have me with controversial views, but I trust Bullet and decide not to make it a big deal. Besides, I'm sure he's steaming since I've disappeared without explanation for a few days, although I did attempt to communicate. My neighbor donning huge head-phones returns to her movie. Occasionally she looks my way to steal a peek of my music list. I kindly and intentionally move my music list to the side to maintain a sense of privacy; if that is possible on a plane.

Nonetheless, I close my eyes as the music places me in a trance. At this point, I imagine how my body is perfectly orchestrated then, with perfect pitch, played to a sensual melody by the touch of his hands. My emotions are equally out of control with thoughts of his gentle touch. Emulating excitement of memories activate my heart to beat faster. Bullets sensuality creates a beat that uncontrollably pounds in my chest, keeping me alive. I can't wait until we make beautiful music with the intertwining of our bodies again.

My neighbor looks my way often. Then she starts to speak. I remove my headphones to make out what she's saying.

"Are you on a business trip?"

"Well, yes, kinda sorta. I'm traveling back home after taking care of business for a friend."

She and I continue to chat about our life and the purpose of our flights. She explains that she is en route to the United States to see an old, outdated boyfriend, however, hoping that the two can rekindle sparks again. The story about her past relationship lasts for about an hour.

Positive, pure instinct gives me good vibes, making it comfortable to open up to her about my life. She completes her story regarding past relationships. After she stops speaking, I can see she wants me to open up about a few things regarding myself. The flight time feels shortened as we continue to talk concerning our relationship woes and situations. I then go in greater detail about my life with Al and Bullet. She is an excellent listener and remains engaged the entire time I speak.

"Al is an artist that is in love with me and pays me substantially to dance and or pose for artistic pictures. Al becomes elaborate with his paintings and is a well-known wealthy artist. We met at an art exhibit that showcased many of his pieces. I took an interest in one of his art pieces twelve years ago, at the time, I had no idea he was the actual painter. We shared a great conversation, wine, and cheese, all while viewing art pieces on display. He formerly offered to do a free painting of me because of how intrigued he was by my beauty and humbled spirit. After that, the relationship grew stronger.

Al became a comfort zone and then trips together to international art shows were in motion. Al always said I was his dime piece and arm trophy companion. I would even assist with business transactions per Al's request. Al then started making huge purchases to compensate for my time towards his business, which I happily accepted. A few of the compensation perks include travels, weekly deposits for basic beauty upkeep, my candy apple colored 911 Carrera 4S Cabriolet Porsche, and the three-tier elegant condo I reside in. Al finances all the aforementioned in exchange for my time, dances, and poses. I was single at the time my union with Al began. I always had 'friends' but never anything substantial until Bullet came into my life. Bullet isn't aware of the union I share with Al. Al would not approve of me being in any serious relationship. Al is a bit controlling. I may have friends, but something serious with another man may discontinue our business and personal relationship. I often travel to promote and advertise my books all from Al's connections and clout. I love Al, he respects me, shows kindness, listens, and never judges. I try to juggle and keep Al and Bullet apart. Confiding with my best friend Dillard is done regularly to keep me grounded and sane. Dillard is my best friend since childhood. He keeps the drama and humor funny regarding my complicated life. He has a way of lightening up the situation. Al finds comfort in sensual hugs and silent moments with me. However, since Bullet has become my love, those times are far and few with Al as I try to avoid jeopardizing my future with Bullet."

My seating companion listens intently before interjecting, "You have a tornado of events in your life. I like Al. It sounds that the two of you should have been in a relationship a long time ago. Have you ever considered being in a relationship with Al when you guys first met?"

"At first, he courted me frequently at local events, meeting prestigious people, and hanging out. He's always been respectful by never attempting to push himself on me. At that time, I started to like Al. He was different, patient, an excellent listener, and romantic. I enjoyed the company and fell in love with him until I discovered Al was seeing another young lady. She would fly in almost every other week. She and Al had known each other way before I was in the picture. Al never mentioned her. One day she came to town to surprise Al, that's when I discovered who she was. Al had left out of town last minute for one of his clients. I was at the house when his then-girlfriend attempted to unlock the door. She had past keys to his house. He had since changed the locks, however, she didn't know."

"Oh my, this is interesting."

"Wait…there is more! I'm not going to go in deep detail about all the in's and out's. To make a long story short, I answered the door because I wanted to see who was trying to come in. At that point, she questioned who I was as I did the same to her. Al and I relationship never became serious. It almost felt like we were in a deep relationship because I had keys to the house, the car, access to his credit cards, and his bank accounts. Oddly, we never became sexual in the beginning of our relationship, although I had sincerely fallen in love with him. The ex-girlfriend's name was Tiff. Tiff and I talked; she explained how long she and Al dated. Tiff revealed how she met Al. She further expressed Al was becoming distant and didn't seem interested in her anymore. Tiff blamed me for taking Al's interest from her. Tiff had plans to marry Al. Al, on the other hand, didn't want to marry Tiff. Tiff stated her last-minute appearance to the house was to surprise Al. She wanted to tell Al that she would be relocating and moving to Louisiana.

Needless to say, that day was bizarre. I could go on and on about that whole incident. But to answer your question, because of that incident with me finding out about Tiff in the manner I did, I felt it necessary to become distant. I pulled away from Al for a long time. I was hurt because he hadn't disclosed any information about Tiff, although he thought it was never a good time. Al proclaimed he loved me from the time we met. He further asserts Tiff never had the advantages that I had. He never shared bank accounts, credit cards, cars, or monies freely with any other woman. I believed him, but all in all, I remained hurt and distant at that time. Over several months I warmed up to him again, started to spend time, and became perfect friends. The travels and other stuff came much later. I truly still love Al, however, we never became involved in an 'official' relationship."

"Sounds like a wholesome relationship possibly without sex or possibly with sex. I'm just meeting you, so I don't know. Either way, it sounds like you have great connections in your little way with both males in your life."

"I never saw it as being in a relationship with Al, but maybe you are right."

The pilot starts to speak in the overhead to prepare us for arrival. That interruption refocuses my neighbor and I on preparing for landing. Our conversation comes to an end. We address each other like we knew one another from a distant past.

I turn to my new friend, "Girl, it's been refreshing talking to you. I've learned so much about you, and I just spilled my guts out about my life."

Speaking cheerfully with a chuckle, "Same here. I adored this little convo we had too."

Landing is soon approaching and welcomed. My new crony and I create a great travel bond. We wish one another good luck with relationship issues. Business for Al is finally done and a success. Tomorrow will be my first day back in the office since the funeral, back to real life again. Bullet has been on my mind consistently, but my flight neighbor has me pondering. Possibly, I have with Al something more serious than I wish to admit.

Chapter 8

HUDDLE

*E*arly morning huddle. Greetings are weak from incomers. There is a side stare from him of a good morning. Tracker is his name, a newbie to the company.

"Morning."

There is small talk with the group about business and the day's plan. Upon the huddle wrap up, there is slow cattle movement to the door to start a day's wage.

"I've missed seeing you around. I opened up to you and you disappeared out of my life. Did I scare you away?" Tracker states as we are walking towards our workplace destination.

"Never that. I had some travels and other business to take care of," I replied.

He reacts with a cavalier grin. Through the blue button-down Armani shirt, Tracker has a pronounced muscular physique. His walk appears to move smoothly and in slow motion. He has big hands, thick thighs, and a soothing voice.

"We need to catch up. I have some business for you."

With a reluctant smile, I respond, "Okay."

He continues to stare with a debonair smile.

"Good morning Indigo. Welcome back. You are always missed. You brighten the office," comments Garret.

"Good morning Garret, you know it's always a pleasure to be in your company."

"By the way, you are gorgeous today and, as always, stunning."

"Thank you, Garrett, you are very handsome as well."

Tracker intercedes while licking his lips, deep-set eyes, perfectly tanned complexion, and side smiles. "Garrett is right about how beautiful you are, but he forgot to mention how good you smell."

Now I'm feeling flushed, legs weak, and a smile plastered on my face. Then I look up to see Dillard watching as this scenario unfolds in the office. Dillard gauzes with low cut eyes, turned up a smile while beckoning with his finger for me to come to his office.

"Good morning Dillard," I smirk and smile. Along with wide eyes without uttering a word, I motion with my mouth, "What's going on?"

"Heifer get yo hot ass up in here, shut the blinds and shut the door."

"What?! I didn't do anything. I don't know what it is, but they all hot this morning."

"Uh, hum. I see exactly what's going on out there, don't even."

"Look, Dillard, I can't help if they all want a sample of this hot sauce." As I lick the tip of my pointer finger, then touch one cheek of my ass.

"Ms. Hot Sauce forget about these men up in here. Let's rewind to the other day, what the hell was all that about with Sky at the funeral? I didn't want to say something too soon, just in case you were still a bit sensitive about the death. Besides, you were in London, and I didn't want you distracted by the information I'm about to tell you. But I just can't hold it in anymore. Now you may feel some type of way when I say what I'm about to say."

"Dillard, Please! You always have something to say. You have created me with tough skin. So what is it?"

Dillard pauses and stares me directly in the eyes, "Okay, let me just dig a bit."

"Dillard!" I shout with high anticipation.

"Okay-okay, at the funeral, did you ever find Bullet?"

"Yea...uh well...no...not really find him." I shrug my shoulders.

Dillard is still staring in my eyes with an anxious stance, "What does that mean? You either found him or not."

I see Dillard is a bit anxious, so I snap immediately with an answer, "I didn't find him, but Bayou told me he saw him talking to Sky, then the two of them left together. Why? What's your point?"

"Hold on, hold on, I'm going to tell you. Just keep listening. I know you must haven't talked to Lex."

"Actually, the only people I spoke with were you, mom, and Al when I was away on business. I did call Bullet, but he didn't answer. Why what's up? Why you mentioned me talking to Lex?"

"Indigo take this at face value. I'm only about to tell you about the conversation I had with Lex for you to keep your eyes open."

"What Dillard? Just tell me for goodness sake."

"Lex said your sister and Bullet pulled up to Sky's house shortly after the funeral. According to Lex, Sky was leaning on Bullet as if she couldn't stand. He was holding her up while rubbing her shoulder, then they both went inside Sky's house."

"Dillard, I already knew he left with Sky. I'm only thinking it over in detail because you know how scandalous Sky can be at times, but to Sky's house? I wouldn't have imagined they would have gone there, and why? Otherwise, this wouldn't even bother me. Maybe I'm overthinking it. Did Lex say if she saw when Bullet left from Sky's house?"

"Lex said she stayed close to the window. Lex claimed she tried calling you, but your phone was going straight to voicemail."

My ears couldn't get enough. My answers are swift in response because I need to hear more.

"I may have had my phone off and didn't see the missed call from Lex. I sure wish I would have known. You know it's funny, I didn't think to just ride over to Sky's house to see if they both were there. Why would I have thought of doing that anyway? I tried calling Sky and Bullet, but neither one would answer my calls until I received a late text from Bullet when he was trippin."

Dillard continues without a pause, "Lex claimed she saw Bullet slap Sky on her ass."

My response is a defense on Bullet's behalf. My mind is geared to this being a fabrication of Lex's imagination, "Dillard, but I don't know how true that may be. Lex may have elaborated a bit, or her vision wasn't clear."

Dillard stops speaking, looks at me without a smile, then proceeds to speak, "How you goin' say her vision wasn't clear? Lex and Sky live practically across the street from each other. Lex window faces Sky's house at a slight diagonal, if she said she saw it, she saw it. Lex isn't known to make up prevarications to make a story sound good."

"Again, did she say what time it was?"

"Naw, that's one thing she did not say…was the exact time. The sun was setting. It was almost dark, according to Lex. Lex said she even walked across the street to Sky's house after Bullet left," continues Dillard.

"Wait. What? What did Lex ask Sky?"

"Lex said she asked Sky why is she messing over you, and what was Bullet doing over there? That's when Lex's Filipino side comes out. You know how Lex can get at times. As you and I are both aware, Lex has always been straightforward with her approach. We all grew up together, and she's been like that forever. Anyway, Lex said Sky admitted to being comforted by a man and Bullet, so happened to be that man at the time. Lex alleged Sky said it with a smirk but didn't say anything thereafter. Lex also stated, Sky stood in the door, stared at Lex, and Lex stared back then turned and walked away back to her house."

At this point, my ears are steaming. I feel myself become frozen with no emotion. Dillard sensing my change in demeanor and hurriedly defends the story.

In a charismatic, gentle tone, Dillard states, "Indi, you know your sister is a liar, so take what was said to Lex with a grain of salt. Sky probably said that because she knows, without a doubt, that Lex is going to tell you exactly what she said. Hell, you know what? I'm getting mad too! Shit, I'm trying to keep game face. But right is right, and wrong is wrong. Don't let Sky get to you. She known to do things like this when it comes to you, but keep your composure. She lied so many times whenever you have something good in your life. Handle it right Indi, just handle it right is all I'm saying."

Dillard turns his head, cracks open the blind and looks out the office window then continues to rant.

With each new word, Dillard's voice fills with disgust every second, "You know I keep it raw and real. While you're comforting your mother, that bitch Sky was all over your man. But hold up! While she's flopping her fat ass all on his shoulder and carrying on, his punk ass rubbing all over her shoulder. You KNOW how this kind of shit drives me crazy! I told Lex she should have recorded what she saw. She said she didn't think about it and was too glued to the window, trying to see if anything else would go down outside."

"Dillard, are you sure? I know Sky dirty, but I can't imagine she took advantage of the situation. It's so funny you saying this because Bullet text me way after the funeral."

"What in the world he had to say?"

He texted me, saying, "Are you good?"

That's when I start scrolling through my phone with puzzled thoughts. I verify the time and show the display to Dillard.

"Look at the time. It's after eight p.m. Then he had the nerve to go off in the text because I never responded. Check this message out from Bullet."

I hope that you are okay. I feel you. I know you have seen me texting, but I guess you have something else going on. You don't ever have to sell me a dream, but I understand now. I give up.

Dillard is looking at me with side-eyes. "Look at this piece of shit here. Did you talk to him yet?"

"Not yet, I had my phone off most of the business trip. On another note, ironically, I did receive a beautiful text from Bullet before I left London yesterday. However, we still haven't spoken over the telephone. But I plan on seeing Bullet tomorrow at the picnic. YOU BETTER BE THERE TOO! I'll keep you updated on any haps."

Dillard sighs, "I'm not saying anything extra. I'm just stating what was said to me. The he-say-she-say is gossip, so doing your own investigation is the best thing. Keep your eyes open, girlfriend. It's probably nothing. But you my Sis. I got your back."

That's one thing about Dillard, he always has my back and will fight in a minute if needed. Which, looking at Dillard, one wouldn't think that, especially with his chill demeanor and model clean-cut appearance. It takes something very personal to get him riled up, otherwise, Dillard doesn't get too involved with drama.

I exchange hugs and cheek-to-cheek kisses to Dillard.

Dillard remains in his office, "Okay, Indi, now I need to get back to my work-face. We will talk some more at a later time away from the job. You know people nosey around here. But if you need to chat some more, I'm here."

Dillard is totally different when he's in the office. He believes in staying professional and proper unless it's just him and me with the door closed. I leave out of Dillard's office to return to my office space. I walk to my headquarters, viewing the stacks of papers placed on my desk in my absence. I try to get back in work mode to counter the news I just received from Dillard. Recollections of the funeral can't escape my thoughts. I begin to reflect on who was present. Of course, Al was there. Al sat in the back. He embraced me so tight when all was over. I remember holding on tight to him as his low and calming words helped relax my trembling body. Now that I think about it, Al has been there for me throughout many of my life's challenging moments. Al loves me.

A warm presence with a penetrating stare in my doorway caught my attention.

"Oh hi, Tracker. I felt your presence at the door."

"There's a whole lot more I want you to feel from me," He murmurs.

"Excuse me. What did you say?"

"Nothing, Nothing."

Dillard walking with steaming coffee in his right hand. Pauses in his steps, he then peeks in my direction with one eyebrow raised.

I take my focus away from Dillard and address Tracker.

"How may I help you, Tracker?" Slightly annoyed with the stare and sly comment.

"I just wanted to offer my assistance, however, you see fit. I admire your work and would be honored to be your gofer or whatever possible. If you don't mind, I would love it if you considered being my mentor. I know it's a lot to ask, but think about it. In the meantime, just call if you need me. Would you like some coffee or tea right now? I'm more than happy to fetch it for you."

"No...no...not right now. But thank you. If anything pops up requiring any assistance, I'll keep you in mind. Right now, I'm good. Thank you, Tracker."

Dillard is passing in front of my office with a grin. "So hot sauce, what's up next?"

"Don't say anything, DILLARD! Close my door!" Laughter exchanges from both of us.

Chapter 9

PICNIC

$\mathcal{I}$'m at my brother's, Bayou, when I hear a buzz on the table. The morning message is from Bullet.

"Good morning baby today I can't wait to see, smell, feel, and be in the presence of you."

I can't respond with merely a text. I call Bullet. On the first ring, he answers.

"Hey, baby."

"Hello, Bullet."

In a firm aggravated tone, I blurt, "Bullet, we need to talk! I'm disturbed about a whole shit load of things! And you know what? Mister, you're a corporate figure in the entire equation. I'm not going to ruin today's picnic because of my mother, but there is a bundle of things that's not clear!"

Bullet response is gentle as he attempts to rectify the situation. "Baby, I already know what you want to talk about. I tried calling you, but you have been ignoring my calls. I even texted you a few days ago again, expressing how much I miss and long for you. I stopped calling. I have been waiting patiently for you to call me. Although, I did receive your text declaring how I make you feel like a Queen. Indi, what's going on with us? You never disappeared on me. Now you're disappearing and not texting back."

"Bullet, I could say the same for you. After my Aunt's funeral, you disappeared and no answer until a late text. There's more about that story I need to address with you too."

"I know Indi, it's about Sky, but baby, please believe I have nothing to hide. I can tell you're upset because of how you're speaking to me. But I want you to rest assure that our talk will be good. I'm still yours and hope you're still mines. Baby, where have you been? What's going on with you? I'm going crazy and I don't want to lose you? Baby, I truly am in love with you. I need you. I can't have you upset with me. We will talk in the manner that pleases you soon. May I still text you and you respond like you normally do? Baby, please. I don't usually ask for anything much, but today I need my old Indigo back. I love you, Indigo. I love you Indigo, I love you, Indigo."

"Yeah, I hear you, Bullet."

"Indigo, let's not fight. I'm going to start our morning off good. I'm going to rewind and text you good morning, and we will continue from there. Indigo, do you love and trust me?"

"Yes, you know, I do."

"Good, that's all I need to hear, so I'm going to hang up. We will talk in person, but for now, I'm going to be the old Bullet and I need the old Indigo just for a moment. I miss your morning erotic text. May I have one to start the day? Did I say I love you already? I miss you too. Who's my one and only? Don't answer because you know it's you. Am I getting a smile yet?"

"Bullet, don't start."

"Indi, I'm trying to lighten the mood because I know, face to face, it's going to be a hot and heated conversation if I know you. Please just this one-time let's be the old us. I promise everything will be good once we talk."

"Okay, send your damn text, let's roll with it."

I can hear the smile emanate from Bullet, "Yes...yes...okay, baby. Love you. Bye."

A second incoming text beeps again from Bullet. This time I anticipate the dialogue.

"Good morning baby today I can't wait to see, smell, feel, and be in the presence of you."

"Good morning, Bae, there are so many things that happened. I can't text everything now, but I want to discuss this with you soon. Bullet, I really need to talk to you. I know you want romance this morning. Now it's just hard for me to play along. I'm sorry I've been out of touch lately. Things with us have been crazy since the last time I visited, then after the funeral, your crazy text messages."

"Baby, we just talked about this, I know. We will talk, but I thought you agreed we would be the old us right now. Please baby. I'm going to try it again, Indi. Good morning my love."

His unceasing request makes me smirk. I look down at the last text with a grin.

"Good morning, the time is approaching soon. I can't wait for you to get here. The day and time of me lying in your arms are nearer every second of the day. What I anticipate most is laying back, you on top, face-to-face, lip-to-lip, and control is yours. Then that moment of entrance to satisfy both yearnings of connection of moistness and stiffness. This thought is continuously on my mind. Slow kisses, lips down my neck, to the breast to the cherries, and to just feel the touch of your hands. I'm going to be your ultimate girl toy for one whole night. The night will be intensified with slippery wet dripping thighs from the rain you create. I know how much you crave red cherries, but this time I want you to enjoy the moistness from my lips to your erotica point of pleasure. You will enjoy many more pleasures to come. Whatever you crave, tonight, I will allow you to have an all-inclusive night to remember. I need an immediate fix for my chronic feening. With strong, passionate anticipation, I'm counting the minutes and seconds to be wrapped in your arms."

Bullet is swift with his response.

"Yes, baby, I can't wait to fulfill all your fantasies. I want to feel your tongue. Slow deep sensual kisses, those that get your Peach Butter flowing. Then I want to sail my ship in your deep ocean. You have me in my feelings right now. You drive me crazy. Can't wait to see you soon."

Text exchanges with Bullet get me excited. Today's picnic is at my brother Bayou's house. Mom is already here. Sky is on her way. I decide I will not confront Sky just yet about the Bullet situation because I know how she lies.

Mom, wiping her hands on her apron, walks in the living area where I'm looking down, reading my text.

"Indigo, what are you doing? Stop playing on that phone and come get some thing's done. You know, once your dad gets here, how things are."

"Ma, you know dad is just a jokester and he's just teasing. By the way, I'm not a child, Ma. I am merely checking my phone."

"You're my child! Don't tell me you're not a child. I hate it when your dad starts teasing about how much longer for the food. So I don't want to get irritated with him. Let's just get all this food done and that's one less annoyance I have to deal with today."

"Alright, but where's Bayou?"

"Bayou is prepping the food for the crawfish boil and BBQ."

"Why is Bayou doing all that by himself? All those sacks of crawfish are heavy. His friends were supposed to be here this morning. He trying to do too much by himself: crawfish, corn, potatoes, turkey necks, and BBQ."

"Indigo, he just prepping! Stop stressing over what Bayou's doing. He does this all the time. You know how your brother is. He always likes to get started early. Just come in here and focus on getting our stuff done."

Mom and I are in the kitchen preparing food. Our alone time is when I feel most comfortable expressing my true feelings with her.

I initiate the conversation with my genuine feelings about Sky. "Sky is always missing while we're getting things together. Watch, she comes in super late. Ma, I can't stand, Sky."

Mother pauses from her current activity of chopping onions to give me her attention. "Indigo, now why would you say that? You and Sky always at each other's throat."

I disregard mother's dumbfounded remark. Mother knows Sky is always getting under my skin. I pretend not to notice my mother looking in my direction. I continue to peel away the husk from the corn. I resume talking without hesitation.

"Ma, Sky just goes too far at times, I'm just sick of her."

"Indi, that's your sister, not today with the two of you. Any other time, but Indi not today. I'm still stressing over everything with my sister. Your dad is going to drive me loony. I'm fragile, Indi. I'm really fragile, so please, whatever you and your sister disagreeing about, don't start it here today. No fighting from either one of you, okay."

"Okay, ma."

"I mean it Indigo. You're my child that has her head on straight. Sky doesn't have it together and she likes to be seen and start drama. I don't want to have to kill Sky today with all that acting out. I'm still frustrated about the scene she caused at the funeral."

"I know Bayou told me what you did at the funeral."

"Indigo, where did Sky come from? She knows not to cut up like that at our family gatherings. She barely was with my sister. I could see if she had a close relationship with Star like you did, but Sky barely opens her mouth around family. That's what made me upset. She wanted attention and Bayou catered just to that. I was a bit annoyed with him too."

"Ma, Bayou is always the peacemaker."

"He and his dad are just alike."

"Baby, whatever Sky did this time, promise me to wait to address it another time. Do that one thing for your mother, please. I love you, baby, and don't let Sky strip you. She always has been jealous of you for whatever reason. Sky is my demon child, but I loved and raised you all the same. Each one of you has your uniqueness and I still love all three of you. One just always wants more attention. I felt bad about speaking about her weight at the funeral, but I was just so angry. Today will be a good day, Indi, right?"

"Yes, Ma, I promise I will not be the cause of any drama with Sky."

No sooner after I promise mom those words, here comes Sky ripping through the kitchen with a grand entrance. She stands tall, showcasing a cut off top, exposing her belly, tights with holes, heels, and fashioned accessories. Sky looks like she is ready for a night on the street corner, awaiting a nightcap pick up. That's one thing that sets mom off is promiscuous dressing from her girls.

In a loud raspy voice, Sky states, "What y'all up in here talking about looking all serious and cozy?"

Mom cuts her eyes in Sky's direction, "Sky, don't play with me! Where have you been? There's a lot that needs to get done and you just flaunting around here. And what is that you have on? Just because it's made in your size doesn't mean you need to buy it, Sky. I have told you that time and time again, wear respectable attire and men will respect you. You know what? I'm drained and really don't care what you wear, but you need to do better, Sky. You need to do better. One more thing, I don't want any scene, drama, acting out, bootie flapping, or any other craziness from you today. I mean it, Sky! I already talked to Indigo about the same and now I'm telling you. We will have a decent gathering today and I will be at peace. I'm demanding it!"

Sky retorts with eyes rolling and a frowned face, "Ma, you always lecture me. I never do anything right to you, from my dress, to just who I am. I was running a lil' late, but I'm still here before the crowd is. Dad hasn't even arrived yet."

"Look, Sky, don't start with your woe-is-me attitude and don't tell me nothing about your father's whereabouts. I'm the mother and you will respect me as such. So get your behind in this kitchen and start helping out, instead of standing asking what me and Indigo is doing. I'm not for it today!"

Sky looks at me then whispers, "She's in a rare mood."

I just stare at Sky with disgust. I'm practically burning up inside. As soon as she walked through that door, my heart skipped a beat out of sheer repugnance and anger. I want to just attack Sky. Mother would kill me if I did what I was thinking. The air is tense. Sky must have sensed the repulsion from me and mother's lecture didn't help create a loving atmosphere.

Sky murmurs, "Y'all both trippin'. Today is goin' be a long day."

"What you said, Sky?!" Mother quickly blurts as she pauses and looks over her shoulder.

"Nothing, ma, I didn't say anything."

Mother looks and rolls her eyes away from Sky then proceeds to prepare for today's event.

The atmosphere in the kitchen eventually begins to lighten up after mom put on some music. The volume went up, coupled with singing and dancing while we cooked. Mom has an angelic voice and is always singing around the house. Mom's hip bumps us occasionally to anchor us to join in karaoke-style singing. Time is moving fast. Before we finish with indoor decorating, dishes, and cleaning, family and friends start to arrive in the backyard.

Bayou's home sits on ten acres. He lives in the country: outdoor DJ speakers, screen patio, built-in pool, BBQ grills, and jumpers for the kids. Along with card and domino tables, alcohol is endless. Picnics at Bayou's place are always the best. Bayou even has four-wheel bikes and horses. The kids and adults both enjoy riding the four-wheelers. Occasionally, he takes the kids out one-by-one to ride on his horses. With the entire set up, Bayou still has much of his manicured land empty. At one time, he rented a portion of his property to a farmer, but something went down approximately two years ago and his extra land has been empty ever since.

Bayou has the music cranking. As folks arrive, they walk to the backyard, grooving in sync with the music. Everyone seems to be happy, bringing extra drinks and a few dishes. Bayou and his partners have grills smoking. The smells emulate the classic backyard picnic. There are pails of crawfish, crabs, turkey necks, corn, sausage, and potatoes. Shrimp and fish are frying too. BBQ chicken, hamburgers, and hotdogs are on the grill. The food Mother, Sky, and I prepared is well over enough to accommodate the entire guest list.

Mom washes up inside before coming to join her guest. I go out first then Sky follows. When mother comes outside, she looks refreshed. She had a few drinks while we were inside cooking, which I think helped loosen her from a bit of stress. Dad greets his wife as soon as she walks outside. The backyard is filling up fast; kids are running around screaming and having a good time. Bullet is here and greets me with a kiss.

"Hey baby, you look nice today," states Bullet.

"Thank you. Bae, I'll be right back. I want to go and greet a friend."

"Okay, I'll just be here with Prox."

Prox is one of Bullet's best friends that occasionally come to our family gatherings. Prox became close with my brother through mutually knowing Bullet. However, Prox and Bayou share a similar interest in the stock market, which led them to a good friendship. At times I see Prox at our family events even when Bullet is out of town.

I depart from Bullet, leaving him with Prox. I see Al and want to say hello. Al is extremely comfortable with my family. He knows all the family very well. However, Al rarely attends big family gatherings. If it's a small immediate family get together, he doesn't mind being present. When my family has condensed family gatherings, Al would stay the duration of the get-together and mingle.

Consequently, when I see Al, I know it will only be a cameo appearance. Al is talking to my father when he spots me walking towards him. Al smiles, takes my hand, and pulls me towards him to give me a big hug.

"Hello, Indigo, everything looks good. Your father was telling me how hard you, your sister, and mother have been working all morning."

My father intervenes then shakes Al's hand firmly, "Al, it's always nice when you come around. Man, you need to come around more often. Some time, you and I can have a few drinks while watching the games. I'm going back over here to see what my wife is getting into. I'll let you and Indigo catch up. Don't be a stranger now, Al. This family always welcomes you."

"Thank you, Bernard. I sincerely appreciate that. I'm going to take you up on that offer one day. By the way, tell your wife Namra hello for me."

"Sure thing Al, I'll let her know you said hello."

As my father walks away, Al displays his white teeth with amusement towards me.

"Sunbeam, it's always nice to see you. It looks like your family has a lot of support from family and friends. There are tons of people here. We still need to celebrate the successful outcome from the meeting you had with the Halo's. Besides, I wanted to show my face because I promised I would come."

I am pleased to see Al also, "I'm happy you're here. Would you like something to eat?"

"Sunbeam, I just wanted to see you. You know I'm not going to stay long. I'm not a fan of hanging at events and so forth. I've seen you, so now I'm going to head out. Walk me to the car."

I walk Al to the front where his vehicle is still hot from parking. Dillard and Arlo are arriving while I am standing in front of Al's car.

"What's up, Al? I haven't had a chance to chop it up with you for a minute. At the funeral, I saw you, but there were so many people there. I couldn't get to you before you disappeared. You look good, man, I'm happy to see you."

Arlo is standing next to Dillard. Mid-speech Arlo interrupts and introduces himself. Arlo is Dillard's new steamy item; they are hot and heavy lately. Arlo is everywhere Dillard is. I figure Dillard loves him incredibly because it's a rarity for Dillard to have one guy with him at all times.

"Hello, I'm Arlo, and YOU ARE Alfonsi Sabbatini! I love your arts!"

Arlo stretches his hand out to shake Al's hand. Al shakes his hand in return. Arlo quickly starts to explain his life before Al can say anything.

"I'm in the art industry as well. Please take my card and check out my work. I would love to hear from you with your expert thoughts on my pieces."

Dillard looks bothered. "Sorry Al, Arlo and I will be leaving you to finish speaking with Indigo. I'll see you around later."

While Dillard is holding Arlo's wrist firmly, I hear the back and forth bickering between them.

Audibly, Arlo tells Dillard, "I didn't know you knew Alfonsi Sabbatini. That's huge! He's the best—"

Next, I hear Dillard whisper firmly, "Stop embarrassing me. He's a good friend."

After their short feud, the two of them disappear into the picnic crowd.

Al just gives a half side smirk at me. "Call me later, Indigo, if not tonight, give me a call soon. I'm not going to keep you away from your family much longer. I'm sure you have other guests to entertain. I love you, Indigo." Al bends down and gives his classic lip-to-lip kiss.

"Al, you don't have to gooooo."

"I know Sunbeam. I like having you alone. I don't want to share your time. I don't want you to stand out here to watch me leave. I want to watch you go back in and enjoy yourself Indigo. I will be waiting to hear from you whenever you get around to calling."

"Okay, be safe, talk to you later, Al."

I wave and walk as he sits in his car, watching. In unison, I see mom and dad line dancing along with most of the guests. I figure Bullet is inside because Prox and Bayou are standing around the grill. Dillard and Arlo are sitting at the table next to Lex, Bam, and Edgewood. Edgewood has some chick I've never seen before at the table. Soon after, I start to look for Sky. Without success, she is nowhere to be found. Subsequently, my mind starts to play tricks. I initially surveyed the picnic and smiled until I had dirty thoughts of where Sky could be. Before my entire thought process of negativity synced in, from behind Bullet grabs my waist sharply.

"RA!" Bullet says as I jump and laugh.

"Where were you?" I ask.

"I went to get something out of the cooler."

As he is talking to me, I see Sky dancing in the backyard. I think to myself, "stop tripping." I don't hint to Bullet my negative thoughts.

"Are you enjoying yourself?" I ask Bullet.

"Yes, it's really nice. You know what else made my day nice?"

"What is that?"

"That morning text I received from my favorite girl."

"Who is your favorite girl?" As my face beams while Bullet is crouching down at me. It feels like no one else is around when he and I are together.

"You...you...you...you are my favorite girl!"

"Is that so?" As he kisses my neck, I begin to giggle.

Bam yells across the yard, "Go get a room!"

We both ignore her and snicker.

Chapter 10

JACUZZI

*B*ullet grabs my hand and escorts me inside the house. "I know you want to talk, that's why I am taking you inside."

Inside is quiet; all the guests are enjoying the food and festivities outside. Bayou's house is huge. I want no interruptions when talking to Bullet. The master guest room will be the most secluded place for privacy. In this particular room mounts a Jacuzzi tub right in the middle. There are small couches and a massive bed.

"Let's go into Bayou's guest room." I take over the lead, and now I am escorting Bullet into the mini-master suite. We sit on the small love seat in the room.

Bullet speaks first, "Okay, let's talk. You start."

"Bullet, what happened with you and Sky? Why did you leave the funeral with her and went to her place? I have more questions, but let's start with those two first."

"Indigo, Sky called me over while I was coming outside to ask you a question. I walked over to her, then she was upset with tears and asked me to take a ride with her. Indigo, I swear I didn't know she was going to her place. We went inside, telling me how she was feeling bad because of your Aunt's passing. She started to drink. I told her I was leaving, but she kept asking me just to listen-"

"Wait...this doesn't make any sense. I'm your girl, and instead of being there for me, you were there for my sister as she's drinking and having a pity party. Then you weren't answering your phone?"

"No, Indi, I didn't know you were calling until later."

"How would you not know I was calling if you were supposed to be with me? This shit is not adding up Bullet. Why would Sky tell Lex she needed comforting from a man and you fulfilled that void?"

"She said what! Indigo, I don't know what Sky told you or Lex, but no void or anything else was fulfilled, I promise you that! When did she say that? I had a feeling this was going to end up with some drama."

While Bullet and I are dialoguing, my mother peeks her head into the guess room. "Indigo, is everything okay? You and Bullet not in here arguing, are you? Indigo, remember what we talked about earlier."

"Yes ma, I know. We are not arguing. We are just talking."

"Okay, both of you need to come out and enjoy the picnic. You two can talk later."

"Alright ma, I'm coming out soon, but please, I just need a few more minutes with Bullet in private. I promise we are not going to argue."

Mother gives me a nod of approval and shuts the door behind her.

I resume the chat, "Bullet, this conversation isn't over. I promised my mother no drama of any sort. I'm very disappointed, but I choose to believe nothing. I can't say where my thoughts are right now, but let's just move on from this for the time being."

"Indigo, before we go back out, may I ask you a question?"

"Yes, what is it?"

"Who was that guy you were talking to in the front of the house?"

"Oh, he's a long time friend."

"Friends kissing you on your lips is okay lately?"

"Bullet, it's not what you think. He's just a friend, and he's always just done that. It's basically nothing." I shrug my shoulder, walk away and then Bullet grabs me.

"Indigo, I trust you, but there's more to this story that needs to be discussed. I don't like it. Why I never knew about this? You have secrets?"

I pose the same question as Bullet did to me earlier, "Do you trust me, Bullet?"

"Yes, I do, Indigo. But I don't trust men."

"Bullet, we both have things we candidly need to discuss. For now, let's get out here before my mother returns. Let you and I continue to trust one another until we can get some things cleared from both sides."

Bullet looks a bit dismayed but says nothing except, "Yes cleared."

As the conversation comes to an end, Bullet reaches out to hold my hand. I place my palm in his as a gesture for a truce. Together hand and hand, we walk toward the door to leave out of the master suite. Still holding hands, Bullet swings me back into the room. He flings me around until my back is pinned against the door. Bullet looks deep into my eyes. I feel the heat of his body as he slowly lowers his head to allow our lips to become adjoined as one. I position my head to greet his kiss. The kiss starts with just a peck, soon after the small peck blossoms into a full-blown tongue exchange. Bullet is kissing me, he locks the door and proceeds to guide me further into the room. Bullets kiss remains locked to my lips as he walks me backward. With continued warmth and loving connections, we are taking small steps in the cozy chamber. Our touches of mouth-to-mouth affection decide to take a break. I then open my eyes. I am in total disbelief when Bullet pulls from his pocket a shriveled up yellow rose petal. The surprise is wrapped in plastic from one of our past dates.

"Baby I placed this in my pocket to always think of you. Indigo, all I think about is you. This yellow rose pedal reminds me of our times together. Not only intimate but laughs shared too."

At this moment, I feel a warm sensation all over. I tune out the sounds from outdoors. I only see and hear Bullet; nothing else matters. The one flower is enough to melt away any distractions. I imagine the room is filled with fresh scented yellow roses.

Bullet removes the yellow rose petal out of the bag and tosses it into the Jacuzzi water. With a flick of a switch, he turns the Jacuzzi to full speed.

I dash over to throw my arms around his neck, giving him another kiss. I turn on the soft sounds of jazz. With only instrumental sounds, Bullet extends his hand to welcome a dance.

He knows I love to dance. I quickly kick off my shoes and then grab his hand. He pulls me in closer as our bodies begin to sway to the tunes of the instruments.

I softly utter, "Bullet, I wish this could go on forever. But we must leave out because my brother or anybody can come knocking at any time."

Bullet hushes my concerns, "Indigo, let's just go with the flow. I've missed you. I'm not worried about any interruptions. For this short moment, I have you in my arms, and I'm not letting go. I need this, even if it's only a few more minutes. Don't worry baby, let me hold you, you take me to that place. In exchange, I hope to take you to another place for just one moment."

Bullet takes the lead and begins to guide my body in the direction he wants it to go. His grip keeps getting tighter as our bodies move in even closer. All of a sudden, I take the lead away from Bullet. Since Bullet commanded control earlier, he doesn't put up any resistance. He allows me to have my way.

We make our way over to the Jacuzzi. I begin to walk him down into the whirlpool bath. Bullet looks down at his soaked pants leg as he slowly emerges in the water. We pause for a moment when we reach the step that enables us to see eye-to-eye. I lean in for yet another kiss, then proceed to walk him down the steps. As my feet submerge into the water, my sundress clings to my body. More of my sundress becomes soaked from the propelling water jets. We are in the middle of the Jacuzzi, fully dressed, kissing, and swaying to the music. I push Bullet back until he sits in the water. Then I kneel until my head is in his chest. I stretch my head up to initiate more kisses. As the kiss becomes more intense, I remove my dress straps off my shoulders slowly one-by-one. I continue until the dress slides off into the water.

My hands glide down under the water to remove the buckle of Bullet's pants. By the expression on his face, I know he has anticipation. I look directly in his eyes without a blink, removing his pants slowly yet eagerly. I manage to pull them off without difficulty. After I'm left with thongs and him in his boxers, I face Bullet then climb in between his legs. I press my uncovered breast up against his chest. Bullet grabs me by the waist and pulls me in. I see Bullet getting ready to exert a word. I slowly place one finger over his lips and say, "Ssshhhhhhhhhhh. No words."

The moment is intense; Bullet follows instructions without uttering a word, things are getting electrifying. As the kissing continues, Bullet softly caresses my breast with his hand. With the desire of his kiss, my head tilts back, causing the ends of my hair to get soaked. Bullets kiss starts at my lips, slowly leading down. The kisses are endless, following a path to the back of my ear. The smooches end back down my neck to greet my breast. At this very moment, he can feel my hand moving inside towards my prizewinner. With a simple touch, I feel how hard I'm commanding his love warrior to a perfect stance. I fully reveal him. The clutch from the palm of my hand becomes firmly positioned around his stiffened pole. My inner portion of my hand continues its unyielding grip by beginning to move in an up and down motion. I raise myself ultimately off his chest, exposing my breast in full sight. Bullet takes one breast in each hand, rubbing them softly. He places each nipple into his mouth in an alternating fashion, allowing a short span of tongue playtime. Besides having my hand continuing with an up and down motion, I softly place my lips, followed by slow swirls of my tongue to the middle of Bullet's chest. This motion of licks and nibbles to his chest reaches up to the peak of his chin. The nips don't cease until I reach around his neck, followed by settling behind his earlobe.

Bullet exclaims, "This feels so good."

I continue by kissing back down his chest. I don't stop. I keep going until I feel slippery leaks from the tip of his penciled point. I take advantage of this moment by rewarding Bullet. My lips lead down to encircle the full head of his shaft. I sense Bullet looking down at me. That's when I know Bullet can feel my lips around the head of his long handle. I glance up to see Bullet focusing his eyes on my lips. I proceed to open my mouth and then slide it into the depths of my throat.

Bullet lets out a loud sigh. This rewarding moment is gifted to Bullet for a few minutes before he rolls me over. Now the roles are reversed; he positions me with my top facing up. Bullet begins to suck my breast, and simultaneously his finger is grazing the inner walls of my love canal. Bullets kisses lead straight to my chest, down to my stomach, then down to my sea of love. Although we are in a Jacuzzi full of water, it is something about his touch. I know he can feel the slippery moisture that is generating from the feelings of sensual gratification.

Bullet faintly states, "Let's get out. I want to taste you."

We don't make it far. The water is dripping off the both of us. I fetch the nearby towels and stack them below us. Eagerly, Bullet takes the drying covering and wraps me dry as he lays me over the small floor pallet. Our love connection continues with Bullet fingers gravitating back into play.

Bullet states, "I finally reached my destination."

Bullet takes my clit, places it between his lips, and occasionally sucks, giving it some attention. I spread my legs as he spread my lips apart to get a more in-depth and better taste.

Bullet murmurs, "I can hear your soft moans. Baby, keep giving it all to me."

Finally, I want more. I take both my hands and wrap them around his head to position him right where I want him to take station.

"Right there, right there," I keep repeating.

This moment is everlasting. Once more, Bullet rises to reach my lips to lock our lips together and, once again, the kisses become very intense. Bullet remains between my legs. I begin to rub my venus butterfly against his hard rod. My cream canal flows laboriously from his love touches, the kisses from his lips, and the hard pointer I always long for entry.

As Bullet prepares to penetrate my wet candy kiss, he begins to thrust in a forward motion.

"I'm ready to have some of that Peach Butter now," Bullet says in a whisper.

My counter movement leads my body down to meet his. There is a sudden exhale that overcomes me. Bullet enters into my Peach Butter. I welcome every bit of it by expelling an unceasing increased amount of love liquids. The juices are an exciting way to express how much his love anchor is missed.

We both begin to motion for the pleasure of one another. As Bullet comes down to position deeper inside, I pull up to welcome every inch. Bullet looks down at my face as we are making love.

I bellow, "This is exactly what I needed, just to feel you. I don't want this ever to end."

We find ourselves in multiple different poses seeking increased feelings of passion. Our love tease began in the Jacuzzi, soon after to the floor, eventually creating new positions in the bed. From the first moment Bullet climbs inside me, our bond becomes interlocked and spiritually stronger. Our love tides are undeniably chained as one. Throughout this union, we switch to different positions ignoring any outside noise from visiting guests. Each time Bullet pulls up, I welcome him back in. Something as simple as small talk became something more with fervor. Being in the presence of Bullet weakens me anytime he touches me.

Finally, we bring our moment of thirsty passion to an end. I straighten up the room so our moment of love will go unnoticed. Bullet and I freshen up before walking out of the room. I tie my hair up to a high bun to camouflage the moisture in my hair. Both of our clothes are damp. My dress is the most notable. However, I ring my sundress out as much as possible. Thereafter, put it back on without a second thought. Bullet and I both look at each other's wet attire and laugh. Bullet grabs my hand again, and this time, we leave the mini-master suite for good.

Bullet and I return outside together, by this time, it's dusk. Mom looks my way and smiles. I walk away for a minute to fetch a needed drink. I see Bullet walk up to Sky with words being exchanged. Sky walks to the front yard while Bullet follows. Once I see those actions, I follow suit to the front yard too. I witness Bullet standing next to his car, speaking firmly to Sky.

I startle both of them when I approach them. "Bullet, what's really going on?" I'm so angry. I feel myself yelling.

"Sky tell your sister the truth!" Shouts Bullet.

Sky stands there with no words. Bullet starts to yell at Sky to stop spreading lies, but Sky remains silent and just stands there. Bayou must have heard some commotion and comes to where the three of us are standing. Bayou sense there is a problem.

"Hey Indi and Sky, Mom in the back talking with her friends. She is tearful right now, talking about her sister. Mother will completely break down if she knows the two of you are out here bickering. Dad will have a fit if he sees this going on. Indigo and Sky stop it!"

Sky just walks off.

I look at Bullet and Bayou.

I tell Bullet, "We will continue later, as stated earlier."

Bullet agrees, "I think it's a good time for me to go Indi. I hate to be lied on."

Bayou shakes Bullet's hand. "Thank you for coming out, man. There's lots of food to take home."

"I'm good, Bayou. Thank you for opening your home. The picnic was nice. Sorry for the late mishap. I don't want to upset anybody."

"Be safe out there on that road. I'll catch up with you later."

Hand departure and half hugs are exchanged with Bayou and Bullet before Bayou heads back to the picnic.

"Baby, I'm sorry about what was told to you. Honestly, I love you, and only you. I don't know what Sky is trying to do. We can talk about anything. I want to have a heart to heart sit down. Baby, we have been distant since our coastal trip. Wedges are being built, and we can't continue this way. As a matter of fact, there's an old school concert coming up. Let's have a date night and start fresh for a day. So Ms. Indigo Trinity Savoy, would you like to go on a date with me? I'll wear my Kango, and you wear your big square hoop earrings. We will get down to Slick Rick, Doug E. Fresh, Dana Dane, and all the old schoolers. Whatcha say? Do I have a date to take with me?"

"Of course you do. I have to go practice my Running Man, and Cabbage Patch moves."

"I love you, baby. Call me when you leave or better yet, you know you can come over anytime too. You have a key."

Bullet whispers in a chuckle, "We can continue what we started earlier tonight."

"Shh..."

I snicker, "Thank you, Bae, maybe. I probably will just stay out here at Bayou's house for tonight. Love you too."

We have an intimate kiss before I return to the picnic. Sky and I make eye contact. She's sitting alone and looks pouty, but I ignore and refuse to allow her to ruin my night. As the picnic begins to come to an end, mom walks up and says I want all my children around me.

Mom is in a happy place.

She looks at us, "I want to thank each of you for making this a good event. There was no confusion amongst us, everyone complimented us on the food, and expressed how much they enjoyed the picnic. My sister would have loved this. She always loved being around people. I know our family isn't perfect, but we family. That's important to know—group hug. I want a sincere hug too. Come on honey, you too. I love every last one of you. I need you guys! Love you."

"Love you too, ma."

Mother with teary eyes goes up to her allocated room. I go to the mini-master suite. Sky decides to leave.

Early the following morning, we all plan to depart from Bayou's country living. No sooner than I am getting ready to leave, Al arrives at my brother's house. I'm startled to see him in the driveway.

I walk up to his car, "Al what are you doing here? I wasn't expecting you."

"Indigo, I just needed to see you."

"Okay, but you drove way out here to see me? I could have just came over, or some other arrangement could have been made."

"Indigo I didn't want it that way. I wanted to see you this way. An unexpected arrival is the best. Indigo, is anybody here with you?"

"No, Al. What are you talking about? I'm at my brother's alone with my family. You're acting strange, Al."

Al has his stern face unmoved by my words. He nods okay then kisses my lips once again. Al says nothing else. He gets in his car, turns on the ignition. Thereafter, he looks at me. With a faint tone, he states, "Love you, Sunbeam." Al departs, before the rest of my family comes outside to notice his presence.

Chapter 11

CONSENT

*B*ullet and I talk about everything, but we never talked, in detail, about the coastal night of rejection or the scar it created for me. Our past discussion about the subject would only consist of him saying, "I just wasn't ready again." Despite that, the previous few nights have been good. We shared a wonderful time at Bayou's picnic. A few days later, we attended an old school concert, went out to eat, playful hugs and kisses, and then fell asleep side-by-side as we cuddled throughout the night.

Today Bullet calls, wanting to speak seriously about the coastal night.

"Indigo, baby, we need to discuss your feelings about that night openly. Things have been different ever since. I want the old us again without friction, doubts, or insecurities."

I listen. After taking note, I take it upon myself to write Bullet a letter before he arrives. Mainly this document is intended to get his manly ego aroused.

"I agree. I anticipate seeing you soon. I have something for you to read once you get here."

"What is it?" I can feel his smile.

"You will see."

Shortly after dialoguing, a few hours later, I hear the key turning to open my door. I see Bullet with a pleasant expression. I have a glass of wine in one hand. I'm barefoot wearing matching bralette and boy-shorts along with a mid-thigh robe. He enters slowly with a cunning smirk.

"Girl, I'm so excited to see you. Oooo, and I miss your sexy ass. Come here."

"Please…you just saw me the other day." While giggling, he runs and picks me up.

"Wait don't, I'm going to spill my drink. Take off your coat. I will deliver your letter shortly."

"I will read that letter later."

"Nope, it's mandatory that you read it now. It can possibly save you from certain fears or discomforts."

"Fears?"

"Yes, fears!"

"Sit back, and I'll give it to you soon."

Bullet sits on the chaise elevating his legs. He takes the letter to read out loud.

Chuckling, "No, read it to yourself please. I already know what it says. Please understand, don't feel any obligation after reading it."

With a smug grin, sunken eyes cut my way. Bullet reads the letter to himself.

> Dear Bullet
> I know it's hard to talk about some things, but I am a
>   great listener. I've heard your concerns about
>   "being ready." Please read and respond on or
>   before the end of today. If you don't want to sign,
>   I understand.
> Love always,
> Indigo

SEXUAL CONSENT FORM

Special Attention

To: Bullet

From: Indigo

·1. **Indigo** presents this Sexual Consent form
to **Bullet** requesting permission to have sex on
multiple occasions.

·2. **Bullet you are not obligated** to sign this
Sexual Consent if you feel any apprehension,
fear, or simply feeling intimidated by any possible
sexual adventures that may be presented
by **Indigo Savoy.**

·3. **Bullet** don't feel obligated or pressured to sign
this Sexual Consent form immediately. Take your
time to contemplate your sexual concerns and
desires.

·4. To be clear with this Sexual Consent form,
foreplay is highly recommended. Occasionally
foreplay can be wavered if warranted.

·5. To avoid any misunderstanding, both
parties, **Indigo and Bullet**, may discuss any
special request ahead of time. This is to assist any
of **Bullet's** uneasy feelings.

·6. **Bullet**, if at any point during the sexual act or
you simply begin with increased anxiety, you may
rescind this Sexual Consent form at any
time. Remember, there will be no pressure from
Indigo. This consent form is to make YOU
comfortable with sexual encounters with Indigo.

·7. To stop the sexual act at any time, let's adopt the

code phrase **FIREBALL**. Fireball will represent 'this is too hot to handle I need to stop NOW!' In other words, which will be understood as **'IMMEDIATE STOP,' 'I CAN'T HANDLE NO MORE,'** and **'I SURRENDER.'**

·8. The above consent is to share open communication regarding sexual encounters between **Indigo and Bullet.**

·9. This Sexual Consent form is a gentle attempt to have mutual respect and assist in placing **Bullet's** emotions in a state of relaxation.

Disclaimer: **DON'T WORRY INDIGO WILL BE GENTLE.**

I **Bullet** hereby declare that I am in sound mind and without pressure or embarrassment give full-unprejudiced consent to **INDIGO** to engage in adventurous sexual intercourse, as mentioned above. I am not under any distress. I am not under any alcohol, drug, or medical influence and have full understanding that the code word **FIREBALL** may be stated by myself **BULLET** at any time to alleviate any possible intimidations I may experience. I **Bullet** understand that this Sexual Consent Form is valid for MULTIPLE sexual encounters, including on a consecutive/concurrent basis between both parties: **BULLET and INDIGO.**

Day 22 Month of June Year 2019
Bullet Signature: **Bullet**   Indigo Signature: **Indigo**

P.s. Hi, Bullet this is Indigo. I know you have voiced
concerns about being ready for our next
encounter, but I promise it's not going to be
anything to fear. I'm your friend first, although
very FIERCE in bed. Therefore, I understand. I
will step it down just a notch to set you a little bit
at ease. I PROMISE!

Love,

Indigo T. Savoy

IMMEDIATELY AFTER READING, BULLET'S HEAD POPS UP. HE RUNS
up to me, tosses me over his shoulder while heading to the
bedroom. He pins me to the bed. I'm laughing so hard,
attempting to fight him off without success. He pins both arms to
my side as he straddles on top, preventing my lower half from
breaking loose.

"Oh you have jokes." Nose-to-nose Bullet is snickering.

"Well, I wasn't sure if you would ever get 'ready,' so I had to
reassure you that you have an escape at any time. You can use 'fireball' and there will never be a misunderstanding ever again."

Bullet keeps his position, "I'll never 'fireball.' You are starting
something that you not goin' be able to turn back from."

My facial expression displays gitty optimism. I look at Bullet
directly in his eyes with a lackadaisical remark, "For some reason,
that is the least of my worries. I'm not the one putting up my arm to
surrender for the night, such as you already know. I'm quite the
opposite. I can never get enough. More and more is my only
vocabulary."

"I got your 'more and more.' I have more and more and more to
give."

"I hear ya talking. I need you to be about your business and act
upon your words. Because at this point, all it is, is just hot air from
your mouth."

At this moment, I feel soft kisses on my neck that lead to my lips.

Surrender is immediate as I wrap my legs around his waist, my arms rubs his back.

He pauses to remove the robe then whispers, "Baby let me give you a massage."

First, the robe, then the twosome garment, is removed. Each rub paralyzes me. The massages are warm with the stroke of his masculine hands. Heated wax drizzles from the nape of my neck down to the middle of my back. This ritual of rubbing, massaging, and touching every crease of my body lasts without end. His touch sets loose the juices, the moistures of my body wanting more. My body is ripe, wishing, waiting, wanting him to take a bite.

He turns me to my back, lifting me to meet him interfaced body to body. Drunken with wine, it feels like I'm floating. Soon after, he pins me against the wall. Thighs to his face, licks of his tongue caress a sample of my cherries. With a long sigh, my head slightly tilts back and my eyes roll-up. I rub his head, wanting this moment never to end; my moans are a sweet harmony. I feel every lick, nibble, and breath. Overly ripe juices leak all over. Down the wall, I slide to greet his entrance. One teardrop falls with the first thrust. His strong arms, legs, and sensual movement make up for any ill past doings. He then brings me to the bed. Through the window, the moonlight creates a shadow of his body.

Touches to my upper inner thigh elevate my anticipation of Kama Sutra positions to follow. I hear deep expirations with every stroke of his hands. The continued upward movement of entrance causes my breaths to escape with loud audible exhales. Like a well-orchestrated dance, slow motion movement rocks my body. Sweat drops cover my frame with heat blazing from our adjoining bodies. I reach for the nearby towel to wipe his forehead, stare for a moment then fall into a deep trance of exhilaration. Our frame becomes one and our soul's interlock; he feels, sees, and is part of me. While rocking and riding, he leans over to nibble my ear, down to my neck, one hand teases my nipples while the other bracing his stance. The night is consumed with lust. The gratifying moments continue. In the transition of our climax recovery, I decided to give him a sensual massage in return.

"Come here, my Stallion. Stretch your body on this couch, close your eyes, and relax."

I remain moist from our earlier ardor, wanting more, but willing to reset the moment. I am in hopes to extend the time we are sharing for more.

Bullet looks, soon surrendering to my request with a beam of delight. Scented rubbing candle oil is the treat in store for him; he rests on his back. One flicker from the candle, the music low, and the atmosphere is erotic. I dip one hand to collect the heated oil. In an opposite circular motion, I caress his chest then slowly glide down the side of his upper body.

"Baby this is the shit! I love this!" Bullet bellows.

Kneeling beside, Bullet suddenly pulls me on top of his oiled body. Our lips connect.

I stop, "No, I want to finish your massage."

With no verbal response, his eyes remain close, broadly smiles, and releases his grip.

"Turn over." I request.

I proceed to climb on top. Simultaneously massaging Bullet's shoulders with warm oil and straddling his back, I lean over to nibble down his ear to his neck. He moans with each rub. My position then reverses to target the lower half of his body. Soon after, I removed myself off his body. Softly requesting, he turns back in his original position, exposing all of him with his face up toward the ceiling. The rubs of hot oil wax start from his neck down to his belly button. Finally, to the part I want the most. I provide warm oil rubs, then succulent kisses, and sucks to follow. The first dip is warm. The wax melts to oil with each massage, engaging both hands as the rub is slow on his skin, caressing each sac one-by-one, then slowly up and down the stiff pole, hoping for a soon entrance into my Peach Butter. Each rub, massage, and caress equates a groan. In addition, with up and down motion, there is growth and widening of his erected pole.

The third rub in, Bullet movements pause. He opens his eyes, looks at me with a dreadful stare. Swiftly asking, "Indi, is that the wax you putting down there?"

I know he is enjoying the pleasure of each caress because of his body response with every touch.

I reply with a loving, "Yes."

Bullet doesn't respond. Instead, he quickly attempts to get off the divan. As an alternative, he is imbalanced and doesn't move with steadiness.

He tumbles off the sofa, runs into the bathroom, yelling, "IT BURNS, IT BURNS!"

In a state of confusion, I hurriedly run behind, asking, "What's wrong!"

He doesn't give a direct response except for the continuous chanting of, "IT BURNS, IT BURNS!"

As soon as he gets a steady grip on the knob, Bullet turns on the cold shower. He jumps in without testing the temperature. Puzzled, I witness the facial contortions of agony.

I run-up to the shower to get a closer peek. Seeing Bullet hold his dick in his hand while his face is parallel to the ceiling, Bullet eyes tightly shut, still chanting, "IT'S STILL BURNING!"

I see the anguish across his face and start to giggle. He tries to laugh too, but pain supersedes the chuckle.

"I'm sorry baby; I didn't know that stuff would burn."

Bullet responds, "But it was feeling so good then all of a sudden the heat became so intense. That shit started feeling like fire!"

With my selfish thoughts, I still didn't want the night to be ruined. "I'm so sorry, but is this it for us tonight? Because I was hoping for a bit more..."

Bullet remains stagnant in the shower; I'm standing outside the shower, still peeking in. He nervously laughs. The burning ultimately starts to subside. I'm uncontrollably laughing. With a wedged walk, Bullet tiptoes out the shower.

"Baby that shit is serious. I didn't think that fire feeling was ever going to leave."

"Ba-by, you moved like the Tasmanian Devil! I'm so weak!"

With a roar, he lets out laughs too. "We never using that shit ever again! That pain is beyond what I ever experienced in my life!"

Bullet heads back in the bedroom. I follow as he goes to dry off.

I draw near, kiss his lips, then proceed to kiss and caress his once burning fire.

Bullet looks at me, "Hey, let's finish part two at my place."

"Tonight?"

"Yes tonight."

"Get dressed, and let's go to my place because I have plans."

"Plans, huh? I'm okay with that."

Chapter 12

FIRES

*U*pon arrival at Bullet's house, it begins to drizzle. The outdoor air remains warm and humid with a soothing breeze. Bullet insists we enter through the backdoor. Claiming he has a bunch of boxes by the front door blocking the entrance. I pay him no attention and follow suit to the back. Instead of going inside, Bullet opens the back screened-in patio. He proceeds to remove altogether the little clothing he had on.

Cackling, "Bullet, what are you doing!"

Maintaining a deep stare at me, without hesitation, Bullet reveals himself to complete nakedness. I don't move. I remain under the covered patio avoiding the slight drizzle and ponder what Bullet has in mind. Bullet runs full speed and jumps in the deepest end of his pool. I can't believe him, folding over with laughter.

My steps become minuscule as I cautiously walk toward the pool. He stays underwater for a long time. Bullet can swim like a fish, so his spontaneous act doesn't surprise me.

"Bullet, it's late, and it will begin to rain at any time. Get out of there before you wake the neighbors."

Now he's at the edge of the pool with only his head peeking up. "Baby, I'm just trying to cool off from YOUR wax earlier today. Come in the water, it feels great. You already know my pool is heated, so what's your excuse?"

"No, no, and no! I am not coming in there. You are crazy! I'll just go over and recline in the chair until you cool off."

Bullet burst, "Are you fireplacing?"

"No, I AM NOT FIREPLACING! First of all, the code word is FIREBALL! NOT FIREPLACING! And no, that's not how it works."

"Sounds like your FIREBALLING to me. From what I remember, the contract had a lot to say about foreplay and everything about Indigo being a BEAST. Well, Miss Indigo Beast, I would conclude your lack of participation is defined as fireplacing."

"It's fireball, fireball, fireball! Stop saying fireplacing!"

"I understand, Indi. You said the code word three times. Yes, I counted them; it was three times. So I clearly understand your surrender and apprehension. Baby, it's okay because this Bullet is some type of beast if I must say so myself. Some…meaning my Indigo even gets intimidated at times."

"Whatever Bullet. You are completely cheating. The contract has a totally different meaning."

"Well, I don't know, Indigo. I only recollect what you said about the fire word. I just remember once the word was said, we both had an understanding. I understand, baby. It's okay. I still love you."

Bullet dips his head back under the water and starts swimming back and forth. I get in closer to place my feet in the water. Especially since I know Bullet may be out here for some time, "cooling off." The outdoor breeze feels good. With tons of humidity, the evaporation from the slight drizzle is a pleasant cooling sensation. Bullet occasionally peeps up. He continually pleads with me, trying to persuade me in the pool. My answer remains a firm no. He shakes his head side-to-side with a cheesy grin then pushes off into a backstroke.

"You fooled me. You just wanted to come take a swim."

"Baby, I wanted us to take a swim."

"Nope, you should have asked, and possibly, just possibly, I would have said 'yes.' Since that wasn't the case, I'll just stay here with my feet submerged in warm water."

Before I could finish, Bullet dips under the water and pops up directly in front of me.

"BULLET DON'T SCARE ME-!"

Next thing I know, Bullet grabs me and plunges me in the water with him. I feel like a drowning cat. Reaching the top felt detrimental to my survival. I push him away to swiftly tread to the edge, anchoring my arms and head up for air.

"You're trying to kill me!"

My airway and speech both fight to come out first. Bullet, on the other hand, thinks the dramatic scene is hilarious. Both my elbows rest on the edge, while my breath catches up with my speeding heart. Bullet approaches me from behind and cradles me completely.

"Baby, you know I'm not going to let anything happen to you."

I shove him off. "Get away! I could have died."

Bullet puts on a comical lip puckered face then starts to speak in a kiddish tone, "Awwh I'm sorry baby for scaring you."

"You are completely naked. Now I have a soaked dress, and my hair is a mess. Bullet! I should…"

"You should what? Miss Indigo, what are you going to do to me? Are you going to make me say fireplace-fireball or whatever? As a matter of fact, that's what I want. Make me surrender to you tonight."

Bullet traps me from behind against the wall pressing his chiseled domineering body next to mine. He then kisses down my neck. My body begins to ease.

"Let's have a repeat of the days before similar to what we did at your brother's house."

"No Bullet," in a whisper. I could barely get the words out, "I want to get out of the pool."

Bullet ignores my barely spoken words and proceeds to enter inside me with his standing stallion from behind. Instantaneously I yelp a loud sigh, not anticipating the sudden entrance. Bullet continues the straddle while I remain against the pool wall. His strokes are firm and robust. With every movement, my uncontrolled cries get louder. Bullet is in rare form; my dress remains in place floating upwards in the glistening blue water. The drizzles start to turn into teardrops of rain. Bullet turns me to face him with an immediate entrance once again.

"You see, the burning stopped, and you getting your more and more as requested."

I have no reply. Except to hold tight around his neck, I'm unable to feel the bottom of the pool. Bullet is my only anchor to remain above water. The strokes from Bullet remain steady and robust. He takes complete charge. I accept what he wants without hesitation. My body doesn't refute any of his actions. Instead, it yearns for more. The rain turns into a downpour. I release my grip off Bullet's shoulder and aim toward a warm house.

"Baby, don't get out the pool. I want some more right here and now."

This time I ignore Bullet; I skip seeking refuge. However, Bullet quickly takes flight behind me. Before reaching the patio, he picks me up over his shoulders, initiating laughter from both of us.

"Put me down! Your naked ass is all out. You have no shame whatsoever!"

"This naked ass is hot for you right now, especially since you set me on fire with wax earlier tonight. Then you had the nerve to have some contract written up for me to sign. I have your contract all right for you tonight. Watch you will see what happens to you soon."

"Bullet!"

"Indigo. Oh, my little Indigo. You just don't know it now, but you have started something all because of that clever contract. No more jokes will be coming from you after tonight."

Bullet puts me on a soaked outside lounger. We both are getting wet from the storm. This man is unfazed by the rain. I'm trapped again, now lying on the lounger and Bullet on top. He rubs my hair back, stares me in the eyes, and kisses my lips once. His straddle is immobilizing.

Low whisper, "I love you, Indigo."

"I love you, Bullet."

My soaked dress is a nuisance to both Bullet and myself. The clinging cotton makes it challenging to touch places Bullet hands desires.

Bullet pops off the lounger and commands, "Don't move Indi."

Bullet runs over to the covered patio and fetches me a towel. "I know you a bit bashful while outside. So let's take off this dress and you keep this towel."

The sticky dress is removed and tossed to the side. Bullet climbs back in place, this time with another immediate entrance into my Peach Butter. The grind and movement are electric. Bullet is forceful yet remains gentle.

"I'm not hurting you am I?" I hear.

"No, of course not Bae. It's okay. You make me feel good."

There is something different this time from Bullet. I love the force, the aggression, and take charge as the raindrops glisten off his mocha skin. I hold him tight to join in unison of each stroke. Our bodies interlock. Every so often, Bullet delivers a tender kiss to my lips. The firm kisses, even command attention, climax happens multiple times, each time Bullet takes notice.

"I can feel when that Peach Butter moistens. Keep it flowing and give me more and more."

The rain causes Bullet to maneuver in different poses to settle himself perfectly on top. The new positions make my kitty purr each time. My hands rub Bullets back, starting from the lower crease reaching up to his broad shoulders.

"Tonight, baby, I'm staying in full control. Am I fully satisfying your every desire? No more contracts, right?"

Bullet continues with strong thrust as he commands my confession of saying no to future contracts. The feeling is hypnotizing. I have no choice but to surrender, "Okay, no more contracts. I promise."

The rain never stops, instead joined with thunder and lightning. At this moment, we both know our night rain rendezvous is coming to a short end. Before going in, Bullet continues with his straddle and gently kisses my lips continuously. His tender kisses are a sweet end to an aggressive love entrance.

We both run under the covered patio, grab some robes, and finally step inside the house.

Bullet politely asks, "Baby, do you want to go in the shower together? I have a little bit more I can share tonight."

"No baby, you go right ahead. I need to get my hair together and will go to the other bathroom to freshen up."

"Okay, if you say so, but I will leave the door unlocked just in case you change your mind."

"Thank you, baby."

I proceed to wash my hair and freshen up. Surprisingly, I finished before Bullet. I get cozy in bed before he gets out of the shower, thinking as I lie in bed.

After arriving at Bullet's place as promised, I received more and more that was given all by him. Once he entered my welcoming juice puddle again, the strokes and moans were swift and aggressive yet with passion. Both sexual encounters were soul connecting, beginning of the night was slow and sensual and to top the night, a little burning wax which brought out the beast in my Bullet.

Before the night ends, I begin to write my feelings and thoughts about Bullet. I barely notice when he joins.

Bullet bends over to read what I'm writing.

I command, "Not yet, it's not for reading."

Bullet smiles, "Okay, Miss Savoy."

"Once I'm done, I'll send it over just for your eyes only."

"Indigo, I will be patiently waiting."

Chapter 13

PEACHES & BUTTER

*B*ullet and I lay in bed knowing eventually we need to get our day started. The girls and I have plans. Bullet states he and Prox have a game to attend. Later that night, Bullet and I are to meet back at his place. Bullet is lying on his back as I'm cradling in his right arm. My back is up against his body. Before making my move out of bed, I turn to look at him. Bullet is staring at the ceiling.

"Deep thoughts. What are you thinking early this morning?" I ask.

"Nothing. I'm just enjoying this moment with you. Having you in my arms is comforting. I'm indulging in the moment, that's all."

"Are you sure that's all you are thinking about?"

"What else is there to think my lil' Indigo?"

"Well, possibly you can be thinking of a variety of things."

"Such as?"

Bullet remains looking at the ceiling with an occasional gaze my way. But he mostly did not budge from the intense stare at the ceiling.

"Since you asked, I'm thinking possibly you have last night on your mind."

"Last night definitely is on my mind."

"I knew it!"

"Then why did you ask, huh huh?"

I smirk with his response, "Did the contract make you feel some kind of way?"

"What? Nope, it sure didn't. Why did you ask me that, Indi?"

"If you ask me, only if you are asking. I'll give you a blunt response. So are you sure you are asking?"

"Yes! Yes! Yes! Little woman speak. I'll say it again. Yes, why are you asking?"

"I would like to just point out after that contract I noticed a different side of you. You put on strong and intense strokes last night. So that being said, in my opinion, my contract has you feeling some kind of way. I know one thing for sure I have no complaints about the outcome of the encounter."

"Is that so? Let me reassure you, your contract did nothing to me. I promise you that. Another promise I can make is that, I bet I can make that Peach Butter flow again even more intense this morning."

"Oh, is that so Mr. Bullet?"

"Yes, that is so Miss Indigo."

"Since you think you know everything, let me inform you of some information you may be unaware of."

"Okay, and what is that Indigo that I'm so unaware of."

"You may be unaware that my Peach Butter is already flowing right at this very moment. Just waiting for you to feel a sample."

Bullet remains on his back, blindly stretches his left hand for a touch of Peach Butter flow.

"Did you need verification, or did you just want to feel a sample?"

He doesn't need to respond with words. I see his gun come to a stiffened full stance. His eyes close as he fondles my Peach Butter. I push his hand to the side to straddle myself on top. This would be an excellent start to our day. I climb in reverse cowgirl while gently placing Bullet inside me. I lower myself slowly into him. Then begin to bounce softly. With a light grasp, Bullet grabs my hips. I proceed to bend over for him to receive a full view from behind, then move my body in a wave motion. It always manages to stimulate my G-spot creating squirts of Peach Butter. Moisture sends Bullet to another level. The more moisture without exception concludes with increased pleasure.

Repeat waves create a deep grunt from Bullet; my moans transform into deep breaths and loud sighs. The ripple is a combination of speeds; his movements meet my sway on point each time. I am in full control, which I love. Neither one of us is speaking a word. We embellish for this moment. I proceed to move my body in a circular motion as I feel Bullet speeding his counter. His peak is soon approaching; grinding circles cause us to meet our climax. I release a long sigh. Bullet remains inside of me while I lay flat on my stomach. I need a moment of stillness before I detach. I face him to position our bellies together. He grabs me tight around my back and kisses my lips.

Bullet blurts. "That was superb, baby!"

"I know, right? This the best way to start our morning."

"I was thinking the same thing."

This morning the moisture equates to puddles. I reach for a towel from the nightstand to wipe first then share with Bullet. I leap off Bullet and proceed to the shower as Bullet joins in. We wash each other. I relish in the morning sponge pamper. My phone interrupts my indulging moment with constant rings back to back. I finish up and leave Bullet in the shower to run and answer my phone. I figure it is one of the girls calling. I know I am running late but didn't realize how late it is. Bullet and I lounged in bed, had a quickie, took a shower, and now the clock reflects 12:45 p.m. I am supposed to meet the girls for lunch. I see the missed call is from Bam. I call her back immediately.

"Hey, Bam, where are you guys?"

"Indigo, we are waiting for you at Lex's place. Do you remember we are supposed to meet at noon? Where are you?"

"I totally didn't forget. I'm at Bullet's house and just lost track of time."

"Bullets house, huh? I know what you must have been doing. Were you doing the butty? Ooooh, I know that's why you late

Indigo. I left my friend's house and could have been doing the butty too. But no, I was trying to meet everybody on time. Since I'm always the last one, but not this time, it's all you Indi. Wait until I tell Lex you over by Bullets house doing the butty." With select words Bam accent is profound.

"Bam! Nobody is doing the butty right now! Anyway, it's pronounced booty. I was doing booty!" I laugh on the phone with Bam.

"Indigo hurry up, we hungry for food. Tell Bullet we know he full from eating you out, but us girls need substance too. So get over here, chica apurado."

I hear Bam yelling, "Lex, Indigo is running late because she is getting some butty from Bullet!"

Lex in the background, "Tell Indigo she always with Bullet. Bullet turn is another time. Tell her to come on. I'm hungry!"

Bam returns to the phone after yelling in my ear, "Oooooo mi amiga get your nasty ass here pronto. We not getting dick, so you can't either. Lex told me to tell you we coming over there to pick your lil' hot ass up. Ha! Indigo on the real, I wish I was getting some dick right now too. Shoot, I'm getting hot just thinking about a little dick inside of all this, Bam!"

Lex must have grabbed the phone from Bam, "Indigo!"

"Oh, hey, Lex!"

"Indigo, now you have Bam feeling all over her body talking about you and Bullet. What's going on? Hurry up! You know Bam is always a hot tamale. We don't want to get her started. Are you really having sex right now?"

"No, Lex! I-AM-NOT-HAVING-SEX-RIGHT-NOW! You and Bam are so dramatic. I'm on my way. Give me no more than thirty minutes tops. I promise I'll be there soon. I'm practically walking out the door as we speak. Bye, sis."

"Okay, sis, see you soon," Lex responds.

I hang up with my girls and laugh to myself. That Bam is always thinking sexually. It doesn't take me long to freshen up, get dressed, and quickly dash out the door. Before leaving, I kiss Bullet goodbye.

"I'll see you tonight, okay, Bae."

"Alright, my love, have fun, and be safe."

"You too, tell Prox I said hello."

No sooner I'm down the street, I see a text message from Lex.

"Meet us at The Jazz Brunch and Spa off Magazine. We will get our table. By the time you get there, we should be seated."

While driving, I just hit 'k' in response to Lex's message.

I manage to keep my word and arrive right at the mark of thirty minutes. Valet parks my car. I see the girls waiting to be placed in the Mardi Gras Spa Room. Coming to The Jazz Brunch and Spa has always been a delicacy treat for a girl's day. We pamper ourselves, chat, eat, and get treated like royalty. This place is phenomenal. Each room has a theme. Once inside your chosen space, everything you need is available for a relaxed day. We mostly always reserve the same package.

Our package entails six hours of pure heavenly treatment, including brunch and jazz. Space consists of a small pool, ice water dipping area, along with an adjacent Jacuzzi. There is a glass ceiling that can open and close per the client's request. Inside there are lounge chairs with décor of the theme room with a touch of French appeal.

We usually decide on the same personal package. The Honey Suckle body wrap is my all-time favorite. It leaves my skin feeling baby soft. The wrap description is best explained by having your body cocooned in a full-body wrap with exfoliating crystals applied to the surface. This rejuvenates my skin. I always leave that extraordinary body wrap for the last sixty minutes of our spa reservation. Therefore, my baby smooth skin lasts for a more extended time. Also included in our package is a sixty-minute massage with warm basalt stones. The ninety-minute rejuvenation glow facial is always a must too. The pool, ice water, and Jacuzzi have a purpose as well. It is included as a complimentary optional therapy known as the Comedy and Tragedy Masks water therapy. The idea is to take a dip in the hot (Tragedy/Melpomene) Jacuzzi then shortly thereafter plunge into the ice-cold water known as Comedy or Thalia. Rarely do I take advantage of this therapy. I always find it challenging to get into the ice water. Therefore, most of the time, I pass on it, although occasionally, the other two girls claim high accolades about their experiences.

Lex spots me first at the door. Her hand raises high to signal their seats.

"Hey, girls."

"You finally made it," Bam exclaims.

"Yes, I told you thirty-minutes tops and see I made it before you guys even went into the Mardi Gras Spa room."

"Luckily, our reservation can be moved back this afternoon. I had to call the Spa once I noticed you were running late. They even waived their normal fee since we are frequent customers," states Lex.

"Thank you, Lex, for being so organized."

Feeling compelled to address my tardiness, "I apologize guys for being late."

Without a filter, Bam barks, "No need! If I was doing what you were doing, trust me, no apology from me. Needs have to be met so you can be in the right frame of mind. Besides Indigo, you know Bullet needs as much fixing as possible. He always yearns for you."

"Bam, what makes you think Bullet always yearns for me? Most couples are this way."

"No, Indigo, I disagree. Most couples are not like you and Bullet. Bullet looks at you a certain way."

"That's why you say he yearns for me because of a look?"

Lex joins in the conversation, "Indi, I would have to agree with Bam on this one. Bullet gazes at you. His eyes can't hide what he feels. I noticed it but never said it to anybody. Indigo, Bullet loves to get fixed by you. That's only my opinion, but eyes don't lie."

In dismay, I respond, sounding shocked, "Oh my goodness! You, ladies, are crazy. I never noticed a certain look from him. But if you guys say so, I guess it may be there."

Before we finish our discussion about Bullet stares, the polite host beckons for our party to enter into the Mardi Gras Spa room. Upon entering our space, we are greeted with white wine, fresh strawberries, and cheese by a well-groomed handsome gentleman. Each one of us is starving. Our decision is always to start with the meal then delight in the package deal. Besides, we have six hours reserved.

"Thank you, sir, for the refreshments," Lex states to the gentleman.

"You are most welcome beautiful," the gentleman states in response.

The guy smiles at Lex as she smiles back in return. Both of them seem to engage well. The young man finally looks at Bam and me and addresses our presence.

"All you ladies are looking lovely today. I hope you enjoy our wonderful Spa experience."

Then he looks back at Lex, "If you need anything, please don't hesitate to contact me. Here's my card please use it at your leisure. I'm always around."

Lex reads his name on the card out loud, "Your name is Cade? Cade Talmadge is very unique. I never met someone with that name. I like it."

"Yes, mam, it is. I look forward to possibly hearing from you. Your name is?"

"I apologize, my name is Lex. These are my other two girlfriends, Bam and Indigo."

"Nice to meet you, Cade." Bam and I say our greetings simultaneously.

Bam then cups her arm into Lex's elbow and addresses Cade.

"Well, Cade, it's a pleasure to have met you, but our time is counting down. We need to get our meal in and start our Spa moment. Lex tuck away Cade's card, and she will call you later. In the meantime, we're starting our spa day."

Cade eagerly apologizes, "Of course I'm sorry if I was holding you ladies up. Please be seated, and I'll assure your waiter will be out to greet you shortly to take orders. By all means, I guarantee your time will not shorten on my account. I make sure all my guests are not shortened by any means."

Bam bluntly asks, "Are you saying you own the place?"

Cade responds with a smile, "Yes, I own it with two other brothers. I occasionally serve my customers when I am in town. That keeps me in touch with what the customers like or dislike. Today I have the pleasure of serving you lovely ladies for a brief moment. However, if any additional services or needs are not met, please do not hesitate to contact me. I gave Lex my personal card."

Bam responds, "Well, well, I'm feeling like we getting the VIP treatment. Thank you, Mister!"

"It's just plain, Cade. You don't have to address me as Mister. But my last name is Talmadge. Again, ladies, it has been a pleasure. Please enjoy your experience. And thank you for being a loyal repeat customer."

I am curious, "How did you know we were repeat customers?"

"It is part of my job to stay aware of my loyal guest. You make this company. We appreciate you."

Cade nods his head to each of us, then, he signals the waiter to come to take our order for lunch.

"Seems like you have an admirer, Lex," I state after Cade leaves.

"He is handsome and has a beautiful smile. His teeth even glowed. You know I love a man with a beautiful smile." Lex states.

"Call him Lex, that's all. If he answers and talks, then feel out his energy. I sure noticed he didn't give us a personal card. Only you, Lex." Bam points out.

"I'll see maybe he's a good guy. I may give him a call." Lex responds.

Subsequently, we seek out getting something to eat. The waiter is kind, and politely takes our orders. Each of us needs some spoiling today.

I love sweets. Dessert first, then my main dish, today's dessert is dulce cheesecake with praline topping. My meal is crawfish stuffed shrimp with creole rice. Most of the time, I don't finish my food because the portions served are always a healthy amount. But this time, I surprised myself and completed every bit. The girls also order seafood but decide to skip on dessert. I feel satisfied, not stuffed. I like to relax while getting all my pampering without the feeling of bloat.

After we finished eating, we sat around for about thirty minutes to allow our food to settle. This is usually the best time for our girl talk. I sip on Conte Priola Pinot Grigio Gold Italian wine, my girls do the same. Hydration is vital before our massage. After girl chat, we hydrate on tons of water. Our first pamper session begins with a facial.

However, before pampering, Bam kicks up the conversation about Bullet again.

"Indigo, I have a question for you."

"I have an answer for you Bam, spit it out."

"Why Bullet calls you Peach Butter?"

"Wait. What?! Where did you hear that?" I was shocked that Bam knew about Bullet calling me Peach Butter. It was nothing I ever shared with the girls. They knew I called myself Peach Butter because that's my signature name for poetry night. However, it's also a name of sensuality between Bullet and myself.

"Come on, Indi. You thought we never heard him whisper to you about Peach Butter in a seductive tone? I know it's your poetry pen name, but Bullet says it differently. It's not like Bullet can whisper very well. I've meant to ask. Since we all here, I'm curious."

Lex joins in, "Yes, Indigo, what's the story behind it?"

"Well, since both of you all in my business, I'll explain where the name Peach Butter came from."

The girls become wholly engaged, waiting to see what I have to say. I poise myself before speaking, look at each one, and we giggle.

I begin my disclosure regarding my signature name.

"The first thing is loyalty and trust before he gets introduced to this Peach Butter. Once all walls have been conquered, and we know where we stand, that's when he gets formally introduced to Peach Butter. When you first meet a guy, that's when both of you are feeling each other out. It's no rush for the goods. For me, it's too much of a bond to exchange on that level of love. Peach Butter is held sacred to me. I honestly can say not many have experienced the true essence of me until we get to another level of Peaches and Butter."

Bam intervenes, "Indigo, I need to be in complete understanding. We are talking about pussy, right? So are you holding out?"

"No, Bam, it's not that I'm holding out. And no, it's not just pussy. Let me finish. I just have to connect with the person I'm with before sharing my Peaches and Butter. See, the difference between you and me is that your hot ass always wants sex. On the other hand, it's not the sex I need or want. I look for that connection. Something lasting. You know something that you can feel. For me, I need it to be palpable then I feel free. I can share everything with whomever once the connection is there."

"Indigo, you have completely lost your damn mind! How you honestly going to say you don't want just plain old hot steamy sex. Especially when they start kissing, feeling, and oooo! I can't resist Indi. I don't know how you do it. But I don't need no connection for some good dick to be up in this!"

Lex is nodding her head side to side in dismay, "Bam, you have to want something more at least every once in a while. I understand where Indi is coming from. I feel that way sometimes too."

"Lex, we know your very conservative ass not giving out nothing too often. There's no need for you to explain your position on this topic. But Indigo?! Chica, I had you read all wrong. I thought you been sharing your Peach Butter a lot more than I thought."

"Maybe I am, and maybe I'm not. We all grown, right? But you right, it's not being shared with many. Thank you very much."

"I don't see why not. I would!"

"Of course, you would," Lex says while rolling her eyes upward.

Lex inquires more, "Indi, how did you come up with Peach Butter?"

"Well, as you all know, Bullet gets a good taste of me every now and then. That translates to him, placing his face, penis, or finger in some slippery places. Peach Butter is how it moistens and allows him to glide right on inside. Sometimes a teaching session is needed. With Bullet, I had to teach him to enjoy the Peach Butter by taking his time and move in slow motion. This makes him crave and moan for it. The Peach Butter drives him crazy. I love producing it because when he goes crazy, it bounces onto me. We have fun with it. That's been my signature name for years. I do know every last ex always remembers my Peach Butter, and don't hesitate to ask for more," smirking.

"Indigo, I love the way you explain it. I'm going to get me a signature name too. I think I will adopt the idea of placing loyalty and trust at the forefront before popping off anything. It's such a basic yet important thing."

"Now, both you bitches tripping!" Blurts Bam.

"For goodness sake, you are not walking down the aisle with every dick. It's mere sexual satisfaction. I fix his or her needs and move on! That's right, got damn it! I said it! It's not a big deal! All this soul connection is way over my head. I guess I'm not at that level fairly yet like the two of you."

"Bam, you do whatever makes you happy. You asked, so I explained why Bullet called me Peach Butter. Although, I introduce myself as Peach Butter every time I recite a poem. However, there is history and a reason. Now both of you know. But I totally understand you, Bam. It's just not my way. However, I'm not saying I wouldn't have a one-night stand. If I ever chose to do it, then I will. Everybody has to live his or her own life. Whatever that may be."

"Now you talking my language Indi. Live your life, baby!" Replies Bam.

"Yes, true, we all have to live our life with our own set of rules," states Lex.

We continue to sip and sit for a second as we reminisce about our old night flings.

Lex looks at her watch, "Okay, ladies, we need to get started on our facials. Our time will move fast. Believe it or not, we been eating and chatting for over an hour and a half. Drink your waters to stay hydrated."

Bam answers, "Okay mom, we will."

"Bam seriously, drink your water, especially you, Bam. We don't want any repeat mishaps." Lex replies.

"I know, Lex, I will. You know I hate to get rid of my buzz, but I already know about hydration, hydration, and hydration. I have it all covered. I promise I will hydrate and not get sick this time."

The last girl outing Bam didn't drink water. She became nauseated, had a headache, and kept stating she felt light-headed after our spa day. Lex attributed her illness to dehydration. Ever since then, Lex makes sure we all drink our water and stay hydrated.

While at the Spa, we continue with girl chat and laughs. The experience is relaxing. Lex speaks about her new guy friend, Elijah, she met a few months ago, and Bam has tons of stories about multiple people in her life. It is all in good fun without judgment; we love each other like sisters. The spa day ends with us meeting up at Lex's place. Of course, we have more drinks, girl chat, and giggles. Around ten p.m., I leave the girls to head back to Bullet's house. He calls to check on me occasionally when I am on the road. When I pull up to Bullet's place, he greets me at the door.

"Baby did you enjoy yourself with the girls?"

"As a matter of fact, I did. I needed that girl time therapy. How about you? Did you enjoy hanging with Prox?"

"Man let me tell you about Prox. This dude had his girl…"

I am so worn-out it seems like Bullet words are hazy.

"Baby, you're tired. You're not even listening to me. After your spa days, you always get drained. I'll run your bath water and wash you down, so all you have to do is sit in the water. I'll take care of the rest."

Bullet leaves my presence. I hear him in the bathroom running the bathwater. I head to the bedroom to undress and put on my robe then lay on the side of the bed to relax for a minute until he is ready for me.

"Okay baby, I'm ready to bath you."

I don't hear Bullet when he comes to fetch me for my bath, nor do I get up. Bullet discovers me crashed across the bed. He realizes how exhausted I am and allows me to remain asleep. I barely remember Bullet coming to bed. Ultimately he cuddles me in his arms for the rest of the night.

Chapter 14

KISSES

I wake up searching for water. Lex was right about the massage dehydrating you. For a moment, I have to gather my thoughts. I feel dazed. I look around and feel Bullet holding me from behind. Then I remembered I came over to Bullet's house after leaving Lex's last night. After the spa, we started drinking more wine by Lex. I guess I didn't drink enough water the second round at Lex's place. I vaguely remember leaving Bam stretch across Lex's sofa. Lex insisted I stay the night, but I decided to drive to Bullet's house anyway. I peek over and see the clock, reads 5:20 a.m. I try to slide out of bed to get some water. My movement in bed does not go unnoticed. Bullet clenches me tight.

"Good morning, baby. I almost thought I was dreaming. What time is it?" Bullet asks.

"Good morning, Bae, go back to sleep it's five a.m. I'm just getting up to get something to drink."

"I have some water over on my side of the bed. All you have to do is climb over me to get it."

"That will not be a problem." I say with a bit of thirst-quenching anticipation.

I see the water Bullet is referring to. There are a few unopened bottles. I lay on top of Bullet to reach for the water as my robe slightly opens. I remain on top of him consuming the whole bottle. Afterward, I stay on top of Bullet to relax for a moment. Bullet unrobes me completely. Then begins to rub the entire backside of my body. We lay against one another. Bullet is bare; the rub of his hand up and down my spine is soothing, sending me back into a deep sleep.

A few hours later, Bullet movements awakened me. I am still lying on top of him when he is attempting to move me to the side. Before he exits out of bed, I ask, "Where are you going?"

"I was going to prepare you some breakfast."

"No, just get back in the bed for a little longer."

Bullet submits to my request and joins me back in bed, wrapping his arms around my waist. I move in closer to enjoy the cuddle time. The first few moments are silent.

I break the silence, "I fell asleep on your story last night. I apologize, but I must have been exhausted."

"Baby that's okay. The story was not important. It was about Prox and his girl. Honestly, I don't even want to talk about Prox right now. He made me so angry with that crazy girl he's dating. She is causing him so much stress. Everything about her is drama. I can say this much, our men's outing was not only with the guys. That's all I'll say about that situation for now. It seemed like you had a better time than me."

"Yesterday is the past, but today will be much better. All my time is dedicated to you, and we will have fun. Forget Prox and his drama girl."

Bullet glares in my direction, "Of course we will have fun. Besides, you have something much more valuable than Prox could ever give."

"Is that so?"

"That is so, period."

Leaning in Bullet advances to give me an early morning kiss. Then pounces on top of me.

"This morning is almost as beautiful as you are, my love."

"You are so kind to me."

I feel my bladder filling up from my early morning hydration. I raise my head and give Bullet a quick peck to the lips.

"Baby I have to go pee. The water caught up with me."

I grab my robe and scurry to the restroom. I take a look behind to see Bullet staring my way as I leap and move with swiftness. When I return to the bedroom, Bullet's position is unchanged. He begins to get up once he notices me entering back in the room. I pause him in his steps to give him a long morning kiss. My robe remains partially draped around me. I then pull him close to me. I lower myself down in bed, simultaneously pulling him on top of me.

Facing each other Bullet, proclaims, "I'm so glad you're here."

"Me too."

Bullet hands gradually go down my side to rub down to my thighs. I lift my leg's up and wrap them around his waist.

"I got you!" I state as I begin to tighten my legs around his waist.

"No you don't!"

Bullet shifts his hands under my arms and begins to tickle me. We start wrestling, rolling around in the bed with laughter. I manage to pin him down. Shortly after, he reverses the pin. I can't control the outburst of laughter as he tickles me under my arms. It's like I'm a little kid being placed in submission to say "uncle."

Pausing, "I miss this Bullet."

"Me too, I miss this a lot. The only reason I let you get me is because you had on red panties last night. You know, I love red."

"No excuses. I beat you fair and square. Give me my props." I state.

A surge of laughter repeats from both of us.

"What do you want to do today?" Bullet asks.

"It doesn't matter."

"I still have that jug." Bullet said with a smile.

"What jug?"

"The one we filled with the different things we could do for a date."

"I thought you would have thrown that away."

"Why would I do that? We can both pick one thing from there and do it." Bullet insists.

"That sounds fun since we never had a chance to play around with it."

"Okay. I'll go get the jug," Bullet continues as he moves toward the closet.

Bullet returns to the bed and lay for a few moments longer. I shift myself close to him to rest in his arms as he begins to open the jar. My head is settled on his chest when I notice his heart racing.

Bragging, "Your heart is beating so fast. I whipped you until your heart is about to jump out your chest."

"No that's just my heart missing you and knowing that its other half is right here on top of me."

"Yeah okay whatever. I know I gave you a bit of a challenge. I can wear you out so quickly."

"Indi, you think you bad, but remember, it was my choice to submit to your pin downs. Don't forget that. I didn't want to bring out the real BULLET in me."

I chuckle and roll my eyes. "Okay mister BULLET. Please don't let that loose."

"Alright as long as you understand that Miss Indigo."

"On that note of me understanding your true BULLET SIDE, let's open our slips to see what's in the jar."

Bullet and I both place our hand in the jar to retrieve a slip of paper. Bullet allows me to read my sheet first, then he follows.

"My slip states 'streetcar adventure.' What does yours say Bullet?"

Bullet pulls the slip out as if he's getting ready to read who won a Grammy award.

"Dunt-tu-d-dun…and my slip reads."

Bullet pauses for a moment.

"For goodness sake, what does the slip say Bullet?"

"Wait, wait, patience, dear. You read your slip your way. Now it's my turn to read my slip my way. And the jar declares the winner of my slip to be, PICNIC!"

"A picnic? I hope the weather will be nice. Well, okay, a picnic it is too. Let me take a quick shower. Then, I'll be ready."

"While you are in the shower, I'll get breakfast started."

"No Bae, it's okay. Let's eat breakfast while we are out. I promise I won't be long, then we out of here."

"Are you sure you not hungry now, Indi?"

"Yes I'm sure. We will find something later."

"If you fine with it, I'm okay too. I'll just go get dressed and be ready when you get done."

"Sounds like a great plan."

Bullet and I start our day after refreshing ourselves. Today will be our date of adventure. I love exploring my city as a tourist. We decide to park our car Uptown on Carrollton Avenue then hop on the streetcar from there. The oak trees keep the area cool. The day is almost perfect, with a slight breeze of wind blowing. After getting on the streetcar, shortly after, I suggest Bullet and I eat at The Camellia Grill for breakfast. The Camellia Grill is packed but well worth the wait. After finishing our breakfast, we hop back on the streetcar. Bullet stretches his hand to greet mine when boarding the trolley. We decide to sit in the middle. He wraps his arm behind my seat. Along the ride, we admire the aged oak trees with our window slightly pushed open.

As we exit, a whisper greets my ear, "I love you, Indigo."

I turn around and smile. We get off the streetcar to arrive at our final destination in the French Quarters. I immediately grab Bullet's hand. The French Market is my first destination. I'm always fascinated to see different things representing my city. Occasionally, I purchase a bag full of gifts. I pretend to be a tourist. As I'm looking around at the various vendor's Bullet disappears for a moment. His disappearance doesn't bother me. I figure he went to get a seat because I look around for long periods.

All of a sudden, Bullet pops up.

"Baby would you like to get some beignets from Café Du Monde for an early morning treat?"

"Bullet I'm still stuffed after eating breakfast from Camellia Grill, BUT you know how much I love beignets. So yes, let's get them to go."

The line at Café Du Monde isn't too long. We agree to get the powdered treat to go. I can't resist taking a few bites of the warm

French doughnuts. Before reaching our next destination, I ate all the beignets. I wipe the sprinkles of powdered sugar that covers my shirt. The day is beautiful. The city is alive as usual. I see the psychics setting up early morning camp. We stroll the area until reaching Royal Street. I look around in many art galleries, sample pralines, and engage with the locals by dancing to street music. After walking so much, Bullet and I decide to rest on a bench near the Riverwalk.

"Indigo are you having a good time?"

"Yes it's a nice day."

"After we break for a while, let's go and relax on the lake to enjoy our picnic."

"Bullet! We forgot to stop and get something for our picnic. What kind of picnic will we have without food? Let's get something to snack on."

"Don't worry, Indigo. I have everything taken care of."

"Oh well, excuse me. I guess you're taking charge of the situation. Let me step back and allow you to be in control of this situation Mr. Bullet."

"Very good, Indigo. You are learning. It's been rough teaching you, but you're learning."

I tap Bullet on his arm.

"Whatever! You can't teach me anything. As you would say, I just submitted because I wanted to."

Bullet and I walk up to Canal Street. Bullet calls for a car service to drive us down to the lake. The driver is talkative and very amusing. She even has complimentary jello-shots for us. The driver keeps us entertained the whole way down to the lake. She drops us off to the lake, where we instantly see a place to use as our temporary home base. Bullet is prepared. To my surprise, in his backpack, he is carrying picnic goods. Bullet takes out a blanket and anchors it to the ground, along with some chocolate-covered strawberries, grapes, and blueberries. In addition to the fruit, Bullet also has a bottle of wine with two wine glasses. Everything is cute. I am proud of him. Lastly, he reaches in his backpack to pull out a Mask and place it on the blanket.

"You bought me a mask?"

"When I left your side, that's when I purchased it for you. I figure since you collect them, you could add one more to your collection. I wanted to surprise you."

"I love it! Thank you!"

"Of course, anything to place a smile on my baby's face."

Bullet and I enjoy a glass of wine. I take small sips as I nibble on the strawberries. Bullet pulls out his Bose speaker to enhance the mood.

"Thank you, baby. I genuinely love this."

"Your welcome, love."

We laugh, sip, and relax; the lake is getting crowded. One particular couple walks by. I hear the lady tell her mate, "That is so romantic. Why don't you have romantic outings like that for me?"

I smile to myself then look in Bullet's direction. He must have heard the same remark and smiles as well. This part of our date is relaxing. The wind feels good until an overcast starts to move in.

"Bullet, it looks like it may rain. Do you think we need to start wrapping up?"

"Just a little longer Indi. I'll call the car service in a few."

"Bullet, I think you need to call the car service now because I feel a slight drizzle."

Bullet is moving slowly to gather everything. So I intervene to assist in moving things along a little faster. The drizzle transforms into an immediate downpour. Thundering starts. Rain soaks us before we finish putting everything away. I run to seek shelter under the nearby gazebo. Bullet runs under to join. He removes his shirt to place over my head.

"Bullet! Eww, your shirt is soaked. Thank you for the offer, but it's useless. I'm going to pass on the shirt."

"Indigo, you know I'm a romantic at heart. This would have been a bit more romantic if my shirt was dry, right?"

"Uh, yes, Bae. But at least you're trying." Laughing as I speak.

Bullet phones the car service. The sky opens up on us even worse. The wind is blowing the rain in both directions, resulting in getting us more soaked. I am eager for the car service to arrive.

Once the driver comes, he has plastic covering on his seat and towels in the back.

"Man thank you for having these towels in here." Bullet addresses the driver.

"I notice the rain is pretty heavy and figured some of my passengers might find the towels useful. I'm happy I could assist in keeping you two dry."

Shivering in his arms, we finally arrive at our parked car. Both of us are drenched. Bullet starts the heater immediately. As we sit in the car, the rain comes down harder. It is to the point that visibility is impossible. The parking lot does not have a single soul here. Bullet decides to sit before departing. He puts on love songs to play repeatedly. Bullet goes into the character of a musician by serenading me with the songs. I love it when he does it. My facial muscles stay fixed in a single position of smiling. While singing, Bullet leans over to give me a couple of kisses.

The rain, music, and heater are running full blast, fogs up the windows. It sets an extreme sensual mood. From a peck, we then go into a full French kiss. Bullet moves in closer to wrap his arm around me. I lean over to make the kiss more accessible. I detect the moment shifting. Bullet glides his hand to my knee as he gradually starts rubbing my leg. The kiss is intense, resulting in me slightly releasing the car seat back.

Bullet hands begin to move further up my sundress, slowly. He maneuvers his hand until he reaches my Peach Butter. With the seat tilted slightly backward, I reposition my body to the edge of the seat and recline back. As Bullet caresses my Peach Butter, he gently spreads my legs further apart.

Bullet whispers, "You don't have any panties on?"

"No. I removed my rain-soaked panties earlier."

Bullet delicately places his hand on my mons pubis, one digit seeks out my clitoris. Immediately the kisses get heavier. As his fingers move down, he gently slides one inside a bit deeper. The kiss stops for a moment. My head leans as I release a low sigh. I proceed by grabbing the lever to lay the car seat all the way back. Bullet's finger starts to move slowly in and out of my Peach Butter, while the other hand begins to stroke my breast. He is sending me in pure excitement.

Bullet slides my sundress up, proceeding to suck on each breast. My hand grasps the back of his head. Bullet makes circular motions over my nipples. While his fingers remain in my Peach Butter, creating more lubrication. Bullet proceeds to move his head between my thighs. With his finger rubbing in and out, he takes his tongue and smoothly runs it across my pencil point, soon after Bullet begins to suck on it. I become a waterfall; the soothing music continues to play in the background while Bullet is rock hard.

Bullet sucks my cherry until my leg begins to shiver. Wanting more, I open up wider. He stops only to launch into kissing me again. As we are kissing, Bullet slides nice and smoothly into my Peach Butter. My wet juices are now flowing all over him while the rain continues to tap on the roof of our car.

The love sounds drowns out the low volume of the music. I place my feet on the dashboard, as our lovemaking becomes more intense. Bullet drives in; I mimic his upward movements as a welcome. We both reach our point of satisfaction. Bullet proceeds to rise, however, I grab him by his lower back and whisper, "Don't move, just stay right here for a second."

Bullet leans in to kiss. I look at Bullet and give off a beaming smile with the rain still beating on the car's roof.

As heavy breathing tames, we decide to tackle the rain cloud-burst and journey home. The weather shifts to a drizzle as we arrive at Bullet's house. I feel sticky, wet, and want to relax. Once we arrive at Bullet's home, he runs over to my side, opens my door, and extends his hand to help me get out of the car.

"I'm going to take a quick shower so I can get comfortable." I say once inside.

"Can I join you?"

"Sure."

We undress and climb into the shower. Bullet has a habit of whenever he touches me, it turns into a massage. Getting into the shower is no different. As he washes my back, he gives me a mini massage as well. We begin to reminisce about the day.

"Indigo, I indeed enjoyed our day."

"Me too, it was very nice."

Once we are done showering, I head to the living room to relax.

"Are you sleepy?" Bullet asks.

"No, just thinking."

Bullet takes my hand to lead me over to the chaise.

"Lay down." Bullet states.

I don't hesitate. I respond by kicking off my slippers and laying across the chaise. Bullet takes out the massaging oil. Once I see the massaging it, I know I am in for a treat. Bullet starts by giving me a deep tissue massage. His massage always relaxes every inch of me.

"You don't have any music on? I'm shocked." I say to Bullet.

"No, just wanted to talk."

"Talk about what?"

"Us and our future."

"Okay."

Before we start the conversation, my phone starts ringing. I pick up my cell, take a look then put it back down. I'm sure Bullet is wondering who is calling me at this time of night even though he doesn't say anything. I can distinguish his demeanor changes. He pauses while giving me a massage then proceeds without a word. It's almost eleven o'clock, and I have no explanation at this time for a late call.

"I thought you wanted to talk," I inquire.

"Nah I'll just talk to you about it later." Bullet states dryly.

Thirty minutes past then Bullet grabs the remote and turns on the music and dimmers the lights. We are enjoying quality time. Interrupting the mood, my phone begins to ring again. I pick it up once more, and without answering it, I put it down.

I look at Bullet and simply say, "It's getting late. I better go."

"Go where? I thought you were staying here."

"No, I'm going by my mother's house. She is expecting me," I state as I'm getting myself together.

I notice the frustration on Bullet's face, but I continue to get dressed for an unexpected departure.

"Don't be angry. I'll call you when I get there. And I will see you tomorrow, okay?" I reassure Bullet.

Bullet hesitantly says, "I guess okay."

It was such a beautiful date today, I'm not eager to leave, but I feel it is necessary. Bullet features of frustration are taking a new shape of anger. He still doesn't say much. He watches me get dress then walks me to the door.

"Are you sure you don't want to stay?" Bullet asks one more time.

"No I'll see you tomorrow."

I kiss Bullet on the lips, but his lips don't respond to my pucker. His face is bland without expression. He tries to remain poised, but the energy in the room is stale. I know he's upset.

Bullet opens the door and watches my car as it drives down the street. Once he goes inside, I know what just transpired will bother Bullet. I'm sure I initiated mixed emotions and deep thoughts for him. I am not able to honor my word to call in the timeframe of thirty minutes. I'm sure Bullet has many thoughts running through his head and will eventually pass by mother's house if I don't make a call. I intend to call as soon as I settle to my next destination. However, for this moment, I can't ponder on Bullet. I have other things on my mind; the calls are unusual. I don't go straight to my mom's house, although, I plan to go eventually before the night is out. Bullet calls me multiple times. I don't answer because I just can't right now.

Bullet leaves a voice message stating, *"Indigo I'm sitting here with many mixed emotions. Thirty minutes have passed, and still no call from you. I begin to worry because your mother only stays a few minutes away. With so many thoughts running through my head, I pick up my phone and dial your number over and over again. I need to know if you have made it safely to your mother's house, and I need to ask you who was calling you so late? I dial your number, but the phone is just ringing and then goes to voicemail. Something is not right. Each time I try to call you, the phone goes to voicemail. Now I'm beginning to worry frantically. Another twenty minutes went by after the first thirty minutes. In my head, I'm saying to myself, "What's going on?" So I get in my car and ride to your mother's house to see if your vehicle is there. To my surprise, there was no car in the driveway. I quickly get out of the car. I could not think straight due to this feeling in my gut. I figured well since you are not at your mother's house, you must have come back to my place. So what do I do? I open my door and maneuver around the house only to see that you are not there. I grab my phone and redial your number. No answer, this voice mail comes on again. Can you please give me a call when you get this message? Indigo, you leave me no choice but to have questions, frustration, and rambling thoughts. Who was that calling you? I need answers, Indigo. Answers."*

Chapter 15

CHOICES

*L*ate-night repetitive calls are unlike AL. I can't let Bullet see I am becoming anxious with the unceasing calls. Once I depart Bullet's house, in a dash, I instantaneously phone Al while in the car but no answer. I continue to call back-to-back and still no response. My original thinking is to call Al, talk about whatever is on his mind then stay at mothers overnight just as I told Bullet. But Al is not picking up after his multiple attempts of calling me. Something has to be wrong. The last time Al made a late-night call, it was for urgent reasons that required overnight hospitalization and thereafter a long recovery in rehab. Worst-case scenario thoughts start to birth in my mind. I can't just ignore the fact he was trying to call me multiple times, especially since it is odd behavior for him. At the moment I decide to go to the city and check on him in person. The drive seems forever. Bullet even calls while I am en route to Al's place. I decide not to answer since I can't clearly explain the situation.

Parking in Al's driveway, I see the house is dark. I notice there are no outside lights on and no lights inside. Before long, it is past midnight. I quickly exit my car, not remembering if I turned off the ignition. Once at the top of Al's stairs, before entering, I look back to make sure my car engine is off.

I enter with cautious call outs, "Al? Al, are you here?"
Silence.

My heart begins palpitating with uncertainty. My palms are becoming sweaty. Beads of sweat develop on my forehead. Suddenly my callouts become louder.

"Al!"

At the very instant I'm yelling out Al's name, my phone begins to ring. I utter a shrill scream. It is Bullet calling again. I look down at the phone and immediately silence the ringer. All at once, I'm shaking; my mind is cloudy with thoughts of fear. I'm sure Bullet is at a loss. I want to explain everything to Bullet, but I just can't at this time. I'm focused on making sure Al is okay. But where is Al?

Gently I'm tiptoeing around the house examining every room. The silence in the house is becoming thicker. My throat is dry, my sweaty palms are growing numb, and I feel empty. Al is not here. Formed thoughts are toying with me. Where is he? Did someone call 911 because he was ill? Did he drive himself to the emergency room? I dial his number repeatedly frantic with no response each time.

Thereafter I text Al, "Please call me immediately."

I turn on lights throughout the house and then contemplate calling Momma Deah. Momma Deah may have some information, but it's late and getting later. I don't want to worry, Momma Deah, especially if it's nothing.

I ponder. I'll give him twenty more minutes before calling Momma Deah.

In the meanwhile, I call Al's phone again, with no response. I start to look around the house to see if I notice anything out of place or any hint of Al even being home. Al's house is tidy, nothing out of place. The bed is made up without a trace of him sleeping in it. I look down at my phone, all I see are the missed calls from Bullet. No message, text, or hint of Al attempting to contact me. It's been twenty minutes now.

Waiting forty-five minutes later, I decided to call Momma Deah. Momma Deah's phone rings several times before her voicemail kicks on.

"Hello, praise the Lord for he has given you breath in your body to make this call, this is Delores Keys. I'm not available now, but maybe later, if the Lord says the same, we will have the conversation you wanted. Until then, have a blessed and glorious day."

I leave a message on Momma Deah's voicemail. "Hello Momma Deah; this is Indigo. I apologize for calling so late. I am just checking on Al. If anything happened, please call me. It's probably nothing. I'll call you in the morning. Love you, Momma Deah. Talk to you later."

After leaving the message, I instantly think, I shouldn't have left a message. Momma Deah never listens to her voicemails anyway. She has Al or me listen, then delete them. I'm the one who helped her set up the original voicemail. What am I thinking of leaving a voicemail for Momma Deah? I am just desperate for answers. Momma Deah will at least see a missed call from me and possibly call if there's anything going on. Now Momma Deah will be worried too if nothing is going on. I'll just call Momma Deah again in the morning if I hear nothing from Al.

As I wait on Al, I go into his room and lay across the neatly organized covers. I start dozing off. I place the phone directly next to me just in case a call or text comes through. The long day with Bullet has me tired, therefore dozing off is easy. A vibration comes across that wakens me. It's an app notification. I look around a bit confused about my whereabouts, and then swiftly remember I'm at Al's place. Eyes blurred, I attempt to focus to see the time on my phone. The time reads 3:42 a.m.

I begin to worry and think. It's after three a.m. and still no hint of Al, especially after his multiple calls.

No soon as I'm looking at the time, I hear the front door opening.

"Indigo?" I hear calling.

I recognize Al's voice then I run to the front door to see what's going on.

"Al?"

Al appears shuffled, eyes red, along with a staggering gait, "Hey Sunbeam."

Al's face tilts to the side, eyebrows raised, and looking puzzled.

"Sunbeam what's wrong? You look troubled."

"Al, what are you talking about? You had me worried! You called me multiple times nonstop. Then when I returned the call, you didn't answer. I thought something was wrong because you never call me late nights, especially repeatedly."

Al just glares at me with a minute grin.

I'm becoming frustrated.

"Al have you been drinking? Why were you calling me? What was that about?"

"Sunbeam, you don't have to worry about me," as Al is staggering toward the living room. Al passes by me and pats my shoulder while keeping his head looking straight ahead. He manages to kick his shoes off while in route of walking.

I blurt, "Al! Are you listening to me?"

I discern Al is not paying attention. He has been drinking and obviously is okay. I intercept Al before he settles to the couch. After that, I manage to escort Al into the bedroom and aid in undressing him for the night. Al has layers of clothes; it is challenging to remove some clothing when he isn't assisting. Finally, I have him down to his underwear and consider my task of undressing complete. I tuck Al under the flush comforter then decide to leave. Al pauses me mid-step by extending his hand to grab mines.

With bloodshot red eyes, Al looks at me, his speech is somewhat slurring, "I love you Sunbeam there is so much I want to tell you, but I just don't know how to say it. I called you tonight for various reasons."

Al's face appears tired and worn. The conversation becomes intriguing. Al manages a smile my way with a glow in his eyes. I reverse my plan to leave then lay on top of Al's covers facing him while he's facing me.

"Sunbeam," Al says almost in a whisper. Then he clears his throat and repeats himself.

"Sunbeam, I love you very dearly. You have to know this already. I have so many things in my life that are positive, including you. But you and I are not on the same page. At times I look for things in other people to replicate what I see in you. Sunbeam, we need to discuss the future. The present is good like it is, but the future is uncertain, meaning business, friendship, or any other possibilities."

The dialogue introduced by Al is unforeseen. Al and I avoid talking about "us" in any form or fashion ever since the one and only try. It's a taboo of some sort. What we have is good. I have always been fearful that our bond will be ruined if we discuss anything regarding our current state of a "relationship." It has no definition. It's almost a tacit knowledge shared amongst us that we will always be what we are without explanation if nothing is ever addressed. My response is not well calculated. It is something that I express from my heart.

"Al, I know you love me, and you have to know I love you too. We have been together for many years in the fashion of 'us.' There is no clear definition of what we share, however, it is unique and sincere. The mutual concern for each other is heartfelt. You know when I'm happy, sad, tired, frustrated, or whatever emotion I may be experiencing without me saying a word. Now that's special. At times I don't know what to define 'us' as either. In the past, we were attempting to make it more, but secrets, should I say, ended that attempt of a union. It's funny because although we went through that sour moment, here we are today."

"Sunbeam, you are right. I know how you think, that's why I never present what I want to you. But this time I am saying something for you to think about. I want you to think about OUR future. Where do you see us going and in what fashion? We will always be special friends. You asked why I called you so late last night, right? Initially, I called because I wanted to talk about business. I received notification from Mr. Halo stating they are interested in signing a huge contract with us. Luca is requesting that you come back to London. He would like you to go back to London to speak to other partners. Hoping to pique their interest also to sign additional contracts. Mr. Halo spoke very highly of you and offered substantial perks if you agreed. I wanted to share that information with you immediately and celebrate. This is what you have been working hard to achieve. You were helping me, but also new avenues and connections began to open for you. I'm so proud of you, Sunbeam. After you didn't answer, I decided to celebrate on my own. I also realized that when you didn't answer, I missed a huge part of my life, which is you. Sunbeam, I love you and want the best for you."

Al's eyes are beginning to get heavy, his word slurring increases, and he can't complete all his statements. I watch him close his eyes and fall into a deep sleep. I still smell the lingering stench of alcohol exhuming from his pores. I don't have an opportunity to lecture him about why he didn't answer any of my calls or at least respond with a text. Neither am I able to express my excitement, joy, enthusiasm, and complete utmost ecstasy about the London deal with Mr. Halo. This is huge! Al believes in me no matter what task or challenge I face in life. He has been by my side this whole ride.

Finally, I've reached a high end, and Al simply wants to share the joy with me. I look at Al and widely smile. I love this man; he wants so much good for me, he's my rock at times and best friend at others. I have it all with Al. I can't even be upset with him. His calls were warranted for fantastic news. My concerns about Al left me staying at his house practically overnight without a simple call or text to Bullet. Al had a point. I need to start thinking about my future. I love Bullet, and I love Al. I'm in love with Bullet, but there's the little issues we face too. Me leaving Bullets house in the middle of the night was crazy. Do I really love Al that much? So much that I left Bullet in the wind? All these thoughts rushed at once as I continue to look at Al with a sense of peace.

I kiss Al on his forehead and decide to go home for the night. For now, there is no explanation about my disappearing act I could even give Bullet. I choose only to text once I arrive home. The rapid disappearance, Al, and not being completely open has been unfair to Bullet. I'm going to have to do better with communication or step away until I can figure out how to balance my life with Al, which I see as my friend, business partner, and heartfelt love.

The statement or question Al present creates an in-depth thought process within me. This day I decide, perhaps I do need a life reflection for my future.

Chapter 16

BULLET

*a*n early morning text awakens me. It's from Indigo. I haven't spoken or seen her since she abruptly fled my house last night.

Incoming text from Indigo reads.

"Bullet, I'm sorry I disappeared in such a hurry. My apologies that I didn't get a chance to suitably say good-bye when I left. Well, anyway, I'm just texting, letting you know that I made it home safely."

As I'm reading the text, I become both angered and happy at the same time. On one hand, I'm glad that Indigo is okay, but mad that she would vanish without a decent explanation. There is no proper way of saying good-bye when leaving abruptly.

I hesitantly text her back, "I'm glad you arrived home, okay."

With an unceasing hurting heart from the night before along with so much confusion going on in my head, that was all I could muster up to say.

"Thank you, Bullet," she replies.

Then there is silence.

Weeks go by, and there isn't much communication between Indigo and myself. Occasionally there is a "good morning" text from time to time. I want to call and investigate our division. I decide to remain silent, hoping I'm allowing time to possibly heal any wounds or ill feelings Indigo may be having. I figure she is still upset about her sister, maybe it's something I said, or perhaps we are drifting apart. I don't push because I don't want to push her away. I have unanswered questions. Every so often, I call, but Indigo speaks briefly then gets off the call. Eventually, Indigo doesn't answer my calls. Business keeps me busy. Texting is the best means of communication with us. Indigo always text back.

I am not alarmed because we have been through a similar division once before when Indigo gets upset with me. The communication slows down, then, texting begins. Eventually, we reunite after Indigo gets over her "stress" moments. However, this separation is becoming different than in past instances. The distance between us is growing longer. It has been a couple of months since I last heard from Indigo. Yet I think about her always. The memories of the beautiful nights we shared stays floating in my head.

I am restless. My mind is full of unsettling thoughts and feelings. Lying in bed and wide-awake is driving me crazy. I try to go to sleep without much success; it's better if I move, I decide to walk outside. Morning dew rests on cars, the grass glistens. Darkness still conceals the sky—a soft, gentle breeze brush across my face. The waft is refreshing. The neighborhood is quiet. As quietness surrounds me, the wind whispers her name, Indigo. Although she is miles away, I begin to feel her presence as if she is next to me.

I can't figure out what has gone wrong that allows Indigo to stay away for so long. Could she have given her love away to another? I often wonder. But how could that be? We have always had such a secure connection with each other. Our relationship grows each time intimacy is exchanged. What we share is real love. I can't imagine Indigo not having the same thoughts I am having. I have constant visions of her lying in my arms. Visuals of how she softly kisses me are permanently etched in my mind. There is confusion in my head. I don't know what transpired between us. I am definitely missing her. Indigo is rare because she connects with my feelings.

Chapter 17

SENSATION

*B*ULLET MONTHS LATER...

AS THE TIME OF INDIGO AND OUR SEPARATION GETS LONGER, THE pain in my heart starts to subside. I declare to myself to stay connected to me and take a hiatus from love. A trip is in desperate need. Relaxation and reflection will do me some good. My passion for Indigo has caused me a great deal of pain. Part of my healing is to spend some time alone. I decide a cruise fits right along with my torn love. This will be my version of therapy; I don't want any company. I title my getaway as a self-healing moment. I have a travel agent make all my arrangements. Love has drained me to the core.

Time for departure arrives swiftly. The seas are calling my name. I wake up early the morning of my bon voyage adventure. I tell no one of my plans, in fear of them wanting to accompany me. Once aboard, I scurry onto the deck to wave to onlookers as our ship begins to drift away.

The atmosphere on the ship is lively. Everyone appears to be happy and cheerful. Inner built-up tension from love heartaches slowly begins releasing its grip. I can feel the layers of stress dissolving.

When I hear the ship horns, I know my relaxation is about to begin. I have a chance to reflect on and understand my current love relationship with Indi. Soon enough, the ship is in motion. The horns blowing are soothing to my ears. I stay on deck, absorbing the relaxed feeling. The wind from taking off has the surrounding kids excited. The playful sounds in the air are healing. Eventually, once the ship sets sail and the winds calm, I head to my room. This is the first time I feel relaxed since my love woes with Indigo. I take this opportunity to rest. A knock on the door awakens me from a sound, peaceful sleep. Upon opening the door, I notice my luggage has arrived. I figure the tap was from the room attendant; my nap was great. I feel refreshed and rejuvenated.

This is the best time to get something to eat. I claim a corner and recline with my food and drink. The horizon is a masterpiece to behold. It's incredible what takes place in your head when you have a clear mind. I have ideas about my future life; I want more. I want Indigo to be a part of my plans. It doesn't matter what Indigo wants, I say to myself. I chuckled as I have that thought come across my mind. But in reality, it does matter. Love is something that cannot be forced. I try to erase those thoughts out of my head. I remind myself that this trip is for me and self-healing. No ideas of Indigo are allowed. She has been the cause of my emotional bruises.

A couple of hours pass. I witness everyone getting into their relaxed moods. The audible sound of children laughing and jumping into the pool is a bonus of happiness in the atmosphere.

As I stand up and walk over to the balcony, I begin to survey the area. Then my eyes fall upon this well-put-together young lady reclining on the deck chair. The two-piece she has on is eye-popping and sexy. Lying face down, I see her mind-blowing hourglass figure. I follow the pattern of her body with my eyes, from the bottom of her toes up to the tip of her hair.

"Damn! She is so sexy." I say to myself.

At that very moment, a fella walks up to the side of her chair with two drinks in his hands.

"That must be her boyfriend," I begin to figure.

Thus I turn and look out to the water for a couple of minutes.

Immediately thoughts of Indigo start running through my head. Looking at that sexy body in the two-piece makes me think about my girl. My memories reflect the night Indigo came to my house and walked around in her red undies. I feel myself getting a little excited about the visuals in my head.

"Down, boy!" I command myself.

I give off a slight chuckle. As I turn back around to get one more glimpse before I leave, the guy is walking off with both drinks still in his hands.

"Well, maybe that is not her boyfriend." I begin to contemplate.

As I swing my head back her way, she lifts to turn over.

"No, this can't be!"

Now I know why looking at this woman reminds me of Indigo, because it is Indigo. How in the hell did she get on this cruise? Emotions begin to rush through me.

I fall back, away from the railing and quickly move towards the elevator. Still in disbelief that she is down there, I hurry back to my room.

"Shit...shit...shit... shit," I begin to talk to myself. I'm glad she didn't see me.

"But this is a five-day cruise. How am I going to avoid running into Indigo?" I start wondering.

"Who has accompanied Indigo on this cruise?"

Now I think back to the fella with the two drinks.

"Could she be with him?"

I kick off my shoes. Then I arrange myself in a supine position across the bed looking up at the ceiling.

"What am I going to do?"

Soon after, the thoughts of her lying there in her bathing suit juggle around in my head.

"Damn, but she looks so good," thinking to myself.

By this time, it's too late. I'm standing at full attention. Now I'm in deep thought. I can feel the head of my pistol thumping. As my hand slowly glides down to touch the head of my penis, I begin to massage it through my shorts. This girl has me on fire, thinking about how sexy her ass is looking. I can't take this anymore! I jump up and strip down to my birthday suit. I walk into the bathroom and turn on the shower. After stepping into the shower, I begin immediately lathering up the soap. I start foaming my body down. With the lather thick and soft, I proceed to place the head of my penis into my hand and slowly start going back and forth with visions of Indigo running in my head. I can see her in my mind bent over the couch with me behind her, slowly stroking from the back. Subsequently, thoughts of Indigo cause my hands to speed the back and forth motions. I am gripping my penis even tighter.

"Damn," I begin to say under a low tone.

I take my thumb and start to rub the head slowly.

"Ohhhhhhhh that sensation!"

My eyes roll back; I can't stop even if I try. My heart is pounding with self-pleasure. All I can think about is her soft and wet Peach Butter cupped around my stiffened pistol. I am having unceasing thoughts of her Peach Butter welcoming me inside with every thrust.

"Oh shit, here it comes!"

I begin to shake, letting my liquid love shoot. With the intense breathing still going on, I lower my head to rest under the downpour from the shower. I stand in the shower to regain my thoughts and process everything that just took place. My heart is still racing. I'm in disbelief that Indigo and I are on the same cruise ship. It has been months since I've seen Indigo. Nervousness and anxiety consume me. I coach myself to calm down.

This act of motion confirms that I'm way overdue for love. I figure my release of self-sexual tension is all part of my self-healing process.

I continue to think, "No matter what I do, I cannot escape thoughts or sights of Indigo. I must pull myself together. This is a long trip, and I can't continue to self-please myself every night. Something has to give."

I decide I will take each moment as it comes. I have to keep my composure. This trip is transforming into a complete U-turn. This is not exactly what I had in mind when I booked my self-healing get-away excursion to heal from Indigo love woes.

Chapter 18

WHIRLWIND

ing, ding, ding, ding, ding…

"Who in the hell is at my door ringing my doorbell like that!"

Ding, ding, ding, ding, ding…

My eyes are barely open. My head is pounding from the sound of the doorbell. I'm so tired because I'm just getting into bed. I glance at my phone for any missed calls. I thought it might have been Bullet after my last night's disappearing act to see Al. The time is 05:45 a.m. There are no new calls or text messages from Bullet. The previous text correspondence between Bullet and myself is less than an hour ago. I texted Bullet after leaving Al's house early in the morning to let him know I was home okay.

My text to Bullet stated, "Sorry I left in such a hurry. My apologies that I didn't get a chance to properly say good-bye when I left. Well, anyway, I'm just texting letting you know that I made it home safely."

Bullet response came through after a few moments of my text, stating, "I'm glad you arrived home okay."

The time of our text messages reflects 05:15 a.m. I just know it's Bullet at my door. He has every right to be outraged after such a beautiful night we shared, then I bluntly vanished.

I grab my robe with thoughts of how I will explain my reasons for leaving. I have many ways to clarify the incident. I start feeling the jitters because Bullet may not understand my relationship with Al. Then I begin contemplating should I mention Al at all.

My mind has a million thoughts as I hobble down the hallway to look out the window. I see nothing.

Ding, ding, ding, ding…

"WHO IS IT!" I scream.

"Bitch open this GOT DAMN door with your scary ass, it's me!"

I swing my door open to see Dillard standing with a smile so wide his face looks like it's cracking.

I smack my lips when I see Dillard.

"Oh, Dillard, it's just you!"

Realizing the time, I scream, "DILLARD What is wrong with you? Why? Let me say it one more time. WHY? Why are you here? You don't know how to call somebody?"

I walk away from Dillard as he continues to stand at the door.

"Well, good morning to you too, miss sunshine," as he closes the front door while he enters.

"You seem to be disappointed to see me."

In a sarcastic tone, Dillard states, "Were you expecting someone else?"

"Let me just tell you, I was not expecting you. That's for sure! I'm going lay back down. I'm tired."

Dillard, still in an upbeat mood, follows behind while talking nonstop. I'm really not paying attention to what he is saying. I'm still half-asleep. My feet are dragging the floor. Mid-step, I stop to look back at Dillard because this is unusual for him to be this happy so early. My head tilts to the side with my eyes cut low towards his direction. I then pose the question.

"Dillard, where are you coming from?"

Dillard pauses, beams, then proceeds to explain his night. "Indi, I had the best night ever. I still haven't gone to sleep. I had to come straight to you and tell you all about my night and early morning."

"Dillard, did it have to include you ringing my bell like a mad man at FIVE FORTY-FIVE in the morning?"

"To answer that question, YES!"

"Well, I'm just getting home myself. This story better be good. My head is in a whirlwind."

Dillard looks up with his eyebrow raised, "Sounds like we have a lot of sharing to do this morning. What or who were you doing that has you just getting in?"

"Dillard, you already know I was with Bullet last night, but…I also was by Al's this morning. It's not what it sounds like, but there is a story attached to it."

Dillard's smile gets even more prominent. "Oh, yes, this will be a good morning. I need details."

"Dillard, if your story is that good, go and get some coffee brewing at least while I go to the bathroom."

"Indigo, don't be too long. I know once you get in the bathroom, you don't like to come out. You take forever in the bathroom. I don't want to be half sleep across your sofa before you come out of there, okay?"

"Damn, Dillard! I CAN go pee, right? You just go make the coffee. I promise I'll be back. DAMN!"

Dillard picks up the mini pillow off the sofa and pitches it at my head, causing my head to bobble. We both laugh.

"Boyyyyy, don't play no!"

"Whatever, skank, go to the bathroom and pee and get your ass back so I can boast about my adventurous night."

The coffee aroma is delightful. I come out to see Dillard humming, placing warm Tastee donuts on saucers. He must have had the donuts in his hands when he came to the door. I was so disappointed it wasn't Bullet, along with being tired I didn't remember seeing him walk inside with a box of donuts. Oddly, I wanted Bullet to be at the door. However, I'm also on the fence about seeing him after last night's craziness. I tell myself I am taking a break from Bullet and Al for some time to think. Funny because if Bullet would have appeared at my door, I don't think I would have been strong enough to tell him I need time to think. Then questions of why and where were you would have followed. I am not ready to answer those questions. That being my thoughts, it's a good thing, it wasn't Bullet at the door. Yet, before going to sit and chat with Dillard, I check my phone one more time to see if Bullet sent a message or possibly called. There is nothing from Bullet. I don't want Dillard to see me checking my phone because he always has something to say. I quickly bounced over to the kitchen and sat to share morning coffee and donuts with Dillard.

Dillard begins to speak about his night, "This is my birthday month, and it's already getting turnt up. I had the best time ever in a long time Indigo. I am really happy with Arlo."

Dillard and Arlo have been getting closer since they've been hot and heavy.

After eating warm, sweet, melting donuts from Tastee's, both our bellies are satisfied. We then move our conversation to the sofa. I'm lying on one end while Dillard is lying on the other end of the couch. My legs are on top of Dillard's legs while I'm snug in my white cotton long bathrobe sipping coffee.

Dillard proceeds to talk about his night while his face lights up, and his eyes sparkle.

"Indigo, first of all, Arlo left a trail of love notes throughout the house for me to scavenge through to start my morning off great. This morning Arlo had six-dozen of roses in the room. Three dozen red roses on each side of the bed along with one huge ass card with a tassel dangling stating 'read me.' I get up, and that's when the scavenger hunt began. The tassel was a love note stating how much he loves me, and I have been the wish that he has wanted his whole life. He said how much I make him happy. Along with this love note, it tells me to go to the microwave. I go to the microwave, and there's another note telling me to go to the refrigerator. In the fridge, there is fresh fruit peeled, cut, and has a toothpick flag stating, "eat me only."

The message continued: "After eating, call this number, allow the phone to ring only three times, and hang up. After you call that number, you have forty-five minutes before a call comes your way. Answer on the second ring, then hang up—say nothing."

I intercede, "Dillard, was Arlo at the house the night before, or did he come in while you were sleeping to get things started?"

"No, Arlo was at the house all night. I'm not sure when he snuck away to get this stuff rolling. But yes, he did leave. You'll know when I finish telling the story. All this was a total shock to me. I love surprising people, but never had it done to me, especially like this."

At this point, the coffee is put away. My slumber is gone, and I am fully alert, listening to Dillard's adventure.

Dillard continues, "Let me backup for a moment. When I went to shower, there was a mini note stating, 'be prepared to be a KING for the day.' Another note instructed me where to find the outfit that is already picked out for me. I showered and was ready in less than thirty minutes. My curiosity was at an all-time high. I sat by the phone, waiting for it to ring. I answered as instructed, allowing it to ring only two times, saying nothing then hanging up. I tell you as soon as I hung up the phone, I mean, as soon as I hung up, the doorbell rang. I answered, and there was a driver with a Phantom outside my door. The driver was clean, professional, and addressed me as KING Dillard."

He stated, "We have orders to escort you to a place undisclosed please oblige and allow me to escort you to your destination. You know I was giddy at this point. I proceeded to walk out, but before I could take a step, the driver and some other assistant ran out and said 'no King Dillard not yet.' Indi, let me tell you I was so confused. The driver beckoned a signal to old chic, she ran and rolled out a red carpet for me to walk on. I said to them, "well, this is all right."

"Dillard, I'm so happy for you. I'm loving this story."

Dillard continues. "When I entered in the Phantom Arlo was sitting there with a smile and one rose. He said, I love you, are you enjoying your adventure?"

"I kissed him like crazy, conveying how much I love him and expressed my morning is beautiful."

My phone rings and interrupts Dillard's story. I ignore the phone initially. I tell Dillard to continue his story. I'll get the phone later. The phone rang again.

Dillard stops and says, "No, Indi see who it is, it may be important."

I get up out of my snug and warm seat and see it was a missed call from Momma Deah. I excuse myself from Dillard for a moment and call Momma Deah back.

Momma Deah answers on the first ring, "Good morning Momma Deah. How you doing?"

"Good morning Indigo. I'm blessed this morning. How are you?"

"Good, Momma Deah."

"Indigo, I saw I have a missed call from you from this morning. Is everything okay? I'm just seeing it. I'm sorry I didn't answer when you called."

"It's okay, Momma Deah. Did you get a chance to listen to your voice message or anything?"

"You know, Indigo, I still haven't figured out how to use this voicemail messaging stuff. I can't listen to any messages. As a matter of fact, I need you or lil' Al to delete anything on the voicemail. I don't even need a voice message. If I don't answer, I just call the number back."

I chuckle.

"I know Momma Deah, it has been a challenge for you to use that voicemail. We have it all set up, but myself or Al will delete the messages for you."

Since Momma Deah admitted to not listening to her voice message, I decide not to disclose why I called her.

"Well, baby, you didn't answer me. Is everything okay?"

"I'm sorry, Momma Deah, yes everything is okay. I accidentally called, and when I realized it, the phone had already gone to voice messaging. So, I'm sorry, Momma Deah, for calling, but everything is okay. Thank you for checking."

"Okay Indigo, if you really need me, you know you can call me anytime."

"I know Momma Deah."

"Have a good day, Indigo, love you."

"You too, Momma Deah, love you too."

I return to the living room to find Dillard half-sleep on the sofa. I shake Dillard to see if he would wake up. Dillard opens his eyes with my first light touch.

"Dillard, do you want to continue the story or rest up a bit, then we continue later?"

Dillard looks up and says, "No, I want to finish my story. These donuts and my wild night have me a little tired, but I want to tell you about most of the night. I may need to continue later if I get too tired."

With fatigue sitting in, he smiles and tells his story in a little less upbeat tone.

"Where was I?"

"You were saying you and Arlo were in the Phantom."

"Oh yea…Arlo had the driver take us along the Bayou. There was a catering truck parked off to the side. Along the Bayou, there was a table for two all set up with servants around the table. The table was covered with white table cloths and chairs adorned with white coverings, a professional photographer capturing every moment, and a warm gourmet breakfast. Arlo even managed to have soothing jazz music in the background. We stayed out there for at least an hour, to an hour in half, as I was catered to the entire time. Some onlookers were staring to see what was going on, but it was just Arlo and myself enjoying the morning together. I gotta show you pics of the whole day. There is so much I need to tell. My day has been so spectacular, Indi. I want to explain every detail. But before I get to all the little ins and outs of my adventurous day. I want to make sure I let you know I was pampered the whole day with servants, food, and love. Let me tell you, not one need went unmet babieee. To top it off, our night ended with passionate lovemaking over and over and over and over again. Arlo was on one last night and trust-you-me he has me wanting more of that again."

"Wait a minute, if you had so much passionate love last night, why are you here early in the morning and not still with Arlo?"

"There you go, Indigo. Let me finish. Then, you will know why."

"Oh, because I'm just saying. That type of night should linger over to the next morning. Well, that's my opinion, anyway."

"If you must know Miss Thang, after our night of passion, Arlo left the house around five-fifteen this morning for an early start of the working life. I couldn't go back to sleep and had to come over here to share my love spell I'm under."

"So, you telling me you been having passionate sex all night. That means your ass still raw and stank, and you're laying your oversexed crack all over my sofa?"

Dillard sits up and swings another pillow across my head while still in his hand.

"That's exactly right! You said it, Miss Indigo. My ass is still raw and wanting more!"

We both started to laugh and start a pillow fight. Both of us are completely up at this point.

Dillard jumps on top of me and starts to command, "Say you sorry!"

While under the pillow, I continuously shake my head side-to-side, gesturing no. Then my muffled outcry says, "Never will I say I'm sorry!"

Dillard lets go of the pillow and grabs under my arm. I hysterically start to say, "No! No! I'm ticklish-no! Okay…okay…okay… I'm sorry your ass is stank!"

Dillard's laughing, "Nope, that's not what I'm looking for!"

I'm uncontrollably laughing, barely speaking, I say, "Sorry!"

Dillard antagonizes the situation while both his hands are parked under both my armpits, "Sorry for what?"

"Sorry, I called your ass raw and stank."

Dillard moves away in slow motion from my arms, looking my way, waiting for me to say something. I say nothing but just look at him with a grin.

"What, what did you say?" Dillard is acting as if he's coming back to tickle me.

"I didn't say anything. You already know."

"What was that? What do I know?"

"Oh nothing." We both smirk and giggle.

Dillard then states, "I do want just a tad bit more of what I had last night, or should I say this morning?

I know the proper way of addressing what I want, let's just say from both last night and this morning."

We both burst into laughter.

"Indigo, we talked about some of my night, now it's your turn."

Dillard sitting up bushy eyed after all the clowning and wrestling on the sofa. I tell Dillard about the event with Bullet, along with my abrupt departure from him. I express to Dillard how I feel. Explaining to Dillard that I'm torn and slowly allowing this 'thing' with Al tear me away from Bullet. The question posed by Al also has me thinking that's the whole reason I feel like I'm in a whirlwind of thoughts, decisions, and a love triangle.

Dillard feels my somber emotions and looks with concern.

Dillard states, "Indigo, I hear everything you're saying, but ultimately, you have to figure out what you want. Don't allow decisions to get you down. Indi, do you see anything further with any of the two guys, if that's even an option? Tell you what, my birthday is coming up in a few days, decide on what you want in life after turning it up over the weekend. After this weekend, your head will be clear, stress will be down, and then we can come together to conclude what's best for my girl 'Indigo.' Love you, chic. Now I'm really getting sleepy. I'm going to crash for a bit in the guest room. I'll show pics of my event later, which is to be continued further this weekend. It's my birthday month, and it will be all that and more. Come here, Indigo."

Dillard reaches for me and gives me a long warm hug as he towers over me. "Everything will work out, Indigo, don't be worried. Now get some sleep too."

Dillard kisses the top of my head and walks off with a drag, which is totally opposite of his entrance. His goal is to seek a couple hours of z's.

I sang out to him and bow at the same time, "Goodnight, your majesty Mr. KING Dee."

Dillard looks back and bows in return, "Goodnight, Ms. Indi" then blows a kiss as if he really is royalty.

At this time of morning, I go tuck away too for a couple hours of rest. I smile to myself with good thoughts about Dillard. For a moment, I feel honored that Dillard wanted to share his story with me before anyone else. That just confirms one of the reasons we have been such best friends for a long time.

Chapter 19

JUDGMENT

"*S*even, please."

The elevator is full. There is silence. I look around, and everyone either has a blank stare or engaged in their electronic devices. I follow suit and keep my eyes on the lit numbers as the elevator stops on each floor. The elevator stops on four when a familiar stranger enters. He smiles my way, and I return the smile. However, I notice he continues to look at me. He's point-blank staring. I say nothing to him as he says nothing to me. The seventh floor light becomes lit. This is my stop. I proceed to exit the elevator. The gentleman steps out to allow my exit off the elevator and smiles again. I return an annoying half fake smile then put a frown to my face when I turn to walk down the hallway. I look back to make sure he's not following me. But, the stranger gets back on the elevator. I know I've seen his face but is puzzled from where. I discount the encounter as nothing and proceed to find door seven thirty-one. I knock a couple of times before hearing, "Come in. It's open." I enter a house full of incense burning with loud rocking club music.

Bam yelling out from the bathroom, "Indigo, is that you?"

"Yes, Bam, it's me! You need to keep your door locked! There are strange people around here!" I yell back.

"Bam, you in the bathroom?"

"Yeah, Indigo, I'll be out in a minute, grab a snack or something. I'm not going to be in here much longer. I'm just getting ready."

I survey Bam's house for a snack and discover some fruit in the refrigerator. I fetch the chilled mango slices. Bam always has the munchies and snacks are always readily available. The house has a stale lingering aroma of herbs. Whenever I leave Bam's house, my clothes always have the smell of herbs, weed, and incense all mixed together. This is not the smell I'm aiming for at Dillard's party. I hope Bam doesn't take a long time to get ready.

"You talked to Dillard lately?" Bam is still yelling from the bathroom.

"Yes, I've been talking to Dillard just about every day this week. He was at my house earlier this week. Not too long ago, we had a morning chat and breakfast together. Why? You haven't been talking to him?" I respond loudly over the music while Bam remains in the bathroom.

"Well, Edgewood said he talked to Dillard a few days ago, but haven't heard from him since. I called, but he didn't answer. He did send me a text after my call, saying he would call me back later, he was out with Arlo. So I wondered if anybody talked to him because I know I didn't talk to him. Although I did get the blast text reminding me about this weekend."

"He's excited about us all hooking up today. I was included in the blast text too. But I did talk to him on the phone this morning as well." I respond.

"Okay, good," Bam states.

Bam remains in the bathroom, still yelling. "Indi, go check out my fit on the bed and tell me what you think?"

On the dresser, I see liquid THC and marijuana wax. Bam has candles all over her bedroom with books about natural health on her dresser. Across the bed, there is a navy blue bodysuit, with gold adornments to the neckline. The front of the bodysuit looks halfway put together. Something looks undone. I pick up the bodysuit, and before I raise it to eye-level Bam comes from behind, "What you think, Mamacita?"

"You wearing this?" I say, puzzled.

"Yea, what's wrong? You don't like it?"

"Bam, I like the color, but it looks half put together. Go try it on, and maybe I can get a better idea of how it will look on you."

"Indigo, I already know you think, it's way too revealing, so just to let you know now. It is!"

"I don't care Bam. I just want to make sure you not looking all hookerish." Then something pops out from the top.

Bam begins to undress, right then and there, to bare flesh and then slips her outfit on.

"Bam, you have no shame, you get buck ass naked in front of anybody, don't you?"

"Yes, mam, we all-natural and should have nothing to hide. Our outer layer should be revealed more often. Society has everybody all worked up about nudity and all things natural."

"Yay, yay, yay, Bam I already know the spill. Please don't start preaching to me today about all the natural stuff."

Bam shrugs me off and continues to adjust her bodysuit. Once the suit is on, Bam looks pretty good in it.

"Bam, it's actually cute," I say surprisingly.

"Told you Indigo, I know how to pick 'em."

"Well, this fit definitely surprised me. Your butt looks huge in this outfit tho."

"EXACTLY! That's how you catch the bees, allowing a bit of honey to sway their way. Then BAM! You have the pick of the litter once you put that sweet-sweet down."

"That's a whole lot of honey," I respond while laughing.

Bam laughs and proceeds to get ready for the night out on Dillard's birthday.

"You took forever in the bathroom. I assume you almost finished getting dolled up."

"I'm almost done, I have to do a few more finishing touches to my hair then I'll be ready. By the way, you are looking like a piece of meat tonight yourself. What you trying to catch? Does Bullet know what you wearing miss chic?"

"Bullet not tripping over what I'm wearing. Besides, I haven't talked to him in a minute."

"What? You and Bullet broke up?"

Bam is looking in the mirror, fixing her hair as she asks questions. Her attention is more on doing her hair then being engaged in my issues with Bullet.

I respond while the question she poses makes me think about how I've missed him. "I don't think so, but I'm really not sure."

"Girl, if he doesn't care about you, then you don't care about him either." Bam nonchalantly proclaims.

I wanted to defend Bullet, but I knew I would be wasting my time. Bam is really not interested in anything else at this moment except looking fresh and delicious for possible bait tonight.

"Bam, it's a little different, but we will talk about all that another time. I'm just ready to enjoy my night with Dillard for his birthday, and as Dillard would say, get it turnt up!"

"Hell yea! Let's turn this bitch up tonight!"

Bam raps her look up with a couple of perfume sprays to her wrist, neck, and in between her legs.

"I'm ready now. All we waiting on is Edgewood to come scoop us up. Indi, when is your dance competition again? Isn't that coming up this week too?"

"It's just a performance, not really a competition. You still coming right? Because I'm riding with you and Edgewood."

"Of course, I'm coming. You know we all come and support you every year. I just wanted to make sure I had my date's right. Everybody just been busy doing their own thing that we haven't been touching bases to confirm past plans."

"Well, consider today confirmed. Everything still booked. We all staying in the same house for the day's event then we head right back. I probably shouldn't drink too much because of the performance, but I'll better judge that as the night passes." I correspond with Bam.

Bam interrupts my conversation, "Hold up, Indigo. Turn down the music that's Edgewood calling."

Bam answers the phone with a nontraditional greeting, "Edgewood, where are you? Shit, me and Indigo are ready. When? Oh, my bad, I must didn't hear it. Let me check. Okay, we heading out now."

Bam gets off the phone, laughing, "Girl, I'm going off, and the boy been texted telling us to come down. He said he texted your phone as well, but none of us responded. He's yelling, and I'm yelling. Girl lets get out of here and go before Dillard starts calling and going off too. You know how he can get."

I look down at my phone and see a few missed calls and text messages.

"Bam, you must have dead zones in your place because I have a few missed calls and text messages too. And, yes, one of those calls is from Dillard. Lex left a text message asking where are we? I'll call Dillard once we get downstairs and text Lex too."

Bam and I get down to see Edgewood completely frustrated. "Why none of y'all answering the phone? I've been out here for about fifteen minutes."

Bam and I both look at each other with our eyebrows puckered. I respond first, "Boy, you need to quit your damn lying because we know so dog' on well it's no way in hell you would sit down here waiting on US that long."

Bam intercedes, "Yay, and why didn't you just simply get out of your car and knock on the door if we weren't answering? Anything could have been going down, and you just sitting down here talking about you texted and called us. Boy, bye!"

Bam looks at me, and we both keep teasing Edgewood.

Edgewood responds, "You know I can't win with both of you girls ganging up on me. Okay, I give up."

Dillard and Lex both are notified that we are on our way, and soon the party is to get started.

We maneuver our way through downtown traffic and arrive at club BLUE EXOTIC. Edgewood utilizes valet service to retrieve his Beamer. Outside the club, I spot Lex with many other faces that weren't familiar to our usual circle. Lex notices us as well and runs over to the car while we exit.

"Hey guys, Dillard is already inside. We have a VIP section too. I was waiting out here since you texted y'all was on the way."

"Lex, who are the rest of those people with you?" asks Bam.

"They here for Dillard, we started talking because we all had the same color wrist band on to represent a VIP party, which is Dillard. I think that's some of Arlo's circle that is invited. But I don't know for sure."

Entering into club BLUE EXOTIC, there's a massive flat water-fall with blue highlights. All the lit areas have a hue of blue lighting. The club is relatively new with a feel of elegance. The place is packed. The VIP section have a private sector with a personal bartender, tables, and is elevated on a stage facing the regular crowd of attendees. A clear sliding plexiglass door sections off the VIP area. The barrier allows options for VIP to either open the door and engage or keep the door closed and stay secluded from the crowd. Additional seclusion also occurs by sliding an extra tinted door allowing the VIP to have a private viewing of the clubbers at will. The tint has a one way viewing for the VIP patrons. The VIP section is very accommodating, fitting approximately fifty people comfortably. Dillard has at least sixty deep joining his party; every-thing is high class. The place has art décor at every angle, from the ceiling to the floor. The walls have all types of videos playing along with the music. Some videos are of water dancing, or music symbols dancing to the music. Unlimited drinking is encouraged; VIP also has mirrors all around. Dillard is already turned up. He runs up with one drink in his hand, smiling and looking tipsy. Dillard hugs me and Bam.

Thereafter Dillard jumps on the table, yelling, "It's my BIRTHDAY lets get started sexy bitches! Yay! Toasts and shots for my peeps!"

Arlo comes over and hugs us, "You know he feeling really good. He's on his third or fourth round of drinks and shots."

We join in and have shots too. Dillard starts dancing in the middle of the floor, spinning, and popping. Then he moves to the top of the table to showcase a few moves pulling on Arlo's arm to encourage him to join. The night is an evening full of drinks, shots, and dancing. The unknowns merge in attempting to grind and dance too. Our VIP plexiglass doors slide open to link with local club-goers. Tracker is even in the club and connects with the party. Bam collects a lot of 'bees' as the party continues. Dillard is out of his element, but he is having a good time drinking and having shots all night long. Lex misses out most of the party due to dozing off from too much alcohol. My night starts to become a blur as it continues. The shots combined with the drinks have me in a perfect place. My attempts to keep my eyes open are failing. Audible sounds become weaker. I recall Tracker holding me up on one side as another guy did the same on the other. Before passing out, I look up to Tracker only to see a perfectly beautiful white smile looking back down at me.

Chapter 20

EXPERIENCES

"Wait, what is that? Oh, no."

I wake up to a pool of wetness; I'm discombobulated. My head is spinning. I look around and see Lex and Bam lying across the bed, still in the same clothes from the night before, when we were at the Blue Exotic. Lex and I are lying side-by-side while Bam is at the end of the bed. I smell a fresh aroma of coffee coming from another room, hear music in the background, and realize I'm at Dillard's crib. I scoot out of bed and run to the bathroom, then plop on the toilet and release a burning urge to pee. I feel ashamed and embarrassed while examining my underwear for any sign of wetness. I take a sigh of relief.

"Nothing, I'm dry."

But the side of my fit is soaked. I jump in Dillard's shower and toss my outfit to the side.

Thinking out loud, I murmur, "Bam or Lex must have peed in the bed."

I wrap in a towel and come out to see Dillard cutting fresh fruit and preparing for breakfast while singing in unison with the background music.

Dillard, see's me from the side, "Morning Ms. Sunshine, did you sleep well?"

"Morning, King Dee, I slept soundly. As a matter of fact, so soundly, I barely remember the end of the night or how we all ended up at your place. So you know that is sound."

"Why you wrapped up in a towel, Indi?"

"I woke up in a pool of piss apparently and nope it's not from me, I checked, the girls still sleeping in it. I think it's from Lex because she and I were side-by-side, and when I tell you, I was soaked. I was soaked!"

"What? So you telling me I have a pissy mattress?!"

"That's exactly what I'm telling you."

"Shit! I just bought that new top cover. That's why I keep a mattress cover. You never know what your guest doing or eliminating while spending a night at your goddamn house. That damn Lex was tore up all night. You know she can't hold too much liquor. I highly doubt Bam with her slushing ass is tipsy because that heifer can hang with the best of them. I should wake they asses up with some ice-cold water."

"Dillard you so crazy, all you have to do is buy a new top cover. The girls and I will pitch in and buy one since it's your birthday week and all. Well, King Dee, did you enjoy yourself?"

"Of course, I did Indigo. I had a blast."

"I know you were turnt up before we even got there. I'm surprised to see you up so early."

"Yea, I had to get up to see Arlo off and then I just stayed awake. Indi go look in my room and find some of my old shorts and t-shirts for you and the other pissy hoes that's sleep. I hear one of them in the bathroom now. I'm sure they're discovering the same damn thing you discovered."

Bam and Lex both wake up to find the same issue I faced upon waking. We all laugh at Lex. She is embarrassed and attempts to plead to not be a normal drinker. We agree to keep her incident private. Dillard cooks breakfast, serves fresh fruit, and gives us fresh-squeezed orange juice. Dillard discloses the agenda for today. This is the last day we are hanging for his birthday weekend celebration before returning to our daily workweek.

Dillard begins explaining our day's plan.

"Today at one p.m. we are going second line starting at St. Charles Ave and Josephine. Joining for the second line will be my day's finale with a perfect rendezvous ending at my favorite restaurant."

After hearing the plan for the day, I decide to head home to freshen up and change into something decent.

As I search the room, I call out to Dillard, "Dillard, do you know where my other shoe and cell phone is at? I can't find it."

"No, I don't remember seeing you with your cell phone, but I'll call it so you can hear it ring."

Bam walks into the room. "Indi last night, you took your shoes off when you were dancing with Tracker. I saw you holding them in your hand while both of you danced all night."

"I danced with Tracker all night?"

"Yes, why you say it like that? You looked happy when you were dancing. He was all over you, and you seemed pleased at the time. Truth be told, you both were booed up."

"Bam, I don't remember dancing with Tracker all night. I think I would have remembered that, are you sure? Were you tipsy when you saw this?"

Bam pulls out her phone and opens up her photos to reveal pictures of Tracker and myself. Just as she stated, we seemed to be enjoying ourselves. He was definitely all over me.

Dillard yells, "Indigo, did you hear your phone ringing? I called it a couple of times."

I yell back to Dillard before responding to Bam, "No, I still haven't found it yet."

I then tone my voice down and look at Bam. "Bam, what made you take these pictures, and did I look like I was drunk or anything? I don't know why I don't remember this."

"Indigo, we were having a good time. We all were tipsy. It isn't a big deal. That's how we ended over at Dillard's house." Bam seems to be nonchalant about the whole night's events.

"How did we end up here?" I question Bam.

"Edgewood met some chic then decided to take her home with him or whatever. Then he told us just to call a car service to escort us home. But Arlo stepped in and insisted we all go together to Dillard's house because you, Dillard, and Lex were lit. I was even a tad bit tipsy. But not even close to y'all tipsy level! So Arlo squeezed all of us in the Range and now here we are. All together this morning."

Lex walks in while Bam telling me about our night. I bend over to look under the bed to continue looking for my shoe and cell phone. Lex comes to her knees next to me to look under the bed too.

Lex speaks in a humble, quiet voice. "Indigo, I hope I didn't get your phone wet."

"Oh no, Lex, I just can't find it. It has nothing to do with you or your accident. Girl, don't worry about that, we were just teasing you. We all have accidents of some sort. Some secretly, some outwardly where everyone is aware. Really, Lex, we were just joking. It's all good."

I hug Lex around her neck. She squeezes back.

"I'm still just so embarrassed, Indi. I really don't remember anything at all. I must have drunk way too much. I'm not doing that again, no time soon."

"Lex, we all had a good time. That's all that really matters."

Bam comes around the bed, "What both of you talking about down there?"

"Nothing Bam, Lex helping me find my stuff."

"INDIGO!" Dillard yelling.

"What Dillard!"

"Come here!"

"Dillard I am looking for my shoes and cell phone, what's up?"

Dillard has his cell phone in his hand and then hands it over to me, "Telephone."

I place the phone to my ear and hear Tracker on the other end.

"Hello. Oh, hello, Tracker." I hold the phone in suspense of what Tracker may say about the night before.

"Hey Indigo, I enjoyed Dillard's party. You know how to have a good time." I can feel Tracker smiling on the other end. I don't want Tracker to know I don't remember half the night, so I just go along with his statement.

"Oh yeah, why do you say that?"

"We just had a great time, that's all. I was feeling you, and I thought you were feeling me too. I would like to continue seeing you again for some more dancing and drinks. Possibly we can discuss hooking up again later."

I respond cautiously, "Tracker, I would love to know what I did to make you enjoy the night so much. Did I say something to you, or was it just the dancing you enjoyed last night?"

"Indigo, it was both," Tracker still smiling on the other end.

"Uh, huh, so I see," I respond.

Tracker intercedes before I could ask another question, "I'm only calling you on Dillard's phone because I have your cell phone. You asked me to hold it last night, and I forgot I had it until I heard it ringing a couple of times. That's what triggered my memory."

"You have my phone! That's great! I was just searching all over the house for it. By any chance, do you have my shoe too?"

"Naw, I don't have your shoe. You were holding them in your hand most of the night. Possibly it's in your car."

"Thank you, Tracker, so much for calling and letting me know you have my phone. I didn't drive, but you have a point it may be in Dillard's truck. I'll look for it right now."

Tracker responds, "Of course, Indigo, you are very welcome. Where would you like to meet to pick it up?"

"I need to call for a car pick up to take me home, go change, then I plan on coming out again to hang with Dillard. All that just to say, once I get my car, I can come over there to your place to pick it up. I'm very appreciative of you having my phone."

Tracker makes another suggestion, "I tell you what, how about I come over to Dillard's house now, bring you your phone, and I can even drop you off at your place? That saves you a lot of hassle. Then, you can have your phone a lot sooner."

I decipher if I want Tracker to know where I live before responding. "Uhmm…I don't know."

"Really Indigo, it's no trouble. I don't mind. Bringing your phone is the least I can do. Besides you need your phone, you never know who's calling. I'm helpless without mine."

"Ok, Tracker. Sure, I'll take you up on your offer."

I hand the phone back to Dillard.

Dillard states, "Hello, and then proceeds to tell Tracker his address."

I inform Dillard of my plans of going home and freshen up. The other girls decide to do the same before heading out for a second lining finale and hanging out once again.

Chapter 21

TRACKER

*T*racker pulls up to Dillard's driveway, as he stated. Before Tracker gets out the car, I say my good-byes to Dillard, Lex, and Bam. I then give my attention to Tracker and proceed to walk to his car. Tracker begins to walk in my direction immediately after he exits out of his car. He smells good, looks handsome, and displays a sexy smile once he sees me. Tracker opens my door, demonstrating how he can be a perfect gentleman.

Tracker and I have a good conversation, but nothing is mentioned regarding the night before at the party. Tracker glances in my direction often and just smiles. I smile in return, although I'm unaware of the purpose of his constant smiles. I do know one thing, his smile is contagious and warm. I feel comfortable next to him. He even has a warm cup of coffee in the car waiting for me. The ride to my house is short. We pull up to my place. Tracker tells me, "Wait, don't touch that door."

Tracker walks around to open the car door. Grabbing my hand, he assists me up the stairs. His whole stance is different. I smile and bathe in all his good manners.

Once at my front door, I assert, "Tracker, you have been so kind today. I want to thank you once again for everything."

"Indigo, is it okay if I come in to use your bathroom?"

When asked the question, I feel funny because I never like anyone in my personal space. However, I convince myself, this is Tracker; he's not exactly a stranger. Besides, the boy drove all the way to Dillard's house to bring me my phone, pick me up, and drop me off home. We had a good conversation; this is Tracker for goodness sake. I'm tripping. My thoughts convince me that it's not a big deal for him to come in. My response of "okay" allows Tracker to enter.

"The bathroom is down the hall and your first right."

Tracker walks to the bathroom while I place my stuff in a small pile on the floor. My shoe was even discovered in the Range. I continue to stand near the front door awaiting him to return for an exit. Tracker takes a while before coming out of the restroom. After about fifteen minutes, I walk toward the bathroom door to check on him.

I hear the water in the bathroom. I knock on the door.

"Tracker, is that the shower I hear running? Are you in my shower!"

"No, I'll be out in a few Indigo. It's taking me longer in here than I thought."

"Tracker, are you okay?"

"Yes, I'm good."

After leaving him in the bathroom, I reach the end of the hallway then hear the bathroom door unlock. My back is towards him. Tracker comes out and approaches me as if we are a couple. I am looking over my shoulder as this ordeal is unfolding. The only thing Tracker is wearing is one of my white towels draped across his shoulder. His abs are chiseled and his body is glistening with a notable full erection. He walks toward me. The scenario feels like it's moving in slow motion; I'm lost for words. I stand there with a long stare. I am not nervous. I feel no emotion. I allow him to come closer. I don't know if I want to see him closer or if I am curious about what is to take place next. For a moment, I freeze. Tracker approaches me from behind, holding my waist tight.

Then whispers, "I want to nimble you up and down, then slowly bite your panties away to share some love I've been longing to give you."

I swiftly turn to face him. As I turn, he leans over and starts to kiss my neck. I quickly pull away, pushing him off. Tracker gingerly grabs my body once again to pull me in close. His bare nakedness is flush against my body. I feel every inch of his inviting big wide prolonged super stiff erection. For some reason, I don't fight. I embrace the few minutes. It feels good. Visually Tracker's body is tempting. His caress feels warm. His voice is soothing. For a moment, he has me considering how it will be if I share intimacy with him. However, I quickly regain my sanity. I can't have an intimate relationship with Tracker. I work with Tracker. This will be a disaster. I simply can't do this. At the moment, Tracker is lusting over me. I'm bathing in the attention. I'm allowing him to feed my ego. My body wants to explore what he has to offer, but my logical side says "no" and wins the battle.

Once my head is clear, my demeanor takes on a different reaction. My trance is broken. Tracker's sexy body is close to mine. I realize I am getting caught up in his web. The feeling of warmth I once was feeling turned into a different reaction. I then figure the only reason Tracker wanted to come over is for some sexual pleasure.

My heart is pounding, and I become enraged, "What the hell are you doing?!" I tell Tracker as I back away.

I say the words without giving it any detail thought. I have to stand my ground; Tracker can't see my weakness. I am falling for his tricks; I want him. I feel guilty; I have Bullet. It is pure necessity that I push Tracker completely away. If not, I don't know if I will be able to resist the temptation. I have to stand my ground.

Tracker looks shocked, "Indigo, what do you mean? Last night?"

"What?! What about last night?!" I continue to yell.

"Indigo, I thought you were feeling me. Last night when I kissed your neck, you seemed to enjoy it. I thought you wanted this or us to go further."

I look at Tracker with anger still burning in my eyes. My blood is boiling for him even to think he was coming over to my place for a quick hookup. I am angrier that I somewhat want him too.

"This is why you wanted to come in?! This is why you were so willing to bring me home?! You thought you were getting you a lil' bit today, I guess, right?!"

"No, no, no, no, Indigo, it's not like that. I didn't think that at all. I just want us to get to know each other better. I knew you were tipsy, but I apologize if I offended you. I guess I read last night all wrong."

"Yes, Tracker, you did. Whatever I did last night, I don't even remember. So whatever was said or done, it wasn't from a sober place. Tracker, did I say anything to you about intimacy or coming over or anything like that?"

"No, Indigo, you just allowed me to embrace you all night with a few kisses to your neck. We danced all night. I tried to kiss your lips several times, but you kept saying 'no', so I left it alone. Indigo, you carried yourself well. I'm feeling you, and I hope one day you give me a chance to show you how much of a good time we could have together."

I feel relieved to know I didn't spread myself wide open with Tracker. He disclosed everything without me even having to ask.

"Tracker, please go. Put your clothes back on, and once you are dressed, I need you to leave."

As Tracker is walking down the hallway, my eyes stay glued in his direction. Damn, he is so sexy. Only if I……damn Tracker you hanging long too…damn and if we didn't work together. We would be explosive!

Tracker looks back once before entering the bathroom. I remain stern. I walk to my front door and open it signaling I still want him to leave. If only he knew what I'm really thinking.

I tell myself, "If Bullet and I don't work out, I know who I have my eye on next." I smirk knowing it was only a fantasy because work and pleasure never mix well.

Tracker comes out of the bathroom, fully dressed. His erection has disappeared. Tracker respects my wishes and walks directly to the front door. He kisses my neck once again.

My heart begins to palpitate faster with his kiss to my neck. I am in heat. Tracker didn't realize it, but he causes my body to react. My panties moisten with his kiss; only Bullet use to possess the power to make my Peach Butter purr. I am surprised my body has this reaction.

After this brief moment, I realize the reason Tracker and I may have connected, at this very minute I have visuals of Bullet. Tracker's arms almost feel like Bullet's warm embrace. No matter, I didn't let on that Tracker is affecting me. If anything, it made me think about Bullet. I want him now. I need him now. My body is hot and thirsting for a quench of satisfaction.

Tracker's words break my momentary trance. "Indigo, whenever you ready, I'll be here."

While the front door is open, I kindly say, "As of now, Tracker hooking up with me would not be a good idea. I have things going on in my life that will not allow me to share myself even if I wanted to. I cannot give you a chance now or anytime soon. Uhmm, how can I say this? It sounds like last night was interesting, to say the least. Last night was me enjoying my best friend's birthday and the party attached to it. Sorry Tracker, if I led you to believe it was anything else, but it wasn't. Be safe, and thank you again for delivering my cell and bringing me home. See you at work, good-bye."

Tracker walks out the door, looks back at me and blows a kiss.

As soon as I close the door, I look through my phone, but no missed calls. It's been several days now, and Bullet has not even ringed my phone once since I left abruptly. I barely call too, so no one is really to blame for the phone call thing. Before freshening up, I stare at my phone and debate should I call Bullet. I start to have jitters. I hold the phone for several minutes, still standing close to the front door. I go to text Bullet, but decide not to send. I convince myself I rather call. I dial Bullet's number. The phone rang two times before I decide to hang up. I stare at the phone again, before putting my phone away I hear a sudden knock at my door.

I look through the peephole to see that Tracker has never left. He's at the door.

I open the front door. "Yes, Tracker, is everything okay?"

Tracker stands at my front door, appearing confused, "Indigo, may I say something to you?"

"Yes, sure, Tracker, go ahead."

"I couldn't leave. I was sitting in my car and decided to come back. Indigo last night was one of the best nights I've had in a long time. I haven't had that feeling of joy like that ever. I wish I could have lived that night forever. Not because of me kissing you but the sincere joy I experienced while we laughed and danced. I want you just to consider to, possibly think about, someday going out with me and enjoy dancing, dinner, and drinks. I made a declaration to myself that whenever I find happiness or something that makes me feel good, I would not let go of it without effort. This is my effort. I'm at least putting it out there for you to consider. Just know I'm not rushing, but whenever you want to hang with a friend, or possibly more, I am available. I just had to say that, then I'm leaving."

Tracker grabs my hand, kisses the back of it, walks away, and gives a wink coupled with a heart-stopping smile.

Blushing, I stand in the doorway without saying a word until Tracker drives off.

My mind is racing with intimate thoughts after Tracker presented his sexy package. I am more in disbelief than tempted. I don't have time to think about this recent event for long. The crew is waiting for me. I still have to change and freshen up my face before meeting up for Dillard's final birthday celebration. Before I start to get ready for the remainder of my day, I sit and think how Trackers caress from behind could have easily been from Bullet.

I imagine Bullet taking his teeth and slowly removing my panties one bite at a time. Followed by licking in between my legs in search of some slippery Peach Butter. I sat back in my chaise with a smirk imagining how our intimate encounter could unfold. I start to talk to myself out loud in a whisper.

If Bullet were here coming out the shower with only a towel around his neck, I would hope to be cradled in his arms with a tight grip. Uhmm, but only for a minute while I would be in the midst of unveiling myself down to nothing. No time for foreplay. I need him to lay me down and give me the pipe the old fashion way but in the new millennium fashion. Would I want it rough? Let me think. Yes, I want this one to be rough, fast, and nasty. I want him to grind this Peach Butter until the juices drip to the floor. I want to feel the moisture. Better yet, I want to hear the moisture. Then I want him to lay me down and get a taste. Taste and nibble me until my moans increase. I'll hold him tight as the sweat of our bodies become one. The sex is rough. My grip is tight. Our final climax comes after Bullet picks me up as my legs are wrapped around his waist. His secure grip holds me up against the wall while my mouth stays open as I exhale long breaths of pleasure. Yeah, I want it just like that right now.

My heart starts to skip a beat with thoughts of the possibilities.

"Damn, I'm horny," I say out loud.

That damn Tracker caused all this steam to rise. I'm yearning for Bullet. My Peach Butter is moistened all over again. My body wants hot, sticky, steamy sex right now.

I have to shower all over again. I freshen up and quickly dress for a day out with my friends. The thoughts are beautiful, but I can't ponder on what I don't have. I phone Dillard to let him know I am on my way back to his place before he starts to call. We meet again at Dillard's house to head out for some second-line festivities, then later eating at Dillard's favorite restaurant.

My day ends with talking to Dillard on the phone after our finale of fun. I decide not to tell Dillard about my earlier experience with Tracker. I figure things will be awkward enough once I see Tracker at work. Dillard may make the situation worse. This time I keep my mouth sealed tight.

Dillard ends our goodnight conversation, "You feel better, Indi? Now that you've decompressed, it gives you a light heart to evaluate life to face personal choices."

Dillard is right. I have to figure out what I am going to do about Al and Bullet. The last thing I need is to add Tracker to this equation. I need to get it together. My body always longs for Bullet. However, my heart also beats for Al. And today, I was lusting over Tracker. Tracker is a null subject. I don't know why Tracker even crossed my mind? I have a tug-of-war with two different emotions.

Something has to give. I have to be honest with myself. Not only that, but I have to be honest with everyone that is a part of my life.

Dillard couldn't have said it better, "It is time for me to evaluate my life to face personal choices."

Dillard is absolutely right, but before I do, I decide to call Tracker one last time. I desire to hear his voice and feel that touch once more. This may complicate my personal choices, but lust has a stronghold on me tonight.

Chapter 22

FOCUS

*D*illard's birthday weekend was a blast, especially for Dillard. The second line was the perfect ending to a beautiful weekend. I feel special to be surrounded by so much love from friends I consider family. The fun is over. Now, it's time to focus on real-life issues. The whole weekend I didn't speak to Al. Al knew it was Dillard's birthday weekend; going out on the town is a yearly ritual whenever Dillard turns a year "younger." I decide to take the day off from work. I just need a day to recoup from my overly excessive alcohol consumption, thoughts, and I sincerely didn't want to see Tracker again this soon after our union. Tracker presented his true feelings. I just need some time to digest everything and enjoy "me" time.

I look at the time. Seven fifty-seven, Dillard should be up and on his way to the office.

I text Dillard. *"Hey D, I'm taking the day off. Don't look for me. I need some 'me' time today."*

Whenever either one of us doesn't go to work, we inform each other, almost like a high school thing. We used to do that then too. But in high school, if Dillard wouldn't come to school, I would try and play hooky, so I didn't have to go either. I guess things haven't changed much in our adult life. After texting Dillard, I sat in bed thinking about my past. I decide I want a change of scenery for the day, somewhat of a staycation. Al has a lakefront condo that he or I hardly go to.

Today I think I'm going to the condo, turn my phone off for a while, think, write, and then go to Al's place and talk to him while he's sober. Possibly the conversation he had with me was from a drunken heart. Regardless, it is something that needs to be addressed.

My phone vibrates while I'm thinking of my day's plan. The call reads, incoming call Dillard.

"Good morning Dillard."

Dillard sounds frazzled and skips the proper morning greeting. "Indigo, why in the hell you not coming to work today? You know today is the big meeting with the international representatives. Did you forget you are one of the key speakers? No, not just you let me rephrase that. We are one of the key speakers. This is a huge contract we are trying to close on."

"What? That's today? Dillard, are you sure? Hold on, let me check my calendar."

Before I could reach for my device, my phone notification starts to alarm. I look down at my phone and see the exact thing Dillard is talking about. Damn Dillard is right, the big meeting is today.

The "relax me" time feeling soon evaporated, and immediately my mind started to race into business mode.

In somewhat of a panic state, I place the phone to my ear, "Dillard you are right. I totally forgot about the meeting today."

"Shit Indigo, are you prepared with your half? You and I present this project together. I know you had it together last week because we reviewed it. Are you still feeling off-balance from my birthday weekend? Damn Indi, if you are, you betta get yo' ass some coffee, red bull, or whatever the hell it takes to get yourself together. I'm going to work and expect you to be here shortly thereafter. We need to review some things before we present. I'm getting off this phone, so you can do WHATEVER needs to be done for you to be right. Get it together, sis, and I'll see you in forty-five minutes, one-hour max! Don't make me come get your ass Indi. We need this contract. I'm counting on you having it together. Now I said what I had to say. I'm not playing, love you, and see you in a few."

Dillard, don't even say goodbye. He just hangs up the phone. That's when I know it's something serious. Dillard has the take-charge personality and now is one of his moments of taking charge.

I immediately put my phone down, open my computer to confirm everything I need is in order. I can't believe I forgot about this presentation today. Thank goodness I texted Dillard early. Everything would have been a disaster. I regroup, review notes, and presentation power points. Everything is in order. I remain at awe that I didn't remember the meeting. Well, my reminder would have at least alerted me. There is so much going on in my head. I allow my professional life to be placed to the side for a moment. I decided the condo and "me" moment will be put on hold. Then I rethink and say "no", I need my "me" time and decide to head to the condo later tonight and stay to the next morning. I'll get to Al later, possibly tonight or tomorrow. For now, I focus on work and getting business complete.

Once I arrive at the office, it is busy. Everyone looks preoccu-pied. Dillard sees when I come in. While walking toward my office, Dillard raises his hand, signaling for me to go to his office instead. Tracker walking in my direction, smiles and greets me with a good morning. Nothing feels strange. He remains professional, and so do I. He is preoccupied with business affairs in preparation for our international guest. I detour my route and walk to Dillard's office.

"Indigo, happy to see you made it here. You even arrived less than an hour. Are you prepared? I have a few more things we need to go over to see if you agree. By the way, your office was taken hostage for a moment, that's why I signaled you over here. Garrett had somewhat of a breakdown. He and Stacy were in your office for some privacy. Don't look at me crazy Indigo. You know how Garrett gets when big projects come our way. Garrett was red and getting loud with everybody. Stacy decided there needed to be some type of intervention. Therefore, your office was the closest. All I saw was Stacey telling Garrett to step in your office; she shut the door, closed the blinds, and went at him. The whole office heard her go off and telling him he needs to calm down and handle pressure better, yelling and getting outraged with everybody will not be tolerated. We all have stress, but some people don't know how to handle it. Stacey is a no-nonsense person, and I guess she got tired of Garrett and his uncontrolled stress behavior. After Stacy reamed him out, Garrett remained in your office for about thirty minutes. He's been quiet and calm ever since that powwow with Stacey. He should be out by now, but I just wanted to update you in case anything is out of order in your office."

"Man, I missed a lot. I'm so happy she took care of that for now. Garrett does act crazy at times when he is under pressure. It's funny because otherwise, Garrett is sweet and low-keyed. We all have our issues. Well, enough about Garrett. Let's get our stuff together and kill this presentation."

"That's my girl. We got this Indi."

Dillard and I go over our presentation before the arrival of our international guest. Once they arrive, the atmosphere in the office is on edge. We all benefit if our international friends sign a contract with our company. The day is long. Dillard and I presentation is beyond excellent. We always work well together, working well back dates to our high school years. We have been hooked at the hip. One of our guests expresses the liking of our presentation. The other guests are stone-faced and unable to be read. After the day's end, there is still no sure answer about the contract partnership with our company. Apparently, they need time to discuss what was presented before making a final decision.

Though there is no formal contract signed, I feel relieved that our international guest's presentation is over from our standpoint. Dillard seems satisfied, as well. It has been a long day at the office.

I invite Dillard to have a drink at the bar before I decide to head to the condo. But he declines and states he has a special night planned, and his unwinding plans are much better than alcohol. I laughed and knew what that meant.

Chapter 23

DISCOVERIES

I am tired and need some time to relax. I decide this is the perfect day for some wine and quiet time. I opt to head to the lakefront condo to enjoy the sound of water and a different scene. I can envision it clearly. I'm going to pop open some wine and relax. I pull up to the lakefront condos on Lakeshore Drive. In the past, Al and I used to visit his waterfront condo often. It was our getaway to do business. The condo has always been a beauty to me. The view of the lake is breathtaking. The high ceilings create a significant dimension of space with the wood-burning fireplace giving that old nostalgic aroma. I decide once settled, I'm going to sit out on the balcony in the quant two-bedroom condo. Even though it's only two bedrooms, the condo's size is always more than enough with a square footage of almost nineteen hundred. This is my home away from home. I need my well deserved, especially after today, "me" time.

Upon entering, I smile to myself. The key entry code still remains the same. Al always keep drinks in the mini winery. I walk in, throw my bags to the side, and take off my shoes.

I turn the dimmers on and survey the room, thinking, "Everything still in order. Man, this feels like old times. Time has flown so fast I can't remember the last time I was here."

Immediately I get comfortable. It is one of those days I want to feel sexy and dainty for myself. I undress to a red sheer lace halter neck bra and matching sheer lace crotchless panties. On these types of days, I call my irresistible sexy gear and pleasure moment, "nasty naughty sweets." My "nasty naughty sweets" is all about self-pleasure, and it's way overdue. Tonight I am going to love on me and fulfill my missing sexual desires. To get started with part one, I pour myself a glass of wine. Thereafter, I throw on my half-opened satin lace robe. I walk outside to the patio with my wine glass in one hand and the remaining bottle in the other. I station myself at the outdoor bistro table. The blowing wind feels refreshing; there is little humidity tonight. I indulge in the breeze while I finish drinking the entire bottle. Once my bottle is done, I return inside.

The dimmers are set low. I am feeling good after completing one bottle of wine. I fetch another bottle and pour another glass to get started on round two. I am ready. In the cabinet, Al has candles stashed to the side. I retrieve six candles, light them up, and turn the dimmers down even lower. In my bag, I pull out part two of "nasty naughty sweets."

I can't have fun all by myself without having toys to join in this monumental moment. Tonight my naughty toys are my six functions dual-action vibrator and last but not least my favorite collectible lifelike vibrating dildo. I lay and get comfortable on the barely touched chaise lounge. The wine loosens any stress I have.

"I'm ready, let the 'nasty naughty sweet' games begin," I say to myself.

At this point, I close my eyes and visualize Bullet entering the door. He comes home to greet me with one long stem red rose in his hand. Bullet sees me lying on the chaise. Before his first kiss, Bullet takes one finger and slides it between my legs with easy access from the revealing sheer crotchless panties. The sheer lace bra is the first to be removed. I visualize him greeting me with a soft kiss to my lips. Then he places his hand to my upper thigh as I feel the unceasing kisses to my neck. With these thoughts in mind, I put my right hand to my inner thigh while caressing and rubbing up to the peak of my clitoris. Slowly I rub back and forth. I place a visual that I'm receiving sexually pleasurable touches from Bullet up and down my body. My other hand shifts back and forth to each tip of my breast. The breast is a sure point to ignite an explosion of pleasure. It doesn't take long before my Peach Butter moistens for more tease. I proceed to take a finger to enter into my Peach Butter and feel the moistness and suction as it cups with every motion. My body joins in movement. My hips wave up and down as my finger moves in and out. I reach over to allow my toys to participate in the fun. I want this moment to last. First, I indulge in a slow, steady clit action using my vibrator. It's relaxing and sensual. My sheer lace panties remain the only item in place before I imagine Bullet removing them for a better taste.

I imagine him saying, "Open wider, I want to taste all of you."

I follow my illusory commands while fully exposing myself. I take the vibrator and rub it close for extreme pleasure, visualizing Bullet getting a taste of my 'nasty naughty sweets.' Soon after, Bullet wants to explore inside my Peach Butter a little deeper. Reaching over for my dual-action vibrator converts the moment to be more exciting.

Bullet whispers, "Turn over. I want to please all of you from behind."

Of course, I beckon to my fantasy of Bullet and proceed to enjoy my signature toy with insertion to satisfy my craving. The vibration is high, coupled with slight anal stimulation, ensuring a definite high climax moment. This is Bullet's favorite position. The Peach Butter is slushing with every vibration. I turn back over to lie flat on my back with thighs wide in the butterfly position. The change in position allows for better control and easier access for breast stimulation. Having the vibrator brush across my clit for extra enjoyment, the explosion is getting closer as I caress my breast to increase moisture. I take pleasure until my climax is reached. My moans are audible, as I enjoy pleasing myself. After climax, I lay for a moment. I continue to take pleasure in my Peach Butter moisture. The 'nasty naughty sweet' game is not over; I want to please myself even more. I relax for a moment to take a sip of wine. I can't resist the ultimate toy. I rub my Peach Butter until it begins to purr for another round of games. I'm still ripe. I quickly grab the deluxe life-like vibrating dildo.

I see Bullet. I feel Bullet. The visual is intense. This is the moment Bullet will enter to connect with my inner soul. I grasp the dildo and place it slowly inside, taking in a deep breath as it fills my canal. Manipulating the toy to create vibrations and movement feels real. It quenches the thirst of my naughty nasty experience. My body moves up and down like a sea of waves. Each thrust I create has me closer and closer to a second climax. My g-spot is discovered. I motion my body with a faster and faster wave, simultaneously pulling in and out with Mr. Real Feel. I picture Bullet as he comes to his climax as I reach mine. It's exciting. I close my legs and rest for a moment; this is a work of art. My sexual desires have been satisfied.

"I love on me," whispering to myself, "Indigo, you know how to make us feel good."

I smile as I imagine Bullet saying similar words. I dry myself off and drape on my satin lace robe. I pour one more glass to top off my second bottle of wine.

Wine in hand with dimmers and candles still flickering, I walk around the condo to place things in order. I want to go and shower upstairs. I plan on possibly having a part three of a "nasty naughty sweet" night. Presently I feel satisfied, but there is always time for continuation. Especially because it's been a while since I've been with Bullet. I decided to go upstairs to check what nighties I have in the drawer. I'm still wearing the same robe as before while climbing up the two-part stairs then stop moving. I think I hear something. I stand dead in my tracks, trying my hardest to decipher what I hear. It is silent for a moment. Then I hear something again. The sound is a faint voice. The words are not clear. I just hear noises or moans of some sort. I become somewhat frightened. I don't know if I should run downstairs to call 911 or keep listening. I hear it again. This time, I recognize the voice. It isn't just any voice, but it's Al's voice. I hear him again. It is Al, but in a low tone. I know his voice. I walk cautiously upstairs. I drape my robe together and tie a bow in the front. The upstairs bedroom door is closed. I place my ear to the door. This time I know the voice is from Al. I turn the doorknob to enter.

Opening the door slowly, "Al?"

I push open the door. Al didn't hear me enter the room. Lights are off, but candles are flickering all over the bedroom. I see Al lying in bed.

I begin to walk toward the bed. I detect that something isn't right. I feel puzzled. Al's arms are above his head. He appears naked and aroused. The room smells good, and a low hint of jazz is playing in the background.

"Al? Hey, what are…"

Before I could approach Al completely, I look to my side and see a man with a groom black Venetian mask. This man is tall, wearing a black bow tie and a black leather jockstrap with a huge front hole. The hole is barely big enough for this mask-wearing man's extreme hard-on.

My surprise entry shocks everyone present. My wine slips out my hand and shatters to the floor. I scream, not knowing if this is in horror or shock. Al wakes from his daze and notices my presence.

Al is startled and yells, "Indigo?!"

The masked man swiftly grabs at some clothes lying on the floor and runs past me, avoiding eye contact, practically knocking me down. I hear him run down the stairs and exit the front door.

Al covers up slightly. I turn on the lights. I have never seen Al at a loss for words.

Al looks at me, "Indigo, I need to explain."

I look at Al with little to say. Al sat in silence. I stand in silence. I walk around the room, spotting cufflinks and a watch. I pick up one of the items the mask-wearing mystery left behind. I stare at the Jellyfish Andrew Logan Swatch watch.

The silence is broken. I stand in the middle of the floor, look at Al directly in his eyes and simply ask, "Al, was it, Dillard?"

Al silence remains. He looks at me after a minute of muteness while we are staring at each other.

"Indigo, I need to tell you some things."

"Al please answer me." One tear falls down my cheek as I'm

holding the watch in one hand, pointing it at Al. "Al please be honest and don't lie to me. This watch is unique, this is Dillard's favorite watch. I know it is because his initials are engraved on the back. Al, I wish you would not have expressed your interest in 'us' becoming an 'us'."

Al remains still for a few more seconds then reaches his hand out to me. "Sunbeam, please come here."

Uncontrollable tears are flowing. "WAS IT DILLARD?!"

Al never answers. Instead, he gets up then clutches me into a hug. "Sunbeam, I love you, and it's not what it seems."

Al's skin is sweaty. His outfit is for a night's tryst with his mystery friend.

I push him off.

Looking back, "Al I'm not mad about your lifestyle choices. I'm hurt."

Stepping over broken glass and red wine, I go down the stairs, gather my toys, and get dressed. With mixed emotions, I depart from what I thought was going to be a relaxed "me" moment. Instead, I leave with feelings of confusion, hurt, and surprises.

Chapter 24

DAZED

"*H*ello, hey, Bam. I'm ready. Just waiting on you guys to get here."

Bam continues to chatter, but I cut the conversation short.

"Bam, you will see me soon. Let me go get a few more things together before you, and Edgewood get here, then we will chat in the car."

Bam always has some adventurous stories to tell, so our long ride to Florida will be exciting. I debate if I should bring up my ordeal with Al to Bam and Edgewood in the car. Lately, things have been so crazy around me. Last night still has me dazed in my feelings. I need my head clear for this Samba competition. I tussle through my numerous suitcases to make sure all my bags are packed, and my Samba costume is ready. Afterward, I survey the house for anything I may have forgotten to pack.

I keep looking out the window for Edgewood's truck. Bam said she and Edgewood weren't too far away. Dillard's truck is in my driveway first, as he's sitting beside Arlo.

As soon as I see Dillard's truck, my heart starts to pound, and my palms begin to sweat. I run to the bathroom and splash water to my face trying to calm myself down. With my bathroom door open, I hear my front door alarm signaling someone entering the house.

Dillard has the code to my house. He has the liberty to walk in whenever, but this time is different; a sickening sensation overtakes me all of a sudden.

Dillard postures himself at the bathroom entry before I can shut the door. "Indi, what's wrong? Are you crying? Are you nervous?"

Dillard appears genuinely concerned. My mouth becomes dry. Instantaneously, I can't find my voice. Dillard stares at me and grabs my shoulders to look at me square.

"Indigo, are you alright?"

Dismissively I respond, "Yes, yes, I'm okay. I guess I have some type of anxiety attack or something. But, uh, yes, yes, I'm okay, Dillard."

I can't look Dillard in the eye. I am still baffled if it was "him" last night with Al. I want to just ask but figure this could get heated, so I avoid the subject.

Dillard continues to look at me with concern.

"Indi don't worry about that competition. You will kill it. It's all in good fun anyway."

"No, no, no Dillard, I'm not too worried about it. I'll just do my best and have fun, that's all."

"That's right! Because my girl will knock all them bitches to the side! Shit, I should have joined and competed this year, let them get a lil' taste of what I have too. You the best, Indigo, and don't you forget it! So shake your ass on that stage and have fun."

Dillard then cradles me with one arm around my right shoulder while we are side-by-side.

He looks down, "Cause you, my girl, I got you."

Dillard kisses my cheek when Bam walks through the front door.

"What in the hell? Y'all having some kinda Kumbaya or something. What's wrong with Indigo?"

"Damn, Bam, nothing's wrong with her. I'm just giving her a pep talk before her competition, so get your nosey ass all up out of our business."

"Indigo, I'm not even entertaining Dillard right now. I just can't. Are you ready?"

"Yes, Bam, I'm ready."

Edgewood now walks in the house.

"Oh Lord, what have I walked into? You know I'm not even going to ask. Indigo is all this stuff that's posted by the door yours to take on the drive?"

"Hey Edgewood, yes." Still cradled in Dillard's one arm, I smile at Edgewood.

Bam, already in the kitchen, grabbing a road snack, yelling, "Let's go everybody!"

Everyone leaves out. I'm the last to exit my front door. I look back inside before locking up and take a deep breath preparing for our road trip ahead.

Edgewood is driving while Bam is in the front seat. I decide to take the backseat to stretch my legs.

"Bam, where's Lex at? I thought she was coming."

"Indigo, she still coming. Apparently, she met some guy or something last night and arrived home late—something like that. Girl, don't have me to start lying because when Lex talks, sometimes I get lost in the story and have no idea what she's talking about. All that to say, yes, she is coming, that's our next stop. After we pick her up, we on the open road."

"Okay cool."

Arlo and Dillard are right behind us. Bam and Edgewood are cranking the music loud. No one is talking, instead listening to music.

We pull up to some unfamiliar neighborhood.

"Why are we here, Edgewood?" I inquire.

Bam replies before Edgewood answers, "Girl didn't I tell you we had to pick up Lex. This is the address she texted me. I told you Lex had some story behind all this."

Edgewood adds a few words, "I just drive and do whatever any of you tell me to do. Lex told me to pick her up here, so here we are."

Lex comes out with her hair flying all over and an overnight bag.

Bam whispers as if Lex could hear her. "Well looks like she did have a night of wild sex. Look...look! Some topless guy at the front door is seeing her off. That's what I'm talking about. Get you a lil' somethin'- somethin' before your long road trip. I'm not even mad at my girl. Finally!"

In unanimity, we gaze at Lex walking toward the car, including Dillard and Arlo behind us. Speechless is an understatement. Edgewood breaks the stillness, while we motionlessly watch Lex get herself together.

"Okay, let's not make her feel uncomfortable, okay, ladies? Indigo and Bam, are you both okay with saying nothing?"

I mutter, "Yea, okay."

Bam hesitates and finally shrugs and gestures with a dismissive response, "Yea uh-huh, whatever Edgewood okay."

Edgewood gets out the truck and opens the door for Lex.

Lex is upbeat and exposes a shiny pearly smile, "Hey guys! Sorry, I was over here, but I still wanted to make it to Indigo's big day."

Bam smirks, "Well good morning Ms. Hoe. I'm sure you're in an excellent mood this morning."

Lex tightens her shoulders and narrows her eyes at Bam then explodes.

"Bam I'm not taking this shit from you today! I'm a grown woman. I do what I want! I don't need you or anybody else judging me! You don't know what I've done! That's no reason for labeling me as a Hoe! You know what, I'm not even riding in the car with you in it!"

Bam, Edgewood, and I are dumbstruck. This is entirely out of character for Lex to go off like this. Bam, for the first time, is at a loss for words.

Edgewood adds his two cents.

"I told you Bam not to say nothing, but you just had to set it off with her. This is new territory for her, as far as we know. She may be sensitive about what people say or think."

"Edgewood, I was just playing with Lex. She knows I do this all day every day, not caring what nobody says. I didn't know she would be all-sensitive about the situation."

"Bam, you need to apologize to Lex and let her know you were just playing. Everybody needs to have good energy for Indigo," chimes in Edgewood.

Lex already walked up to Dillard's truck and hobbled to the back seat. Bam walks up to the truck to signal Dillard to put the windows down.

"Lex I was just kidding, no judgment, I'm sorry if my comment offended you."

For the first time, I witness Bam apologize. This is uncharted territory. Dillard quirks an eyebrow at me with a puzzled look through the window, I shrug my shoulders.

Lex peeps her head up and only states, "Okay."

Lex slumps back down and becomes silent.

Bam gets back in the car with a surge of dread. Edgewood gives Bam that "I told you so" look again. And as for me, I sit in the back-seat listening to Edgewood's blasting music with pondering thoughts of my life up to this point.

The ride to Florida is relaxing. Ironically Bam doesn't say much on the trip. I think Lex getting angry bothered her. I've never seen Lex get upset or better yet speak her mind to anyone.

I didn't feel bad for Bam, it wasn't that big of a deal what she said. Lex is probably just going through some things, and that one comment from Bam just sent her over the edge. We all have those moments, is the way I look at it.

We congregate in one huge house rental, with more than enough room for all of us. There is a pool in the backyard with a nice grill. Everybody wants to unwind after our long journey on the road.

Dillard and Arlo take the master bedroom. My bedroom is the smallest, closest to the pool on the first floor. Edgewood, Lex, and Bam decide to take the rooms upstairs. I didn't mind taking the smaller place, I am grateful they all decided to come and support my competition the following day.

Dillard calls us to the living room to play games, talk, and share a few drinks. Initially, there is a hint of tension in the house with Bam and Lex. Snippet thoughts of the other night also have me at odds with Dillard, but he doesn't know. Edgewood notices the uptight atmosphere with Bam and Lex. Therefore, he turns on some music and starts to dance. Edgewood grabs both girls' hands, moving each of their arms in rhythm until they quit protesting and snap-on beat. It didn't take much for Dillard to zap up and showcase his signature moves. Shortly Dillard conquers his quest, having Arlo join in the fun too.

After a few sips of wine, I did a couple of two-step moves as well. The tense atmosphere is completely broken once we start karaoke night. First girls against boys, with each of us doing a solo with the others as background singers. Bam led the first song. Edgewood starts the guys out. Karaoke goes on for a long time before I witness the overly consumed alcohol version of my friends. Arlo, beyond his tipping point, slurring continuously, telling Dillard how much he loves him. The drama of love is quite amusing to watch between those two already, but the alcohol sets the dramatization over the top. Edgewood and Bam look like they are having heart-to-heart convos, almost like they are mesmerized with one another.

The whole night is crazy and fun. Lex and I have a girl chat. She and I both are the soberest of the crew. I have a big day the next morning, and Lex vows not to have another "accident" from alcohol. I open up to Lex about what happened the night before with Al. Al even called a few times. He left only one message wishing me good luck. He also requested I call him as soon as the competition is over so that we can have a deep needed conversation. Also, I disclose to Lex about Dillard's watch and cufflinks being with Al. Lex plunges forward in her chair in disbelief. She insists I bring it up to Dillard and point-blank ask. Skittish about Dillard's reaction while we all together, I tell her this isn't a good time. Lex is convinced if it were Dillard, he would have said something immediately. Curiosity is prickling Lex and me. What stuns me the most is Dillard doesn't act strangely. He is the same Dillard and never mentions anything about last night.

As the night becomes later, the rest of the crew becomes rowdier. I hear Arlo jump in the pool outside. Dillard is saying he wants something from the grill. Bam has her "dose of medicine" lit.

Edgewood is mellow, drinking his mix of alcohol. Lex and I sat next to each other, laughing at our drunken high friends.

Lex leans in and whispers, "Ask Dillard now while he's a bit tipsy."

"No, Lex, I'm not bringing it up. Now is not the time."

"Indigo, just don't let it slide. If it bothers you, speak up about it. You know he would do the same. Besides, both of you are the best of friends. It's just mere communication."

"I know Lex, but it's a sensitive issue. You just don't understand everything. Dillard does, though. I promise I will have a conversation with him later, just not now. Lex promise me you will not mention anything we talked about to anyone. I'm going in to get some sleep, so that I'll be ready for tomorrow."

Lex nods a yes and states, "Of course Indi, I would never mention this to anybody. Especially after you asking me not to, this is your deal, no one else's business. Besides, later, I need to talk to you about me as well. I need you to keep my secret to yourself only."

I pause all movement and look at Lex, "Do you want to talk about it now?"

"Thank you, Indigo, but like you, now is not a good time for me. Soon, but not today."

"Of course, Lex, I understand. And yes, your secret will be secure with me. Love you, Chica."

Lex displays a bright smile, "Love you too, Indi."

I hug Lex, get up, and make a few short steps towards my door.

"Goodnight, everybody," I yell.

From a distance, Dillard responds, "Indi, if you going in, I think I'll turn it in too. We all have to get up early."

Everybody starts to gather their belongings and retreat inside to get ready for the next morning. Goodnights are exchanged, thereafter, everyone resorts to their rooms and the house is quiet.

Chapter 25

ALARMS

*D*eep into sleep, I hear my name being called out.
"Indigo, Indigo!"

Still groggy in a stupor of sleep, I begin to feel my bed shaking.

"Indigo, please wake up! Indigo!" The audible voice is an aggressive whisper.

I look up to see Lex standing over me. "Lex, what? What is it?"

"Indigo, remember I said I needed to talk to you about something?"

"Yes Lex, yes, what's going on?"

"Well Indigo, I was pregnant and had an abortion yesterday."

"Wait, what? Lex, what are you talking about?"

Lex speaking nervously, "Indigo I'm bleeding all over and can't stop. Please, I need your help. I don't know what to do?"

I sit straight up in bed to see Lex's color is pale. Her nighties are bloody, with a bloody towel snuggled between her legs. I focus immediately.

Instantly I get chills, "Lex you're bleeding out too much. I need you to lie down. I'm calling 9-1-1!"

"No, Indigo, I'll be okay."

Lex color turns even paler, her legs weaken and give way right before she passes out on the floor next to my bed. I panic and start to scream her name. Lex isn't answering. My scream causes Dillard to sprint into my room.

Breathing shakily, "Dillard, call 9-1-1!"

Dillard calls 9-1-1 without hesitation. The blood is nonstop. Dillard clinches my hand. Dillard kneels face-to-face with Lex.

"Lex! Lex!" he continues to call her name, attempting to wake her up.

Dillard looks up to me, remaining kneeled in the pool of blood. In a panic, I can hear the tremble in Dillard's voice.

"Indi what's going on? Will Lex be okay?"

While positioning myself to kneel next to Lex, I stare blankly at Dillard.

A nauseous panic overtakes me, "Dillard I hope so. That's all I can say. Dillard, just pray, please; prayer is all we have to lean on right now."

By this time, Bam and Edgewood are standing at the door while Dillard and I are kneeling next to unresponsive Lex. She appears dead. Her color is pale, and her pulse is weak.

I continue to talk to Lex, "Sis you will be okay. Hang in there. Lex, please hang in there."

I bend down to kiss Lex's forehead as I swipe her hair back. Dillard remains on the opposite side of Lex until help arrives.

Once the paramedics arrive, I jump in the back with Lex while the others follow behind.

"Please Lex, wake up, you will be okay," I continue to chant the same statement continuously over her head. My prayers for Lex remain constant. Lex remains lifeless, no matter how loud my cries are.

Chapter 26

SIESTA

*L*ex has emergency surgery. The night is short. The morning rolls in. However, Lex is barely awake. I'm the first to visit.

"Lex, how you doing?" Tenderly spoken.

"Hey, Indigo, I'm doing fine. I could be better," she rustles softly. "Indigo, your competition? Did I ruin it?"

"No, Lex, not at all. You are much more important than any competition. There will be many others. I refuse to leave this hospital until I knew you were okay."

"Do the others know what happened?" Lex asks in a somber demeanor.

"Nope, not from me, they don't. Everyone just knows you lost a lot of blood. But I did not mention anything else."

"Indi I should tell you who the father is-"

"Lex, no, please don't. This is not the time. All I need you to do is heal and get better. One day the time will come, and when you are truly ready or if, you can open up at that time. But now, no, please just heal. It's not important. What is important, is you right now."

No further words are exchanged. Lex looks at me with sunken

weak eyes. She musters up a partial enfeebled smile before her eyes seal together.

Lex stays in the hospital for five days. The gang is genuinely concerned. Everybody comes to visit. Each had a one to one time with Lex. Once the crew realizes that Lex is over the life-threatening medical issues, they each decide to go back home. The others have to get back to New Orleans. I choose to stay behind with Lex until she is discharged. I stare at Lex in a hypnotic trance. I can't believe we almost lost Lex. One doctor comes to visit Lex multiple times; he is in dismay. He explains to me each time he visits, that Lex lost so much blood requiring a lot of volume replacement. The blood loss was so extensive he didn't think she would survive due to her unstable vital signs. He gives a friendly smile and says, "she's a miracle." I then realize how life is so unpredictable. Lex is able to rest quite a bit while in the hospital. Her color remains slightly pale, but at least she is okay. During this time, while Lex sleeps, I seize the opportunity to talk with Al. I decide Al and I need to meet up soon to discuss many emotions. I miss Bullet at this moment too. I want our old self again. I wonder if he even thought about me lately. He still hasn't called in a while. I sat aside my anxiety and dial Bullet's number, but I have no answer. Bullet's phone goes directly to voicemail. I call again and straight to voicemail once more. I decide I will call one more time, just to discover the voicemail greeting again.

I leave a simple voice message, "hi Bullet, this is Indigo," before sadly hanging up.

I have wishful thinking that he will call me back immediately. But that call never comes through.

The day of Lex's discharge is hectic. Arranging transportation, getting airline clearance to fly, and monitoring Lex's care is exhausting. The discharge doesn't occur until late afternoon, which causes the rush to begin. Our flight is scheduled to leave at three p.m. but, we don't leave the hospital until twelve-thirty p.m. Talk about pushing for time. It is an insane experience, to say the least. Lex is still weak and tired, so we don't talk much. I allow her to rest.

Chapter 27

ABSENCE

*O*nce back home, I make sure Lex is okay, then the squad comes to visit. The house is clean. Soup, snacks, tons of flowers, and balloons greet us when we walk through the front door. Lex is surprised and spurts joy. She is showered with tons of love at home. Bam is the first to give Lex the most prolonged and most heartfelt hug.

Bam shrills, "Welcome home, Sis! We love you and happy to see you're back!"

Lex holding back tears, "Thank you Bam, I love you and everybody in this room. You all are making me feel so loved."

Amid the festive welcome back for Lex, I feel my phone vibrating. When I look down, I notice I have two missed calls from Bullet. I immediately excuse myself from the welcome back party to go outside to call Bullet back. I instantaneously have a smile across my face, just dialing his number.

"Hello." I hear from the other end.

"Hey, it's me Indigo, how are you doing Bullet?"

"Hi Indigo, I'm doing good."

I quickly respond, "I uhmm been meaning to call you because I've missed you--- Hello...hello?"

The phone just cuts off. In a flash, I call Bullet back, but the phone goes straight to voicemail. I call a couple of times, but it continues to do the same thing. Since Bullet didn't answer, I decide to send him the poem I was writing the night he tried to have a glimpse many days ago.

Text message reads.

"Bullet, this is a little something I wanted to share with you. I call this poem Moments."

MOMENTS

There are moments when I miss you most
I then search and reminisce of your existence
I cow down and thumb through past pictures

At that time, I study the way your eyes speak to the
    camera
At times I see joy, but on the other, I also see mystery
I know both stares oh so well

It's one of the little things I miss about you
Not to mention the soft caressing touches as we lay
    beside one another
The soft kisses to greet my return were always a
    sweet treat

Or simply the detailed way of assuring dinner was
    soon to be avail
The early morning pleaser was a welcomed ending
    before your departure

Making love is a thought that remains a constant
    memory
and desire since your absence

Soon someday, I'll have you back in my arms again,
    and we can dance, drink,

make love, or simply have small chatter

Whatever or whenever that time comes,
I will welcome the warmth of your hugs and kisses
    with a gleeful heart.
I miss and love you sincerely, my love, my comforter,
my King, my safe haven, my EVERYTHING.

I FIGURE HE WILL CALL ME BACK. I PRESUME HE IS JUST AS
excited to talk too. On the other hand, I really couldn't tell because
the conversation was cut short. I stay outside for a few more
minutes, waiting to see if he will phone back. When I don't get a
return call, I take it upon myself and dial his number. Still all and
all, the phone goes straight to voicemail once again. I go back inside
to rejoin the others. I turn my ringer on to make sure it is in reach in
hopes of "that" call from Bullet.

"Lex, what did the doctor say?" ask Bam.

I intercede with a swift answer, "The doctors said Lex's vitals
were unstable, and she needed a lot of volume replacement."

"Yea, I figured she lost a lot of blood. Any word on what caused
any of your sudden symptoms?" Bam is redirecting the question
to Lex.

Dillard notices that Lex isn't answering, then adds his few words.
"Bam, let Lex rest. Indigo and Lex are probably tired. Medical
details are not important. All that is important is, Lex is back home
recovering to good health. Right, Lex?"

Lex looks at Dillard with a half-grin of gratitude and says "yes"
softly.

Bam with a stab of regret approaches, "Lex, about earlier in the
week, I'm sorry if I came across harsh or whatever. But you know I
meant no harm."

"It's okay, Bam. It's not a big deal. Thank you, Bam."

The two hug once more.

I discern everybody is in their feelings since Lex's medical issues.

Dillard pulls me to the side then tugs my shirt to signal for me to go in the kitchen. He and I are alone.

Dillard starts first, "Indi, how are you?! You seem a bit distant since you walked in the house. Are you okay?"

"Yes, Dillard, I'm doing okay."

"Well, what's wrong then? You are not acting like yourself. You even acting stand-offish with me. Did I say or do something to make you angry?"

"No not really Dillard I'm just tired, that's all."

Dillard continues to dig, "Are you sure that's it?"

"Yes, Dillard, I'm sure."

I don't want to bring up the Al situation. I simply am not in the mood. I have no energy for any possible explanation or debate that may give birth from the conversation.

Unsurely, Dillard looks at me and says, "Alright, Indigo, if you say so."

"Yes, Dillard, I say so."

I walk out of the kitchen to find the others surrounded by Lex. Dillard follows suit.

I am ready to get back to my comfort zone and bed to just relax after the long days of the past. I hug and kiss Lex on the cheek.

I whisper, "Call me if you need anything. I love you, chic. I'm leaving you in the hands of Dillard for tonight."

Lex nods, "Thank you, Indigo, for being there. Love you, and I'll call you later."

"Yes, of course, we sisters. I wouldn't have had it any other way."

The others stay to keep Lex company and make sure she's okay. However, Dillard plan on staying overnight for Lex's first day back home.

Edgewood escorts me home before returning to Lex's place.

As I'm stepping out of the truck, Edgewood blurts out, "So Indigo, what's really going on with Lex? I notice she's not saying much. Do you know anything?"

"Edgewood, now you know so damn well if I know something I will not put all her business out there. But anyway, no, I don't know anything. Whatever is going on with Lex, Lex will let us know when she's ready."

"Now that's a shady answer, Indi. I know you know. I respect it, though. I knew Lex was going through something when she snapped. Indi, you know, on the real, I'm just happy that she's okay. No matter what she's going through, Lex is my girl. You did your part, so we all stepping up to support her too. You knew I was going to ask more questions to see what you knew. But one day she will tell you, and all of us what she's dealing with like you just said. Until then, we just have to be good friends."

"Edgewood, you couldn't have said that any better. You are unequivocally right."

"Alright, Indi, see you later."

"See ya, Edgewood."

Edgewood waits until I am inside before leaving out the driveway.

"Home sweet home," I mutter to myself.

I set my phone down on the kitchen counter then I have a slew of text messages come through all at once. When I look, there are tons of text messages from Mr. Halo. The times and dates are random. My phone didn't have good reception in the hospital, causing a possible delay in messaging. Al also texted, asking me to contact Lian. Lian is also another one of my London connections. Al never texts, so I am a bit shocked to see his request. I must not have had phone service; that's the only explanation of Al texting me.

I sat on the edge of the sofa to call Lian.

The phone barely rang before Lian picked up the other line. "Indigo Savoy! Hello hello...I need to see you and discuss some major businesses."

"Hello Lian, I hear in your voice that you have some exciting news or endeavors coming up."

"Yes...yes...yes, Indigo, all the time with you. Yes!"

Lian is one of the upbeat, hip, modern-day London connections. I am blessed to have interaction with him. Lian is always fun. When first meeting Lian he made the meeting comfortable and amusing. His look on life is exciting. He believes in making the most of each moment with happiness and joy.

"Sorry, Lian, I missed all your text messages. I was in the hospital-"

"Hospital? Are you okay, Indigo?"

"Oooo, it wasn't for me. I was there supporting a friend. While I was there, I didn't have the best cell reception."

"I knew something was wrong. I didn't want to frazzle my feathers over it. I figured you would get the voice messages and call back."

"Wait, Lian, I didn't get any of your voice messages. My phone has been acting up lately."

"Well, Ms. Savoy, I would like to talk to you face-to-face to make some possible deals that can make you and me possibly a lot of money. I called Alfonso, he requested all negotiations go through you. I explained to him the importance of the meeting, however, he insisted you were the lady I needed to talk to."

"Lian speaking in person would not be a problem. I can get to London in a few days if the meeting is urgent."

Lian is silent for a few seconds before responding, "Tell you what Indigo, instead of you coming to London, how about we make this a fun adventure."

"O-kay, I'm listening."

"Indigo, I'm in much need of relaxation. Business always comes first, but we can make this meeting a celebration slash getaway meeting. I'm that confident about my offer. How about I come to your end for a short three or possibly five-day cruise to basically nowhere? We will be away from cell phones and outside disturbances. Feel free to bring a friend if you choose. I may bring my companion, but that's still up in the air."

"Lian, I like your thinking. A mini getaway couldn't come at a better time for me. Let's make it happen."

"Great Indigo! Let's make deals and enjoy the pleasures of the waters. I can't wait to see your pretty little smile. I'll schedule the cruise and see you in a few days on the waters. We will both have our own rooms. Should you decide to bring a friend, please email me their name and information within the next hour. Otherwise, I'll email the cruise confirmations to you by the end of the day."

"Absolutely Lian, I'm looking forward to seeing you too. Cheers."

"Same here, Indigo. Cheers."

Chapter 28

REST

*S*hortly after my conversation with Lian, I phone Al with the news. Al didn't seem the least bit surprised. Al's voice is monotone.

In a relentless tone, Al states, "I just need to see you, Indigo."

"Okay, Al, I'll come over tomorrow, and we can talk then."

I need today just to unwind. I still didn't get any rest after the previous long days with Lex. This is my time. The weekend is quickly approaching. I feel disconnected. People I love have been questionable in my life. Bullet and I are not talking regularly. Al has a secret life. It is so much to take in. I call mom to check on her; it has been forever since I spoke to her.

"Hello, hey, Ma. How are you and how's dad?"

"Indigo, hey. Baby things around here have been nonstop lately. Your dad and his new boat have been driving me up the wall. Every chance he's inviting people over to see the boat, come in the boat, look at this or that. All this traffic in and out of the house is driving me crazy. I'm trying to let him enjoy his boat and all without me complaining. But I'm getting close to the edge Indi. You would be proud of me because all I do is just smile and don't say anything. I don't know how long this will last."

"Ma, you doing a good thing for dad. You know he loves entertaining and having company. Sounds like dad is doing well then."

"Yes, all is good over here. Sky been Sky. I noticed you haven't been coming around lately. Is it because of Sky?"

"Ma, it's a combination of Sky, and I've been busy too. You know Lex was in the hospital for a week. I was there with her while she was hospitalized."

"Is she okay Indigo? I was trying to call you a few days ago, and your phone was going straight to voicemail. I left you a message. I called Dillard, and he told me where you were. I was calling to see how your competition turned out."

"Yes, Lex is okay. I ended up not competing because of her situation. I wanted to let you know I'm going on a business cruise too in about a week or so."

"A business cruise with who? What are the exact dates and exact locations?"

"It's with Lian. He and I have business tides. He's from London. The dates I'm not sure yet. I'm waiting for him to email me later today. If you need any details while I'm gone, Al knows the people I'm dealing with. Call him too, Ma, if you ever need information about anything regarding me traveling to Europe. Ma, I have to catch the call on the other line. Love you. Kiss, dad, for me. I'll call you later."

"Okay, bye, Indi, I love you too."

The call on the other end was from Lian, but he hung up before I answered.

Lian sent a text immediately, "Check your email. Details of the cruise have been scheduled."

My email has all cruise information scheduled for the next day. Lian is serious about getting together immediately. I scramble around to pack for the cruise. I have a voice message from Al. He must have called while I was on the phone with Mom, all while Lian was calling too.

Al voice message states, "Indigo, do you need me to get anything for you tomorrow? I want our talk to be undisturbed. If there's anything you need, please call and let me know. See you tomorrow."

Aw man, I'm not going to be able to see Al tomorrow. The cruise is tomorrow.

I call Al, but he isn't available, his phone has no answer. I call several times with no response each time. I decided not to leave a voice message. I'll just ride over to see Al later today after I finish packing. Today ends up not being a day of rest. My agenda has made a drastic U-turn from relaxing to high gear packing and going out to meet Al.

After packing, I decide to put all my packed items in the car and head to Al's house. Al isn't home when I arrive. Momma Deah has food out for Al. She must have just left because the food is still warm and the house smells good. I invite myself to fix a plate. I have a belly full before falling asleep on the loveseat.

"Indigo. Indigo. Indigo, wake up and come to bed."

"Huh, Al? What are you doing here?"

Al chuckle, "Indigo, you're at my house. You must have been here for a while. Come to bed."

"Al, what time is it? I am supposed to be on a cruise."

"Indigo, what cruise? It's two a.m. I really don't think you are supposed to be on a cruise right now."

"No, Al, I have a cruise with Lian. Is it Thursday?"

"Yes, Indigo, it's Thursday morning. You and Lian are going on a cruise? Why?"

Still groggy, I attempt to explain the cruise to Al, "Oh, it was his idea for us to discuss business. That's why I came over to talk to you today, but you weren't answering, so I just came over."

Al picks me up and carries me to my room. "Get some sleep, Indigo we will figure your cruise out in the morning."

Al kisses my forehead and walks out of the room.

The next morning I hear Momma Deah shuffling pots around cooking breakfast. I wake up refreshed. I must have been exhausted last night. After I ate at Al's house, I don't remember much of anything after that. I arrived at Al's house at seven p.m. and must have slept throughout the night.

Al is already awake. I am the last to get up. "Good morning." I greet Momma Deah and Al.

"Good morning," they both reply.

It is seven a.m., and breakfast is ready to be served.

"Indigo, did you sleep well?" Momma Deah asks.

"Yes I did, thank you for asking Momma Deah."

"I came over yesterday night because I left behind my extra keys, and you were sleeping so soundly last night. I cleaned up the kitchen and put the food away and you never moved a muscle. I'm happy you got some good rest. Well, Indigo, I have something planned for today and have to leave you two early. Hope both of you have a good day, and I'll see you both later on."

"Thank you, Momma Deah. You have a wonderful blessed day."

Al walks Momma Deah to the door and kisses her cheek before she leaves.

Al comes back, "Indigo last night you said you're going on a cruise with Lian. Was that correctly stated?"

"Yes, Lian stated he contacted you about a potentially great deal, but you referenced him to me. Therefore, he came up with the idea of going on a cruise for business and pleasure."

"Pleasure? Did Lian make a pass at you?"

"Al, I don't think it's anything like that. There's no strings attached. It's all business. He even extended the offer for me to bring a friend if I choose to. He and I spoke yesterday and he actually scheduled the cruise immediately for today. I had no time to do anything. That's why I packed as soon as I was aware of the cruise and came over here to talk. Especially since I knew I wasn't going to be able to talk tonight as originally planned."

"Okay Indigo. No worries. We will have our time. I'll bring you to your port and upon your return, let's schedule another day and time to have a heart to heart."

"You are always very understanding, Al. I'll go freshen up, and then I'll be ready to head out."

I hug Al before getting myself ready for a much needed relaxing getaway.

Chapter 29

ENCOUNTERS

*I*t's a beautiful blistering windy day. The shining sun creates a slight sizzle on my skin. Affirmation of beautiful weather confirms today is going to be a great day. I'm rested, ready for moneymaking beginnings, all while having a mini vacation. My life couldn't get any better than this present moment. Boarding is smooth. Lian books a large suite with lots of extra amenities.

Giggling and dancing by myself, "Five days on the sea. YES!"

A knock at the door interrupts my self-motivated private celebration, which I presume is Lian. As assumed, it is.

"Good morning Lian. It's a beautiful day."

"Indigo, you are absolutely correct with that statement. It is definitely a beautiful day. I hope you're pleased with your accommodations."

"Yes, of course, I couldn't have asked for anything better. It's too bad I'm here solo, but being solo isn't always a bad thing. It just means I'll get a lot of work done. Wait, excuse me, let me rephrase that. Not a lot of work, more like needed rest and relaxation."

"That's right, Indigo. I'm thinking on our first day on the ship; let's get situated and enjoy a bit of relaxation before getting to business. I'm planning that tomorrow we can meet up after breakfast on the Lido deck and talk about my propositions and get some feedback from you. I promise it will be a stress-free meeting. Mostly we will talk a few numbers but nothing too hot and heavy. Alfonso called me this morning already and I ran the proposition with him over the telephone. He's all in. You and I are going through formalities to ensure you agree as well. Alfonso did remind me, although he agrees, you are the final decision maker in this deal. Alfonso also wanted to make sure you will be well taken care of while on the ship and no other intent is coming from me. I reassured him our encounter is strictly business."

"Lian. Al...I mean, Alfonso can be a bit protective, so I apologize if he offended you. I have no concerns and know our meeting is totally professional. Tomorrow will be a great time to meet up. I think I'm going to put my bikini on now and head to the deck for some sun."

"Indigo, it's perfectly okay. I was not offended. Al is merely protecting you. I get it."

Lian gets up to exit when a male walks up to the doorway.

"Indigo, I would like you to meet Ury. Ury is in training. He will be joining our meeting tomorrow. Ury will be another contactor that will start communications with you and Alfonso sometime in the near future."

I extend my hand to greet Ury. Instead, Ury takes my hand and kisses the top of it.

Ury with a British accent states, "Nice to finally meet you, Indigo. My coworkers have had many interactions with you. I see your name in many of our files."

"Pleasure to meet you as well, Ury. I'm eager to work with you. All my interactions have been positive with our fellow London friends. Well, if both of you will excuse me, I'm going to get ready to enjoy the sun while it's still out shining."

Ury responds in agreement, "That sounds like a good idea. I may do the same thing. Hope to see you around Indigo."

"Yes, of course, see you guys later. If not today, I will definitely see you tomorrow, and I'm sure the next four days."

Happy faces surround the ship. I discover an empty chair and plant myself in the middle of the busy deck. I decide to claim this chair as my relaxing zone. I have my music in my ears and a towel to cover my face. I couldn't wait to show off my new gold-adorned bikini. I've been working-out religiously so it can fit perfectly. The sun has this orange-yellowish hue glistening, highlighting portions of my bathing suit. I lay on the long cushioned deckchair face down. Even the sweltering sun isn't going to keep me inside my room. I tune out any on-lookers to relish in my bubble of a world relaxing on the waters.

Eventually, everything around me is muted out. Right, when I am completely comfortable and relaxed, soon to follow, Ury taps my shoulder.

"Hello Indigo, I see you made it down and camping out. When I was passing, I had a drink for Lian and myself, but I decided to stop and see if you wanted one of the drinks. I can always go back and get myself another drink."

"Ury, you are too kind. What kind of drink is it?"

"Both of these are Patron pineapple. You may like it. The tequila gets you feeling good immediately."

"Ury, I don't do too well with any type of tequila drink, so I'm going to pass on this one. I appreciate the offer. I'm more of a daiquiri or rum type drinker."

"Would you like me to fetch you a daiquiri? It will be no trouble at all."

"Uhmmm...maybe, I will accept your offer."

"What type of daiquiri would you like?"

"I'll have a piña colada with whip cream topped over the drink. Thank you, Ury."

"No problem, I'll bring it right over in a few."

Ury walks away with the original drinks in his hand. I remove the cover from my face and then sit up for a few to survey all the cheerful faces. It's been a few hours, and already you can see some cruisers a little tipsy. Everyone needs a getaway. I cover up with my swimsuit over-lay, sit up, and continue to enjoy my headset. Ury and Lian both return with my daiquiri. The two of them joined me for a few hours as we sat in our own world, not talking to one another, but enjoying the essence of relaxation. Eventually, Lian starts to chat. Ury and I become engaged in the conversation. One-by-one, we all depart our separate ways. Sunlight slowly vanishes. I figure it is time for eveningwear.

Halfway to my room, I realized I left my beach bag near my chair outside on the deck. I immediately remove my headphones and run back to the deck to find my bag is gone. My heart starts to pound wildly. I look around to see if anyone is walking away with my bag, but I don't see it.

As I'm walking to the elevator, someone from behind grabs my hand tightly. I let out a startling scream and looked to my side to see Bullet.

"Bullet! What-"

Bullet had a smile ear to ear. His face is close to mine. He pulls my hand closer to his body.

"Did you lose this?"

"My bag! Yes! How did you see me? Where? How did you know I was missing my bag?"

At a point, I am lost for words. As we are standing in front of the elevator, Bullet hugs me tightly. The grasp is felt deep within.

Bullet pulls himself back slightly, "Indigo, I've missed you so much. What happened to us?"

My heart is pounding and I'm shaking with jitters. I feel like a high school girl meeting the crush of her life for the first time. I stare at Bullet for a minute with just a smile. I ponder what's the chance of Bullet and I to encounter each other on a cruise?

"Bullet, I can't believe you are here…at the same time, I'm here. Are you here alone?"

Bullet grabs my face and kisses my lips very softly.

"Does that answer your question?"

"Yes."

"Indigo, do you have a minute we can talk alone?"

As the "talk" question is brought up, I feel a pang to my chest. "Yea, uhmm yeah, I was just heading to my room to change. Would you like to meet me somewhere, or possibly you can come to my room now."

"I would like to come to your room now, of course, if that's okay with you or your company?"

"Okay, okay, well, just follow me."

I remain a bit nervous. I don't know why. All types of thoughts are rushing in my head. I have been eager to just talk to Bullet, but now, he's in my presence. This is even better than talking over the telephone. He doesn't seem upset with me; time has passed between us. Our phone calls have been hit or miss. I don't know if he is seeing somebody else. Is there still even an "us"?

All of these thoughts are rushing in my mind at once as I escort Bullet to my suite. Bullet keeps a tight clench to my hand. I feel his body next to mine the whole time we are walking. Sneaking a few long stares his way, quickly reminds me how his brown eyes glow. Merely looking in his eyes gets me wet and wanting him. My body misses all of him. Instantaneously my body is reacting to his voice, touch, and his look. It has been a while. But no, Bullet always has this effect on me.

I welcome Bullet into my chambers.

"This is a nice room, Indigo. Are you sure it's okay for me to be in here?"

Wanting to devour him whole, I gaze at Bullet while he speaks. "Yes, what was that you were saying, Bullet?"

"I said, are you alone on this trip? I saw a guy bring two drinks your way then he left with both in his hand. Are you on this trip with him?"

"No, well, yes, I am."

"Which one is it? Yes or no?"

"It's a business trip, so yes, I'm here with business partners, but overall I'm staying in my room alone."

Bullet perches himself on the bed, smiles, and progresses to ask questions.

"Indigo, what happened between us? You disappeared then blocked my calls. I talked to you briefly the other day, but you hung up on me and I couldn't reach you since your phone was going straight to voicemail."

"Bullet, I never blocked your calls. Recently my phone has been delayed in sending me messages. My mom and friends all said my phone was going to voicemail too. I called several times but thought you didn't want to talk. I would ring your phone, but I never received a call back from you either. I'm sorry I left you hanging, but there is a lot I need to share with you."

Bullet beckon for me to come near him on the bed, "Indigo whatever it is, we will talk about it later. For now, let's enjoy this time we have together on this cruise. I have really missed you. I saw you from the pier and couldn't believe it was you. I was nervous and aroused all at the same time. You do something to me, and I love it. I haven't been with anybody else because I can't get you off my mind. When you called, I may have been on business, therefore, my phone was possibly off. Why didn't you just call the business line? I always answer that phone. By the way, you look very beautiful in your swimsuit. For old time sakes, do you mind if I give you a massage? It relaxes you and me at the same time."

"Bullet, I really should take a shower first."

Bullet responds with a grin, "Before you do that, I need to go in first."

His response puzzles me but piques my interest by the way he looks.

"Okay go right ahead."

Bullet isn't in the bathroom very long, but he leaves me a love note near the face bowl.

"Indigo, you know you are not right. But you look so good in that two-piece. I love it!

Wit yo sexy ass!

I want to make love to your mind until your brain ejaculates the thoughts that it possesses so we can be on one accord.

I then want to make love to your heart, penetrating deep inside of it until our souls are intertwined as one.

Lastly, I want to kiss your lips and allow my hands to trace every curve of your sexy body.

Until your body yearns for me to give it more, and your canal is overfilling with the moistures of pleasure.

And then for me to explore your love tunnel and sink deep into your soul."

His written surprise has me yearning for his touch. I shower to ensure every crevice of my body is clean. We share the same desire. I long for him to trace every part of my body so we can intertwine as one once again too.

Once I step out the bathroom, Bullet has bright lights off, windows covered, and only leaving one distant lamp expelling a shimmer of ray. With my towel still wrapped around, Bullet takes my hand and requests I take position face down. The first touch is a soft kiss behind my ear then another kiss down my neck. I melt in the bed as I feel the warmth of his lips to my skin. Bullet rises and begins the massage. He knows a massage is a soft spot for me. He's the best and because it comes from him, the most sensual touch I ever experience. The massage always begins with my shoulders, extends to my arms, my hands and fingers, down my torso, legs, feet, butt. However, depending on the mood, the front portion of my body equally gets a warm rub down too.

Bullet whispers gently in my ear, "You doing okay?"

Melting in his arms, I respond with a whisper, "Yes, I'm doing fine."

Bullet hands move up both my inner thighs to give a gentle massage. His classic clever maneuvers of his fingers gingerly graze my explosive juicy canal. I hear him moan with pleasure as his only focus remains in the inner part of my Peach Butter. The sounds of slush begin to get him more aroused. His fingers start to move in and out as my body motions with the rhythm of his fingers.

"Turn over," Bullet whispers.

Bullet advances to remove the half-worn towel draped over me completely.

Bullet asserts, "I've missed my cherries so much."

Thenceforth, he opens my legs wide to massage my clitoris with his tongue. Bullet then grabs the lower part of my back and raises me to a sitting position.

"I need you to sit all over my face."

I oblige to his request, becoming his apple so he can take a bite wherever he chooses. He licks from front to back without skipping a beat.

I begin caressing my swollen nipples then reveal, "Baby I needed this. This is the best I ever had."

Bullet never responds but continues to eat, suck, and massage every part of the wide opening that welcomes him in. The tongue massage is accompanied by a finger caress in and out. The pleasure is erotic.

Cooing, gasping for breath, I exert, "BABY I never remember it feeling this damn good! I guess I forgot how much of a master you are at making me feel so goddamn virtuous!" His licks cause my inner thigh to shiver nonstop.

Later, Bullet flattens me to the bed. Flat on my back, Bullet drives himself inside tenderly. The inner connection triggers my heart rate to surge. As he strokes and kisses my breast, my grip around his back remains firm, never wanting this sensation to go away. The emotion is so high it sparks a tear to fall from one eye. Bullet kisses my lips passionately along with rubbing my body with endearment.

I look up at Bullet and repeat his classic saying, "I feel you."

"Baby I feel you too. I want to feel you today and forever, Indi. Forever."

Our lovemaking session lasts all night. Repeat acts of passion, kissing, touching, and just holding one another is never enough.

The next morning is the meeting with London connects, Lian and Ury. Coffee is a must beverage to keep my eyes open. Bullet washes me in the shower then leaves out and brings me some freshly brewed coffee to help me become more alert.

Bullet and I pick up from where we left off, but even better. The emotions are fiercer. His touches are deeper and intense. I can't pinpoint all emotions, but I sense it's something more there with Bullet. He has something to say, but, for some reason, doesn't disclose all his thoughts. We both pledge to relish the cruise without any heavy thoughts or burdens on one another. Bullet looks at me differently. He is even more engaging than I ever experienced. I roll with it and enjoy all the attention he gives.

Lian and Ury present an unbelievable offer that can't be denied. Al and I will come out, making a lot of money signing a two-year contract to do business with them exclusively. I already know Al agrees. I decide to sign the contract and move forward with the proposition.

Bullet and I spend the remainder of the cruise together with endless nights of lovemaking and cuddling. It is catch up time and we do just that.

I see Lian and Ury the duration of our trip on the sea. We chose to eat dinner together on the last night of the cruise. To complete the deal, I still must fly to London. Lian request, the sooner I can come, the better. I decide to make plans to depart within the next twenty-four hours. I figure this deal is too great to linger without making it final. Lian and Ury are both pleased and extend their hospitality once I arrive in London.

Before leaving off the ship, I have a video message from Dillard. Notifications from Dillard are via video and voice messages. My excitement to spend time with Bullet outweighed logic. I usually listen to messages in private. This time is an exception. I open the video chat and place it on speaker.

I see Dillard at his desk in the office while he records the message.

"Indigo T. Savoy, what the hell is going on with YOU, Miss Hot Sauce and Tracker? This man is going manic, asking about your whereabouts. Now Indigo talk to me! Something is up. You are not disclosing full details. No..."

I turn off the speaker and close the message immediately before I finish viewing and listening to the message. Bullet looks up into my direction. I sense the atmosphere change. I turn away from Bullet to hide my guilt and especially to avoid eye contact with my all-night lover.

Chapter 30

VOWS

*B*ullet and I leave the cruise ship together.

Bullet speaks first, "Indigo, what was Dillard talking about? Better yet, whom was Dillard talking about?"

Dismissively I answer, "Bullet nothing. It's office issues."

"Office issues?"

"Yes, office issues, Bullet."

"Indigo change of subject then, when will I see you again? I'm not allowing us to disconnect like we did ever again. Let's make vows to communicate no matter the situation. No more tearing the walls of love and no secrets."

Bullet is sincere in his declaration, "Yes, I vow to communicate at all times."

"Indigo, are you going to give me an answer on when we can see each other and have a sit-down? I have a lot I want to say to you."

I look directly into his mesmerizing brown eyes, "I have a lot to say too. May I ask if my key still works to the house?"

Bullet chuckles, nodding, "Yes, Indigo, your key still works. I always wished you had used it and surprised me one day. But I wasn't so lucky to have that happen. So yes, Indigo, your key still works."

I giggle. Turning towards him, "In that case, how about sometime next week after returning from London? So let's just say next Tuesday. Does that work for you? You can call me anytime and of course, I'll at least text. I promise I will not disappear. I'm sticking to the vow I made."

Nodding, in agreement, Bullet responds with a short "okay."

Bullet ensures I get home by having his driver bring me to my house. I leave to London the following day and make a quicker turnaround than I expected. My plane lands Sunday night. I decide to surprise Bullet the night I land instead of Tuesday as originally planned. I try to enter quietly through the front door. Upon my entering, the lights are dim. Bullet has his back facing my way.

I place my hand on his back and say, "Hey, baby, what are you doing?"

Bullet is flabbergasted.

The night Bullet and I share is beautiful. We clarify what we both want. But I know it's vital to tell Bullet about Al. I hate to ruin such a good night with something Bullet may take out of context. It is a discussion that has to take place. Bullet agrees that he will postpone the conversation until today. Therefore, I have to honor my words and stay open and honest.

I decide to talk about Al early the next morning. Get it over with and move forward. Besides, Al is part of my life, especially after this big business contract. That solidified our union. Business tides are connected between Al and me for at least another two years. After some discoveries about Al and other unknowns, I know Al and I will never have a romantic relationship. Bullet is my connection and always has been. I yearned for him for so long. Only he makes me feel like a high school girl all over again.

Bullet remains resting in bed. I decide to cook breakfast along with fresh-squeezed orange juice. This will set the mood right for a morning discussion. Bullet wakens before breakfast is complete.

I hear his footsteps getting closer while I'm in the kitchen. From behind, Bullet grabs my waist, "Morning baby."

"Good morning Bae, did you sleep well?"

"Yes, I slept EXCELLENTLY! How about you?"

"I slept just as excellent too, Bae. Go back to bed so I can cater to you this morning and feed you breakfast."

"What? I get V.I.P. treatment this morning? What caused this great honor for all this?"

"Stop it! Just go back to bed, and I'll be in shortly with breakfast and our little talk that was postponed until today.

"Indigo, this must be serious. Nothing bad, huh? You haven't been intimate with some other man, have you?"

"Bullet, it's none of those things, it's just us talking."

"As long as that ass is only for me, nothing can get me upset. I'll retreat to bed, but to let you know, I'm being buck as naked too."

I chuckle at Bullet and wave my hand to shoo him away, "Whatever, do whatever you want."

Bullet laughs in unison and walks back to the room. Bullet has all the covers removed, laying buck ass naked as he declared earlier with a hard sticking straight up.

With a delighted grin, I tell Bullet, "Put that thing away. I have a serious conversation here."

Bullet displays a devilish smile, "You sure about that lil' lady? I hate to put it away when you can enjoy much pleasure before the day begins."

Uncontrollably laughing, "Baby, I'm sure."

I toss the comforter over him while commanding him to sit up as I feed him his morning breakfast.

Bullet notices I have something on my mind.

He becomes serious too, "Indigo, what is it that you need to tell me?"

I open up to Bullet about everything regarding Al. I even explained to him about the night I left him to go and check on Al. Nothing is a secret. He is made aware of when Al came to Bayou's house and the history my family has with Al. I leave no stone unturned. I don't want any more secrets or barriers between Bullet and I. Bullet sat on the side of the bed in silence before uttering a word. Bullet's first spoken word is faint as if he needs to clear his throat. The conversation seems to take him by surprise.

Piercing the long silence, "So Indigo, you had or have a real connection with this man? Does he have a stronghold on your heart that may potentially cause us not to be together?"

Reassuringly I answer. "No, I promise Al and I will not have an intimate relationship. Al is like family to a certain degree."

"Let me get this straight, all your traveling and even the recent travel was because of business with this dude name Al?"

"Yes, Al helped me become prosperous to a certain degree before I met you. I promise Al will not interfere between you and I."

I don't disclose Al's lifestyle to Bullet. I feel that it is personal for Al. Bullet had heard of Al due to his popularity but never realized the connection Al and I shared. Bullet looks distant and disappointed. There is a bit of tension in the air.

Dead serious, Bullet states, "We will get through this. I have no further questions right now. I just need to let everything sink in."

Bullet looks at me while still on the side of the bed and continues, "Indigo just tell me one thing, do you love me?"

"Yes, Bullet, you know I do."

"Indigo, you know I love you. Since you love me, and I love you, we will get through anything that comes our way."

Bullet pulls me close to him and hugs me very tightly.

He kisses my forehead and whispers, "You have my heart Indigo. I'm never letting you go."

We embrace each other. The energy lightens up for a moment.

Before I leave, Bullet kisses and hugs me, saying, "You know you stuck with me for the rest of your life. I love you, Indigo. I want you to understand that I really love you."

"I love you too, Bullet."

Bullet watches my every move, as to question my sincerity. I know all my secrets are not completely revealed. I have questions of my own to myself. Am I candid with Bullet? I honestly can't answer the question. I only can give Bullet what I want my truth to be. I convince myself I am doing the right thing. Shit Bullet has secrets. I'm more than sure some link is missing in this equation from Bullet's standpoint as well. Why should I put all my cards out when there are different sides to Bullet I'm learning about?

Bullet face looks thoughtless as mine do too. I take my thoughts to paper. Tonight had me questioning my true feelings.

TRUE FEELINGS

It changes daily, from moment to moment
At times I embrace the good so tight that it turns into
    a corpse by my side
Resurrection soon follows suit to give birth to this
    decay
I once walked away from

Darkness and light battles for attention
Darkness demands to be respected as light gingerly
    softens the heart
This dual of feelings bruises and breaks invisible
    walls of strong stances

Feel...feel...feel...pause to silence
Stillness conveys the true feelings to grant the golden
    reward
to either darkness or light to win the race of truth in
    regards to...
One's deepest unchallengeable undeniable realistic
    true feelings

Chapter 31

CONTINUATION

$\mathcal{A}$fter leaving Bullet, my day is full. Leaving no time to talk with Bullet since that morning. Late evening I notice I have a few missed calls, one being Bullet. It's after nine p.m. I text him right away to let him know I'll call him once I get settled in from a busy day.

I want to talk to Bullet before calling it a night. Once I call, we are on the phone talking about our day. Not once did the previous night's conversation surface. It's always been easy to talk to him. He is a great listener, especially since I always have something to say. I love that about Bullet. He genuinely cares about what I have to say. Surprisingly he has a great memory about everything that always pertains to "us".

I have an idea but don't want Bullet to know I am aware of his schedule.

"What time do you go to work tomorrow?"

Bullet replies, "I have an online conference meeting and one major late-night conference call. I should be finished all work-related issues no later than eleven p.m."

"Oh okay."

"Why? What's up?"

I explode with a giggle, "Nothing I just wanted to know."

It's essential that we say our goodbyes for the night. We have early morning schedules we are obligated to. Both of us don't want to hang up, stating we will talk "five more minutes." After talking, "five more minutes" that same, "five more minutes" escapes our awareness. Turning that "five more minutes" more equivalent to a couple of hours later.

The next morning I decide to phone Bullet early in hopes he hasn't started any of his conference calls. He and I chat for a few minutes; he tells me his daily plans have changed. He and some other associates will meet tonight, having the late conference call only. That meant Bullet will be away from home until later tonight. He reassures me he will be back home by eleven p.m.

"If it's not too late, Indigo, I'll call you when I'm heading home."

"Bullet, that will be great. Possibly you can stop here when you're done. Wait, no, instead, just call me. I'll be awake. I forgot about something."

"What did you forget? You don't want me over there, Indigo? Are you hiding something, Ms. little Indigo?" As he chuckles a bit while speaking.

"Nope, not hiding anything. You just call that's all."

"Al-right lil lady, you just be ready for big daddy's phone call."

"Big Daddy, uh? Oh, okay, Big Daddy, I'll be ready."

The time Bullet is away passes fast. Before I know, it is at the end of the day. Bullet rings my phone, but I don't answer. Bullet calls three times back-to-back, but no answer from me either time.

Immediately, I receive a text from Bullet.

"I know it's late, and maybe you have gone to bed already. I didn't get a chance to call from work because the meeting was so intense. So I'm going to take a slow ride home just listening to my music and thinking about you."

Purposely, I don't respond to his text.

Bullet arrives home. The first thing I hear is Bullet pulling up to the driveway and getting out of the car. I have the music softly playing inside as he approaches his front door. Bullet has no idea I am going to be at his house when he arrives. I park my car in the garage, which Bullet never uses.

I can tell the front door is opened slowly and cautiously. I have all lights off with candles illuminating the whole house. Bullet is now in the house, not saying a word. I hear the opening and closing of every room door.

The bathroom is the last door before his bedroom. When he opens the bathroom door, Bullet discovers candles ordained throughout. There was a bubbly tub of water, a bucket of ice with a bottle of wine stationed in place, and two wine glasses sitting on the mantle.

His bedroom door is the last door to get opened. I welcome Bullet's entrance. I lay across the bed in a silk robe. Bullet quickly makes his way over to where I'm settled to greet me with a kiss.

Biting his bottom lip, he remarks excitingly, "Baby! When did you get here? That explains why you were not answering the phone. I knew something was strange. I couldn't remember if I left the music on when I left the house earlier. Hearing the music when I first walked up to the door had me confused. But once I opened it, I knew you had a hand in this entire set up. The smell in the house is refreshing, with all these candles lit. Baby, I love this."

I get out the bed, "Come with me. I have a surprise for you."

Bullet says nothing, instead extends his hand for me. I grab Bullet by the hand and lead him back to the bathroom.

"Don't say a word, just listen, okay?"

"Okay," Bullet replies.

I remain covered in a slinky silk robe. I guide Bullet to the bubbly foam bath while I remain standing near the tub. He undresses then steps in the water. I notice Bullet shoulders are tense.

"Just relax for a minute," I utter delicately.

Bullet leans his head back and just closes his eyes.

I reach for the remote to increase background music. The tune is soothing and mellow.

Bullet attempts to speak. "Where did you find that?"

"Shhh, remember no talking, just listen."

I pour two glasses of red wine, handing one over to him. Bullet's body is immersed under white bubbles. I begin to dance to the sound of the music.

I move my body like a work of art, purposefully allowing peeks of my silhouette from the candle flames' flickers. I sway from side-to-side, occasionally turning for a birds-eye view from the back.

The dance lasts until the song ends. With my back turned to Bullet, and my head turned around looking at him, I loosen my robe's belt, allowing it to stretch open. I observe Bullet become aroused from the enjoyment of watching me dance.

I grab the wine and take another sip before allowing the robe to slide off my shoulders onto the floor.

Turning on the jacuzzi jets, I climb into the tub to join my hypnotic brown-eyed lover. I fold over to place my soft lips against his. We begin to kiss as I feel his tongue rolling around in my mouth. I glide my body right between his legs. The kiss intensifies. He takes his hand and softly rubs it across my nipple; the touch creates stiffness to the tip. I subsequently turn to face Bullet so that the kisses can be more accessible. With both his hands full of my breast, he begins to kiss me down my neck. I lean my head in closer. He reaches one arm around my back and pulls me in, even more. From the back, he begins to massage my ass. With both hands, he continues to caress my body.

He takes his fingers to spread my cheeks apart. On one accord, I proceed to take my hand and reach down in the water to grab his love pistol, stroking it up and down. My legs spread apart to welcome his finger inside.

Although we are in the water, Bullet proclaims, "I can feel your juices flowing. It is so slippery."

I begin to ride his finger, going up and down. I just can't take it anymore; I want more. With my breast in his mouth, I take his hard measurement of love to slide it into my ever-waiting love cave. I push him back so that he's almost lying down in the water. Both my arms are placed on each side of the tub to position myself to ride that horse to ecstasy.

I can hear my ass darting on the water every time I come down to receive him internally. With him responding with an upward thrust every time I settle down. He hears my moans of fulfillment; I am feeling him. The water is splattering all over, neither one of us cares.

"I want to find that G-spot, so I can feel you explode! Fuck me, baby," Bullet softly whispers.

"Fuck me baby, ohhhhhhh," he repeats.

The repetitive motion continues until I get up and step out of the tub. Bullet remains sitting.

That's when I lean over the side of the tub, look back, then tell Bullet, "Now it's your turn. Fuck me, big daddy."

Chapter 32

ILLUMINATIONS

*B*ullet and I are back in good graces. I feel the authen-
ticity of his love, and I love showing him my sincerity.
The last couple of nights with Bullet are intense and what my body
has been longing for. I clarify some misconceptions of thoughts and
feelings regarding the relationship we share. After leaving Bullet's
place, the next morning, past issues need to be addressed. Al has
been waiting to speak to me. It's way overdue for me to talk to
Dillard. I conclude I don't care if the mystery man is Dillard or not
anymore.

Secrets can be revealed without me feeling bound to deception. I
figure we have our own life to live, no need to hide anything from
me. All these thoughts, as I decide to work it off at the gym. A good
workout will set additional endorphins of stress-free if I have any
still hidden from myself.

The gym gives me just what I long for. I'm cranked on a natural
high. My day is starting great. As I'm leaving the gym's parking lot,
outcomes a car zooming past startling me, practically running me
over. It triggers me, and some other vehicles, to come to a complete
stop. It seems that this car is trying to leave in a hurry. Another car
soon follows moving just as fast. I don't move. I look around to
ensure no additional cars are in pursuit. The two vehicles create

such a commotion. Eventually, it is safe to drive. The two automobiles disappear out of sight. Riding down the side street, I stop at the local market to pick up a few things. But I see those two cars again, this time both of them are parked in the market's parking lot. I look over with curiosity. I notice, what I think, is a familiar face. I continue to stare while I remain in my car. I'm being nosey.

What in the hell has the two of them zooming out of a gym's parking lot like that? I see two men out of the car. The first face I see is definitely one I don't know, however, the other guy looks familiar. The conversation seems intense.

I can't quite tell who this other guy is and where I have seen him before, but I brush it off and keep looking. None of the cars are familiar to me, so I am only looking out of pure marvel. I cancel the idea of knowing either one of the guys. My vision isn't clear enough. I wish I could hear what they are saying. Their argument caught the attention of other onlookers too. I witness people looking back and some point-blank stop to look.

My phone rings, "Hello?"

"Hey Indigo, what are you doing today?"

"Dillard, right now, I'm at the market watching a juicy heated argument. I think blows about to start. Wait, no! Hold on, Dillard. No, no, let me call you back."

I hang up the phone with Dillard because I see another car pull up. Out comes another dude walking up to the whole ordeal. My phone rings again, it reads, "Dillard." I don't answer since I remain engaged in the quarrel. I unquestionably know the new face that pulls up. This is the face of Arlo pulling up.

I think to myself, "Now what in the world is Arlo doing pulling up to this?"

The car Arlo is driving is unfamiliar. This car is an Audi S5 Coupe. That sucker is black and sparkling clean. I even have to say, "Damn! I like that."

Dillard calls me again right in the midst of me talking to myself and trying to engage in what's to happen next.

I answer this time with a distant greeting, "Yea, Dillard."

"Yea, Dillard? Indi what you doing? Who is fighting?"

"I told you I am at the market. Oh, Dillard, did Arlo get a new car?"

Before Dillard answers me, as I still gawk over at the guys, Arlo steps out the car and grabs one of the unfamiliar faces then he starts to give him a deep kiss right then and there. The other guy tries to grab the guy Arlo started to kiss, but he pulls from him, then jumps in his car and pulls off.

I become frozen. I know it is Arlo. What in the hell? Dillard is talking, but I don't remember what he's saying.

"Dillard? What?"

Dillard with an elevated tone, "Indigo, what are you doing?! I said Arlo doesn't have a new car. What made you ask that?"

"Yea, okay. Where's Arlo now, Dillard?"

"He's at work. Why? What's going on, Indi?"

"Nothing. I need to come see you. I was going to call you right before you called me. See you in a bit." I say hurriedly.

I am trying to get off the phone with Dillard. I don't want him to ask me any additional questions.

"Indi are you still watching a fight wherever you at?"

"No, no fight. It's over now."

"Since you at the market bring me some fresh squeezed OJ," Dillard states.

"Dillard I'll bring it another time."

"Bring it now, you said you at the market, right?"

"Yes, I did say that, but I have to run back to the gym immediately. I left something. So I'm not getting out to go inside the market. Dillard, I gotta go. I'm going to see you soon. Bye."

Dillard just will keep asking questions. I remain stunned. Besides, I want to keep looking to see what Arlo is doing with this new face. I am numb. Dillard seems to have no clue either. Arlo gets in his car, and the other guy gets in his car after the two of them kiss and embrace one another. Arlo passes right in front of my car. That's when I know for sure it is him. My vision is clear and identifies his face with no question. I slump down in my driver seat when I see his car approaching my way. I am so happy he doesn't realize it is my car. I guess he is on an adrenaline high with his lil' boo.

I can't believe I see all this action early in the morning. I sit in my car, shocked. Now I start questioning everything.

"Arlo has a new car or somebody's car, a new side thing? Dillard has no clue, or I'm just tripping? Possibly Dillard is doing his thing, and Arlo does his thing too. But there is the issue of Dillard and Al, possibly, right?"

I try to make sense of everything. I take a long scenic ride to Dillard's place. I lied to Dillard about going back to the gym. I just wanted to get off the phone and think for a minute. I am too numb to go to the market. After all this craziness, I figure everybody's wearing a mask of some sort. I pull up to Dillard's place and just walk in the house.

"Dillard? I'm here. Dillard?"

Dillard comes from the back with his phone glued to his ear. He signals for me to be quiet while he's on the line then goes back into another room to finish his conversation.

For the first time, I don't just sit down. I put my purse down and study Dillard's place. I mean, I look at everything around me. I walk up to pictures around the house to look at faces. I see a picture of Arlo.

I glare at his face, questioning, "What or who else are you doing?"

Things are mysterious, but Dillard and I have been besties our whole life. I'm point blank asking questions. Enough of me with all these questions in my head. I know if the shoe were on the other foot, Dillard would not hesitate in one second to ask straight-up questions to me.

Dillard is on his phone call for a while. I walk to Dillard's bedroom, searching for his Jellyfish Andrew Logan Swatch. Dillard loves that watch and keeps it in the same place at all times. I know because he always shares his display of new adornments with me. Half the time, I am there when he purchases his embellishments. Dillard walks in his room as I'm perusing through his trinkets.

"Indigo whatcha doing?"

I turn back fast, "Dillard, I didn't hear you come in."

"I bet you didn't. You like a two-year-old getting into something you not supposed to. Are you looking for something?"

I look at Dillard stoned faced then bluntly ask, "Are you fucking Al?"

Dillard looks dumbfounded, "WHAT? WAIT! Indigo, what did you just ask me?"

"Dillard, don't play around. I need the honest truth. We have no secrets, remember? You know EVERYTHING about me!"

"Indigo did you just ask me, am I fucking Al? Are you serious?"

"Dillard, where is your Jellyfish Andrew Logan Swatch? You love that thing. I'm only asking because I'm tired of deceitfulness and lies. Al has not been straightforward with me, so I'm coming to you."

"Al? What you mean Al has not been straightforward with you? Hold up! Hold up! What does Al not being straightforward has anything to do with me? INDIGO what is really going on?"

Dillard's face turns red. His face is scowling with astonishment when I turn to him with a response, "Dillard, I saw your watch. It was at Al's condo off the lake."

"Indigo that couldn't have been my watch, I'm pretty sure of it. Al has exquisite taste too. Indigo, you know that could be Al's watch. Did Al mention my name or something?"

"Dillard I knew it was your watch because your initials were engraved on the back, unique to only you. In addition to the watch, I saw your cufflinks. Dillard, both your items were there, and you say it wasn't you? I saw you when you ran past me. Dillard just say it. It hurt me at first because I felt you betrayed me knowing the history Al and I shared. Especially sneaking behind my back was the worst. You know you could tell me anything, and I'm very understanding. I would have never betrayed your trust."

"Indigo STOP! JUST STOP! What is Al doing with my stuff? You said you saw me, then why didn't you stop me?"

I look at Dillard with his continued twist of disbelief, "Dillard was it you?"

"Indigo straight up I swear whatever you saw, it was not me."

Now I'm sitting there baffled. Dillard seems to be candidly confused about what I'm talking about.

A low mutter blurts from my mouth, "Possibly Dillard, it wasn't you then. The person I saw was wearing a mask and ran so fast by me. Dillard, I swear it looked like your body frame. When I confronted Al and asked if it was you, he remained silent as if he didn't want the secret revealed."

"He remained silent?! There was no reason his ass remained silent! He should have told you right then and there, it wasn't me! Shit! Now you coming up in here playing inspector gadget and shit accusing me of fucking Al, looking like some got damn crazy woman! You have my heart racing a mile a minute, trying to figure out what the hell Al doing with MY SHIT! Al needs to man up and SAY SOMETHING! Call his ASS now! You know what, betta yet, we taking a ride to his silent ass house right now! We are nipping this shit up TODAY! Mother...you got my blood pressure high! Indigo I don't like this shit, especially when my name is connected!"

Dillard is in rare form. Before I could refute going to Al's house, Dillard already has his keys in hand, demanding to leave now. Dillard drives his car. Al's car is home.

"Dillard, before we go in here, please don't go crazy. I still need to talk to Al about some things that are not clear between us."

Dillard looks straight ahead through his windshield. Dillard is speaking as if he is coaching himself to be calm, "Indigo, I don't care what you and Al have going on. All I want is my shit, and my name cleared."

"Dillard, like I said, Al didn't really say it was you. So your name is clear."

"Indigo, if my got damn name was clear then we wouldn't be at this got damn silent ass man front door, now would we?! By him not saying it wasn't me then, THEREFORE, MY NAME IS NOT CLEAR! Indigo I don't have time to discuss this with you. Get your-ass-out-my-car, and let's clarify ALLLLL this shit today!"

Dillard is in an irrational mode. My movements aren't as swift as Dillard. I am still walking up the stairs while Dillard is banging on the door and ringing the doorbell. Momma Deah opens the door; she greets me with a hug and kiss as usual.

Dillard greets Momma Deah dry and sharply, "Good morning Momma D! Where's Al?"

Momma Deah responds, "Well hello there, Dillard I haven't seen you in such a long time. You looking—"

Before Momma Deah finishes her greeting to Dillard, Dillard cut Momma Deah's conversation short, "Uh huh Momma D, yeah... yeah, nice to see you and everything, but where is AL!"

Momma Deah steps back, possibly sensing the urgency in Dillard's voice. Momma Deah walks away, calling out for Al. Al comes to the front. "Momma Deah what's wrong? Why are you yelling?"

Al walks to where Momma Deah stands with concern when he sees Dillard and me in the living room.

"Indigo, hello. Hello, Dillard." I could tell Al is puzzled.

I interject before Dillard can say anything. Momma Deah steps out of the room and I no longer see her this visit.

"I know it's early, Al, but Dillard and I were talking. I kinda asked him about his cufflinks."

Dillard is disgusted by how I introduce our presence, "Al, Indigo, and I are here because she is confused about something pertaining to my cufflinks and watch. First of all, why do you have my cufflinks and watch? Second of all, why is it that when Indigo confronted you about me, you had no answer? Today we clarifying the air, and I'm getting my shit back, TODAY!"

Al's face looks deflated. Al remains calm, although Dillard is on level one hundred ready to set anything off at any minute.

"Both of you, please take a seat. Indigo, I wanted us to talk, which I hope we do soon."

"Yes, Al, we can still talk. I'm sorry this issue has been brought to your attention this way."

Dillard looks at me with a crazy stare, "Indigo, we here to clear the air! Your ass should have thought about bringing up issues and shit before you came to my house with all your accusations. You apologizing to him! Where's my got damn apology? Shit on all that!

Al speak up. You have the floor again. INDIGO WILL NOT SAY A WORD UNTIL YOU'RE DONE, RIGHT INDIGO!"

"Right, please, Al continue. Sorry, Dillard."

Brazenly Dillard states, "Whatever Indigo, let the man speak PLEASE! Leave all that sentimental talk for another time."

Al takes the floor proceeding to explain, "Indigo, the night you came to the condo was not for you to witness. Dillard, the cufflinks and watch belongs to you. I did not know it did. I had no part in taking it from you. The items were left behind when Indigo startled my night."

Dillard's heated demeanor calms to a level seventy, "Left behind by who? I don't even remember misplacing them. Al, who are you referring to?"

Al has a gloomy face then sighs before speaking, "Dillard, Indigo, the guy I was with was Arlo. Arlo must have taken Dillard's belongings, not realizing he left them behind. Arlo flew by you Indigo because I assume he didn't want you to identify him. Dillard, Arlo approached me after the picnic when he introduced himself, he continued to hound me, asking me to mentor him. The night Indigo found us was the first night we were going to be together. By Indigo coming in, nothing happened. As it happens, Arlo has never called for your belongings. I have them in my room. I was going to talk to Indigo, then give them to her, but we never had a chance to speak yet. I'm sorry, Dillard. Arlo was very persistent in the chase, which is no excuse. I should have said no, then none of this would have taken place."

With a cold stare, Dillard snaps, "You got damn right about that!"

Al gets up after talking with a somber demeanor stepping away to retrieve Dillard's belongings. I hug Dillard while we sit in silence. Dillard places his face in his hands. The news shocks me with a double whammy, especially since I just saw Arlo boo'd up with somebody else.

Piercing the dark silence, I turn to Dillard, "Dillard this is a straight-up moment with clarity, no deceptions, no secrets, right?"

Dillard looks at me, "Indigo?"

"Dillard, I'm saying this raw with no lubricant. I saw Arlo today in the Audi, I questioned you about, with another man. He kissed him. Apparently, they looked like they were in a relationship of some sort. Dillard, Arlo is not what you think he is. I'm truly sorry, my friend. I wanted to tell you the whole story while I was at the market when I was witnessing everything. I was speechless. I didn't know how to tell you that's why I hung up so quickly with you. I asked you about Arlo's whereabouts for a reason, the car too. Arlo initially wasn't in the part of the quarrel when you first called but later arrived and swept one of the guys that were arguing away with him. I convinced myself that you and Arlo are practicing an open relationship. I was going to talk to you later about what I saw, but the conversation led into a different direction when I tried to clarify the relationship with you and Al."

Dillard stays silent.

I embrace Dillard tightly. Al hands me Dillard belongings, then I give them to Dillard. Dillard takes a stand, straightens himself up, then stands more erect.

Dillard, one-by-one, looks at Al first then me, "Thank you for clarity. Indigo, I need to take a ride alone."

Al states, "Indigo stay here so we can talk. I'll bring you to your car if that's okay with you."

I see Dillard needs time and space. Therefore, I stay behind with Al allowing Dillard to have his requested alone time.

I hug Dillard tightly again, asking, "Are you sure you want to be alone?"

Dillard nods, "yes." Dillard looks dazed but seems to be calm when he departs Al's place.

Chapter 33

MASQUE

*A*fter Dillard leaves, I stand outside, looking down the street until Dillard's car is no longer visible. Once Dillard makes a turn, that's it. I can only imagine what is going through his mind. Dillard isn't one to be silent. But for that moment after the shocking news from Al, then from me, silence is precisely what Dillard displayed. Al comes to the door where I'm standing. The shutters tremble with each gust of wind.

"Indigo, come inside out of this windy weather."

I shut the door slowly. Everything seems surreal. I feel completely like an ass after accusing Dillard of something with Al. When this whole time, Dillard is the one getting the worst affliction from this unfolding nightmare.

Even now, I can visualize Dillard's face clearly when I confronted him. Dillard, my best friend, how could I think that was him? For Dillard to run pass me wouldn't have been his nature. Dillard would have owned up to the situation right at that moment. I of all people knew this about Dillard too. Why was I tripping?

In my muddle of thoughts, out the blue, Al begins speaking. "I know you are concerned about Dillard. I didn't want to break the news to him that way. I never wanted him to know about that night. I was going to only tell you things about me, but since Arlo left

Dillard's stuff, it made the situation awkward when you insisted on having an answer. You were determined that Arlo was Dillard. I was lost for a word, that's why I couldn't answer you at the time. It was never my place to say anything about whom I was with to you or anybody else. The watch undoubtedly needed an explanation of discovery."

"Al, it's okay. You don't need to explain anything to me about that night. The person who needed to know now knows what type of person he's dealing with. I only wished it wasn't Arlo. You and Dillard, I thought, were cool with one another. I wouldn't have imagined. I guess you never know, right?"

"No, Indigo, that's not an accurate statement. It's not like that at all. I—"

I sense Al is getting ready to get into an in-depth explanation. I put my finger to my lips to shish his continued vindication. I'm concurrently shaking my head side-to-side with a "no" pattern of movement.

I stop him before hearing anymore, "Al, really, it's okay. No more, okay. Really it's okay. You don't have to explain Dillard's painful situation to me. I feel bad because I accused him in my mind all this time before asking. I know Dillard. I should've known better to understand he wouldn't have run past me or leave behind his favorite watch for me or anybody else. Then to witness the event I saw today and break down some additional ruthless news? My friend probably has so many unsettling reflections going through his head. One of those thoughts is more likely, me and my accusations. All that to say, Al, you owe me no explanation. I'm very grateful you were honest and disclosed the truth to Dillard. Thank you for that. I'm thinking about Dillard, but I'm sure you have thoughts as well. Since we are being open, I too want to disclose something to you."

Al looks intently and serious, "Indigo, please speak."

I unveil my relationship with Bullet to Al. I explain to Al that I love him, but I'm in love with Bullet.

"Al, you and I have a great connection. After walking into your nightcap that night, I reflected on 'myself' even deeper. I was hurt, really hurt, and honestly, I shouldn't have been. Al, you and I have no committed intimacy. I know you love me, but I felt something that night seeing you with somebody else for some reason. It didn't matter if it was a man or a woman. It was the fact that it was somebody. It's quite selfish of me to have felt those feelings because I have an intimate life outside of you. It's crazy, Al, just crazy. I guess subconsciously, I never wanted to see you with anybody. I wanted you to be Al, and I be Indigo, that's it. Whatever we had, I wanted it for a lifetime, an unspoken 'us'. I wanted neither one of us to flaunt another companion around one another. I wanted this forever. We kinda sorta had it for a long time, five-plus years easily. Yet, life changes along with circumstances. I get it. At the time, my emotions took the better side of me. I juggled you and Bullet as long as there were no boundaries crossed. But you know boundaries were being crossed the whole time. Secrets were the boundaries. I wore whatever mask suited me for the situation. I had no quarrels with it and assumed you didn't either."

Looking directly into my eyes, Al grabs both my hands then leans forward to speak to me. The hairs on my arm stand to attention; the chills crawl down my spine. My heart melts like butter while he is completely engaged. Warmth in the room is tangible— shaking shutters and strong whistling windbreaks the quietude in the room. Dancing leafs occasionally beat on the window, desiring entrance from the snare of the breeze.

Al assents, "Indigo, I wanted the same thing you wanted. If you hadn't ever come to the condo that night, we still would have it, I honestly believe. That one night turned into an ugly situation in many ways. Indigo, my lifestyle was something I kept to myself. I never involved you in any of my relationships outside of you. As it happens, you coming in may have been a good thing in hindsight. Eventually, if one of us were to fall in love with someone outside of 'us', then what? The transition of openness, including someone 'serious', would have been challenging to accept for me. Indigo, I knew you had guy friends, possibly even a boyfriend. I was okay with that as long as it wasn't serious. You said it was selfish of you to have your feelings. On the other hand, I had it worse than you. Seeing you with another would have torn me apart. Indigo, I have always loved and respected you. I always wanted more but knew I had to be honest with myself. The past issue with Tiff tore us apart right from the beginning. At that time, I was already breaking up with Tiff before you and I experienced any intimacy. Indigo I tried to explain to you then that Tiff was not who I wanted, and I'll explain it to you now, there is no one I want. I loved you then and still love you now. Looking back on everything I put you through, I know I have to let you be free. I can't continue with the feelings I have for you. No matter who was to come in my life, you are always my priority. Yes, Indigo, I have intimacy outside of 'us', but I never paraded it in your face and never would have. Indigo, I want you to be happy. If you are happy, I share your happiness with you. When you spoke about your friend, I see that you were happy talking about him."

My eyes are filling up with tears as Al speaks to me. I undergo a sense of relief that we can be open about our lives. Al and I have an unspoken love and union.

I know it, and so does he. "Al I love you. We needed to have this talk. It has been somewhat an elephant in the room. I knew how you felt, although it was never said. Now I know why I knew, it is because I feel the same way. Recently I told Bullet about you. You were part of my masked life. I juggled both of you to keep bliss on both ends. I never told you this, but I stopped seeing Bullet because of you. My plan wasn't to stop seeing him, though, I did."

Al responds, "Indigo, I never knew. I didn't ask--"

"I know, Al, I know. It was the night you paged me late. I left Bullet's place abruptly for you. Thereafter, Bullet and I became estranged. The story is longer, nonetheless, that's the short and sweet of it. I'm only telling you this because ironically, I saw Bullet for the first time since that night. He was unexpectedly on the cruise while I was doing business with Lian. I spoke to Bullet once we were shore side. Thereafter, I knew I needed to talk to you. It was time."

Al's eyes wander to the side, looking off in space, "Did you hear that?"

Pausing in position, "I hear it. It sounds like the wind beating on the windows."

Beating is heard again, now in a constant rhythm.

Al jumps up, "That's somebody at the front door."

I overhear commotion at the front door, shouting out, "Al is everything okay?"

Al steps outside before answering. I sat for a while, figuring it is nothing.

There is a nauseous panic of yelling outside. Retreating to the door, I witness Arlo in a hysterical state. Arlo had pulled into Al's driveway with his new Audi, which is still running. Arlo façade is in disarray, a totally different exterior from earlier today. Arlo appears out of breath while talking as if he just ran a marathon. Al is standing with an impartial posture. I hear Al respond to Arlo, "the truth."

The driveway is too distant for me to hear anything else Al is saying. Al's speech is monotone. Arlo is flapping his arms side to side out-of-control. It looks like Arlo is going to snap at any moment. Al is not one bit moved by Arlo's theatrics; Al stays committed to his stance. Arlo is pacing back and forth in front of Al.

I march down to where both Arlo and Al are standing, "What's going on down here? What's all the commotion about Arlo?"

Arlo's expression is edgy; he doesn't remedy my inquiry. Al looks at me from the side and shrugs his shoulders. My facial countenance is perplexed.

Dillard pulls in hot, speeding up to the driveway blocking Arlo in. He pitches a hard rock bar of soap aimed at Arlo with a dangling string wrapped around the soap. Large print displays, "GO WASH YA ASS!"

Dillard steps back in his car, staring at Arlo from the car window a good five seconds, before getting out to stand against his car door. Al stands rock solid, examining everything in reserve. Arlo stares back at Dillard in a frozen stance. Dillard's face is a mixture of rage and repulsion. I run up to Dillard to encourage him to enlighten me on what's going on.

Dillard reels in a forward fumed slow march toward Arlo, allowing his gaze to remain on Arlo, leaving me behind. He's speaking to me but pointing his finger high and direct while yelling with brazen words directed at Arlo.

"Indi, I found out this hoe ass bitch standing in the driveway been trickin' all over the Crescent City! Enough to bring back some disease to me! He knows so damn well I don't play that kinda shit!"

I talk to Dillard in a soft motherly calming tone. At the same time, I cradle my arm into his. If anybody can calm Dillard down, it's me.

"Dillard let's all talk about everything. Did you investigate properly? This could all be speculation. Let's get in your car and head home."

Dillard allows me to escort him back towards the direction of his car.

Dillard rocks his head, side-to-side in frustration.

"Let's go, Dillard. He's not worth the trouble or you getting all worked up over. Let's go. I'm just goin' run inside to get my purse and phone. I'll be right back immediately, then, we will leave, okay?"

Dillard says nothing except gestures with a slight head tilt agreeing to wait for me to get my belongings. The nod is a mutual understanding of "okay." After that, we will leave.

I sprint in the house, grab my purse and phone then dart back down the stairs to the car. Dillard is standing outside his vehicle on the passenger side, waiting for me. His posture is guarded and he's still on edge. Dillard's cold eagle stare remains on Arlo; he doesn't utter a word. Dillard opens my door for me to get in.

I lip to Al, "I'll call you later."

Al nods on his way back in the house.

I perceive Arlo's anxiety becomes reduced while he continues to stand outside beside his car. I wonder why he even came to Al's house in the first place. I suppose he is asking Al what was said to Dillard earlier today. That was only a hypothesis in my mind since I heard Al stating "the truth." Arlo appears to muster a backbone all of a sudden since Dillard is in the car, not saying anything.

Out of nowhere, I see Arlo pointing and waving his hand towards Dillard.

Suddenly, in a taunting manner, Arlo burst out, "That's right BITCH. I sure did make my rounds! I'm not scared of you! I'm well taken care of!"

I can't move; Arlo must be on a suicide mission. My eyes darted to see Dillard. I am in disbelief that Arlo has the nerve to say what he just said in the midst of him still standing in the driveway. My passenger door is already shut. Arlo is acting cocky, after his spoken declaration, he just stands arrogantly, looking at Dillard. I'm clenching my teeth, stiffened with unknowns that can take place. I survey Dillard's every move with a peripheral view of Arlo.

Dillard is walking leisurely toward the driver's door as if he isn't fazed by Arlo's words. Dillard opens his driver's door, indicating he is getting in the car. Astonishingly, instead, Dillard charges like a roaring lion in a rampage hunt toward Arlo. He then blatantly punches Arlo directly across the face. I don't think Arlo was expecting that type of reaction since Dillard appears so chill. With that direct blow, Arlo stance breaks resulting in a hefty face fall.

The incident occurs extremely fast. It startles me, crafting a chilling scream, "DILLARD!"

Dillard never looks up at me. Instead, he displays the persona of a man with boiled up madness. Gentleman went out the window in a one-two count. He starts kicking Arlo uncontrollably. I ran up to Dillard in an effort to stop his spectacle of wrath.

Dillard hollering at Arlo, "Who the bitch na?!"

Anything else Dillard is saying I can't fathom. I am busy trying to wrench Dillard away from Arlo. My tugs are useless, Dillard doesn't budge. Al comes running out to my aide. Al is able to grab Dillard off Arlo.

Dillard yanks Al off him, "Get yo motherfuckin' hands off me bitch! You part of this shit too! I should whip yo ass along with this hoe ass bitch!"

Arlo is lying in a fetal position. I see blood on the pavement along with what appears to be a tooth missing. Abruptly Dillard runs back to Arlo and kicks him as hard as he can in between his legs. Dillard then takes off his hard steel shoe, trying to break the windshield. His attempts to break the windshield has minimal victory. A crack to the windshield is noted. When Dillard realizes the windshield mission is in vain, he hits the driver's mirror, successfully breaking it to a dangle on Arlo's new Audi.

I start to yell, "Lets go Dillard now before the police come out here!"

Dillard looks my way infuriated. I repeat the phrase louder, "LET'S GO before these white folks call the police!"

Dillard concludes his mission of trying to sabotage Arlo's car. Dillard gets in the car with straight arms. Every vein in his arm is popping out. Sweat drenches him while he's taking deep breaths. Dillard holds the steering wheel firm. The shockwave of events has my adrenaline high.

I beg, "Dillard please let me drive."

Dillard dismisses my plea, "No, I got this!"

My hands are shaking; my heart is racing. Dillard backs out with a loud skid from his wheels. Al is still outside bent down, trying to talk to Arlo. I decline to say goodbye to Al. There is not even any eye contact. I want Dillard to remove himself from the scene; too many heated emotions are flying around. Dillard drives erratic. He ultimately pulls up to a coffee shop to pause for a moment. Dillard removes himself from the driver's seat then signals for me to take the wheel. Neither one of us says a word. I drive Dillard and I to his place with a soft hint of jazz music in the background. For this moment, silence is best. Soothing sounds of jazz alleviates my inner anxiety and likewise seems to do the same for Dillard momentarily.

Chapter 34

NO QUESTION

*W*e enter the still house. The eeriness is a familiar visitor lately. Moments ago, I was condemning Dillard of one thing, now we both at the house with different realities. Dillard waste no time heading for the shower.

Dillard is weary. In his drained voice, Dillard states, "Indi I'm going take a shower then lay down for a minute. You staying or leaving?"

Dillard is in no shape to be alone. I don't know what happened to Arlo, nor his intentions. Dillard did some damage to Arlo's car, not to mention Arlo himself. I know I am not leaving Dillard for one minute. If Arlo shows up to Dillard's place, I think somebody may die tonight. Maybe Arlo wants sweet revenge and will call the authorities on Dillard. I am unsure of any of those things. The only thing I am sure of, is that I am not leaving.

"Dillard, I'm not going anywhere. Rest as long as you want. I'll relax and cook us up something by the time you wake up."

Dillard's pace is slow and slumber. Dillard responds, "Okay."

Wiped out, Dillard turns on the water. I figure a hot shower is a good start to help calm his nerves. I lay across the sofa, getting my thoughts together too. I am unnerved about what may happen next. I wait to call Al to see if Arlo is still there. I don't want Dillard to hear me on the phone with Al. I listen intently to hear when the shower will end. Dillard showers at least thirty to forty minutes easily. At least that's how long the shower runs. Finally, when the downfall of water turns off, it's a matter of counting down before I think Dillard will doze off. I sit there and wait thirty more minutes. I figure approximately fifteen more minutes will be an accurate estimation for him to be completely out. I plan on peaking in the room. The fifteen minutes haven't come to pass before my phone rings. Across the screen is Bullet's name.

I answer in a tense low tone, "Hello Bullet."

"Hey, Love, I want to see you. Do you think you have time to fit me in your schedule today?"

"Today? Well, maybe, but at this very moment, I can't get out."

"Indigo, what's wrong, you sound funny? Are you okay?"

"Yes, I'm okay. Dillard had an altercation with Arlo, that's why I may sound different. The incident was a lot to take in for one day. That's the reason my time is dedicated to Dillard at this present moment."

"What kind of altercation? Is Dillard okay?"

"Yeah, yeah, Dillard is okay too. It's a long dramatic story, nothing I want to talk about. What Dillard went through is painful and personal. I was just there to witness it all. He needs me right now, although he's asleep. I'm not at liberty to leave him alone."

"Do you know how long you plan on being there?"

"You know, I'm not sure. I guess I may be here pretty much all night, now that I'm thinking about it. Instead of meeting me out, how about you stop for a few by Dillard's? Dillard is sleeping, therefore, you can come to keep me company while I get something burning on the stove before Dillard wakes up."

"That will not be a problem. I'll be over there in a few. Do you need me to bring anything?" Bullet asks.

"Bring whatever you want as long as you bring yourself. I'll text you Dillard's address. I need to make a few phone calls so I'll see you soon. Call me if you get lost."

"Okay, my love, love you."

"Love you too, Bullet."

The conversation with Bullet ate up some time. My fifteen-minute grace period for Dillard to fall asleep has long passed. I tiptoe to Dillard's door to confirm if he is sleeping. Audible snoring outside the door proves Dillard is out for the count. This is the opportunity I have been waiting for. Al is on my mind to check on Arlo. Al answers the phone on the first ring.

"Hey, Al."

Tenderly Al answers, "Hello Indigo, I wanted to call, but the situation is fragile. Me calling may have escalated an already out of control situation."

I quickly rebuttal to avoid a long conversation, "Al, I'm at Dillard's place now. I don't want him to catch me checking on you and Arlo. The conversation will be brief. Mainly I don't care anything about Arlo. My primary concern is if Arlo called the police to report Dillard."

Al sighs heavily, "Well, Indi, Arlo didn't call the police, but my neighbor did. My neighbor shouted, 'Al, the police is on their way!' Once Arlo heard that he gathered himself quickly to jet out. The good thing, Arlo left shortly after you guys pulled off. I had my concerns. Arlo wasn't in the best of shape. Arlo, for some reason, didn't want to come in contact with the police. I'm more than sure once he left, no police were notified from Arlo. Unfortunately, there's no way I could one hundred percent affirm that notion."

"Al, when the police arrived, did you say anything?"

"Indi, I said nothing. My neighbor complained about the noise she heard. My neighbor, Sue, was unable to give a thorough report of the incident because she didn't see it. By the time she came out, you guys had already pulled off, however, she saw Arlo on the ground and made her own conclusions. Oddly, Sue thought Arlo attacked me. She figured I protected myself and Arlo was an intruder. The police asked me a few questions regarding my safety. The encounter with the police was no big deal. I'm hoping no one witnessed anything and reports the incident independently. As both, you and I know cameras, eyes, or whatever is always watching, especially where I reside."

"You are absolutely right, Al. I appreciate you so dearly. You received an impact of Dillard's anger too. Did Arlo lash out to you as well?"

"Arlo, like I said, left so quickly if he wanted to lash out he couldn't. What Dillard said to me was every bit deserved on my part. I crossed lines. I feel extremely guilty about that. I truly am sorry for my part in this hurricane situation. I'm partly the cause of his pain. Someday soon I hope to sincerely apologize to Dillard once things cool down a little bit more."

"Al, I think that's an excellent idea. Thank you again for updates from your end. You take care of yourself. I'll call you later. Please keep Arlo away from your house. That man is trouble. I wouldn't have imagined, but sometimes people shock us in crazy ways. The worst thing about it is, Dillard really loved him. Your suggestion of apologizing would be an excellent gesture someday. Talk to you later, Al."

"Cheers, Indigo."

Al sounds genuinely sorrowful. Al was out of line, putting himself in that position with Arlo, knowing that was Dillard's mate. I didn't know what Al was thinking either. I was determined not to ponder on the situation all day.

I see Edgewood's text message, "Call me Indigo as soon as you see this text. Your phone is going straight to voicemail."

I look down at my phone. I have no missed calls, which means nothing. If it's a dead zone, my phone doesn't ring. I call Edgewood.

Edgewood answers hastily, "Indigo, where's Dillard?!"

"Edgewood Dillard is sleep. Why what's the panic about?"

"Arlo called me proclaiming he just fought with Dillard and threatening to file charges with the police if Dillard doesn't give him all of his belongings out the house."

"Arlo called you? Why would he threaten Dillard by calling you? I have Dillard's phone on the table. Arlo not once called Dillard's line to request anything. What stuff is he referring to anyway? Do you know? Besides, we arrived home not too long ago. Arlo is starting shit all over again. Tell you what, whenever you talk to Arlo, tell him he can have his stuff. Dillard doesn't want or need it. The less Dillard deals with Arlo, the better. I'm answering for

Dillard. When Dillard wakes up, I'll gather it all by the end of the week. Arlo can retrieve it from you or some other spot at that time."

"Indigo, I have no problem with that. Dillard doing okay? Arlo called me pretty much saying Dillard destroyed his car and punched him for no reason."

"Boy-boy-boy, Arlo is a liar too. Edgewood, there's a lot more to that story. The true portion is that Dillard did kick his ass and put a few bumps and bruises to his new car. Which was all warranted if you ask my opinion."

"Indi, so what exactly happened? Why Dillard and Arlo beefing?"

"Edgewood, you know so damn well I'm not going in detail about that issue. Dillard will need to disclose anything he wants y'all to know. The last thing I need is Dillard hearing Indigo said, 'blah-blah-blah.' Rumors spread fast, besides I prefer people to exploit their business if they choose to."

"Indigo, I can never get anything out you. Okay, so Dillard straight then, right?"

"Well...I didn't say all that. I will say he's asleep resting now."

"Hold on, Indi, that's Bam on the other line."

"Okay."

Still on hold, no sooner do I see Bam calling my other line.

Clicking over, I hear Bam loudmouth, "Ms. Indigo, I have Edge-wood on the line too."

I address Edgewood, "Edgewood, you had me on hold and now you on a conference call with Bam. What did you tell Bam?"

"He didn't have to tell me much for me to know we need a group gathering of love. Me and Edgewood heading over there, we making Dillard feel better from whatever went down today. If he needs us, you know I'm down to go look for sorry ass, Arlo. I'll kick his ass myself, messing with my friend Dillard. Do you want any particular daiquiri? I'm bringing a couple gallons. I have a feeling we will need every drop after today."

Edgewood interjects, "How about we fry some shrimp and fish. Let's make some po'boys along with other finger snacks. I'll even stop to pick up the ingredients to make Dillard's favorite dessert, peach cobbler. Dillard loves my peach cobbler."

Bam loves the idea, "That's what I'm talking about, we 'bout to get crunk up in here. Get double portions to make that peach cobbler. I may want to bring me a big chunk home for myself. Edgewood, pick me up when you heading out."

Edgewood wisecrack at Bam, "Chick be ready! I'm on my way in about fifteen minutes. Be ready, BEFORE I get there."

"Edgewood, you think I'm worried about what you say. I'll be ready when I'm ready. I know you better be parked outside my place by the time I AM READY!"

Bam and Edgewood act like an old married couple. I know my cue to get off the phone. "Well, okay, you two. I will see both of you when you get here. I think I'll call Lex and invite her too."

Bam spurts, "Too late! I texted her while we were all talking. She texted back, saying she will bring healthy snacks like fruits, veggies, and a cheese platter."

Things are set, sounds like there is going to be a friend fun love intervention for Dillard without him even being aware. I tell both Edgewood and Bam, "Goodbye see you guys soon."

I begin to straighten up and clear the front area for pending arrivals. Lex arrives first; everyone else comes approximately at the same time.

Bullet greets me with a kiss.

Stunned, Lex states, "Bullet? Wow, I haven't seen you in forever. Nice to see you again."

Everybody greets Bullet since they haven't seen him for a long time. Bullet takes over frying the fish and shrimp, and Edgewood tackles the peach cobbler. Bam has the drinks service on lock. I coach the guys to keep the noise to a minimum since Dillard is asleep in the other room.

Edgewood peach cobbler is the world's best. The aroma of the mixture of sweet peaches and cinnamon livens the house up. Everybody is salivating for a taste of his finished cobbler. The smell wakens Dillard from a sound sleep.

Hearing Dillard's door open, he comes around the wall with his eyes half-open adjusting to the room lighting. Lex jumps up to embrace Dillard tightly around his neck. Dillard has no choice but to return the hug. We stand up with a word and join Lex to give a group hug. The hugs touch Dillard to the point of one tear falling down his face. The love is strong in the room. One by one, we embrace Dillard.

Dillard expresses, "I truly love each and every one of you."

I inquire gingerly, "Do you feel rested?"

"Indigo, I feel more than rested. I feel refreshed. That peach cobbler smell awakened my inner bear from hibernation. I know my senses weren't deceiving me. I can identify Edgewood's peach cobbler anywhere. No gloomy faces allowed. Y'all got it smelling good up in here and couldn't have picked a better time to come. I'm hungry, rejuvenated, and ready to be around people who love me. If the food and cobbler are done, let's grub!"

Dillard initially doesn't pay attention to Bullet.

When he notices Bullet, he states, "Bullet! Man, how's it going? It's nice to see you. I'm happy to see you and Indigo talking again."

"I'm happy to be around all you guys again. This lady here is the inner light that keeps me going. I love this woman. I always did. It never stopped. I promise my absence will never take place again if I have anything to do with it. Indigo is not getting out my grips ever again."

Bullet stares straight into my eyes across the table, "Nothing is stopping me from fighting for you. I know what I want."

Bullets affirmation of love shocks me in front of my friends. I am somewhat embarrassed. Everybody looks in my direction to view my reaction. The crew is quiet with giddy facial expressions. My response is a glowing smile. For some reason, my friends want more than just a smile. But that is all I have to give under unexpected circumstances.

"Okay y'all can stop staring my way. I love Bullet too."

Lex and her drama, "Awhhh...I love you guys."

Dillard takes a seat in front of Lex. Lex began to massage his shoulders. Dillard indulges in the comforting massage by rolling his eyes and rolling his head to get a better feel with each tender squeeze.

Bam on her second thirty-two ounce daiquiri sat across from Dillard blabbers, "Indigo, so that means you must be back in the rodeo again, huh chic? I know you riding that horse again! Getty-up!"

Lex stops massaging Dillard's shoulders for a second with a curious expression, "Bam, what does that suppose to mean?"

Dillard opens his eyes, hunches his shoulder, signaling for Lex to keep massaging, "Damn it, Lex! That means Indigo getting sum dick again."

The light flickers in Lex's head, "Oh...ooooo. I knew that much when I saw Bullet here. Indigo bouncing around a tad more cheerful than usual since Bullets in the room."

I look over to Lex as she avoids looking in my direction, "Lex!"

"Indi, you know it's true. I can't lie. I love when you have 'you know what in your life' you are a little less cranky and laid back during those times."

I notice I am the brunt of everybody's laughter.

Bam exclaims, "This feels good having all of us back together in good graces again. Dillard, we came together for a friendship love intervention. I feel the love from all of us. I want us always to keep our bond together."

All of us nod and agree.

I smirk, "Bam, you hit that right on the nose, which gives me an idea. Tell me what y'all think about this. I would like to have a masquerade party. However, this masquerade party will be unique. The theme will be 'Confront or Confess.' The party requires everyone to come in costume. However, this party is for all unseen masks to be revealed—any issue you have with someone you confront him or her.

Or on the other hand, any issue you have with someone and want others to know as well because you tired of keeping it a secret, therefore, you confess. The venue will have a stage. The option is up to each individual to keep it personal or broadcast for everyone to hear on stage. There will also be note cards for the less brave. You may write confessions to whomever you like. The host will deliver to your requested individual. The party is to take place in a few weeks. Therefore, get shopping for your 'Confront or Confess' costume. Also get your situations in order and be ready for a full night of 'Confront or Confess'."

The masquerade party becomes the topic of our night. Everyone is on board expressing excitement to attend. The night will be a night of fun with family and friends to build us stronger together.

Chapter 35

NINTH HOUR

'Confront or Confess' masquerade party is in motion. I wear a partial eye-covering mask. I have my costume custom-tailored; it's red and gold with sparkles of glistening imitation diamonds. The chosen venue is showcasing everything perfectly. Mild wind creates a cool breeze in the air, reflecting a beautiful evening. Costumes of all types cascade the floor; many are mysterious. Totally painted, each a different color, aerial dancers hang and perform from above. The ribbons match the color of their painted bodies as a hint of light illuminates each vertical dancer. Waiters, waitresses, and the bartender are all in costume.

Al declines to attend. I know he prefers to stay away from crowds. Al wishes me well and demands I take a lot of pictures.

My family is in attendance. Mom, Dad, Bayou, and Sky enter together.

My mother spots me as soon as she walks in, then starts to walk in my direction.

My mother went into character, looking good. "Indigo, this is very nice. I like this. I see the bartenders shaking up the drinks. You have waiters and waitresses serving drinks concurrently with another waiter walking around with finger foods. I feel like I'm at a

V.I.P. event. You really outdid yourself. Are you doing this for a client or something?"

"No, Ma, I did this for us. For family and friends. I figured the mask disguise would give each individual a chance to unveil his or her truth about oneself. It's a reality to keep honesty in check when you love each other, you know."

My mother grabs my face to kiss my cheek. "Baby, I'm proud of you. This is very beautiful. Good job. Now, let me find your daddy so I can 'confront' some stuff." She laughs then trots her way across the room.

Each friend comes to greet me with a kiss as they enter. Dillard is the first to tap my shoulder from behind, grabbing and hugging me.

"Dillard, baby, you looking good!"

"Thank you, darling. You outdid yourself this time, sister. This is me all day!"

"Dillard, who is that over there?"

Dillard chuckles, "Chile, that's my lil' friend. Indi, he's just a friend, but we been chilling out lately."

"Dillard, that's good! We haven't been chatting lately since this the first I'm hearing about this new friend and everything."

"Na Indi, don't get all excited too fast. But I'm happy."

Reaching in my pocket, I hand Dillard a folded card with the *"Confront or Confess"* logo stamped across. "Dillard, this is for you. Possibly it could stack on some happiness in your life as well."

Dillard unfolds the card then begins to read out loud. "Dillard, I never apologized adequately to you. I tainted our friendship with betrayal. I take full responsibility for my actions. Since that day of confession, I have visions of your hurt etched in my memory. I'm asking you to accept my token of apology. I know this doesn't change the past, but if I could bring you a glimmer of joy, that alone will help alleviate some of my guilt. Money doesn't remove past actions. I'm only hoping that this could soften the blow. Dillard, I'm genuinely sorry for any pain that I may have caused you to experience. Love Al"

Inside Dillard's card, he pulls out two paid tickets for a two-week vacation in the Cook Islands. A small note inside reads, "Schedule your getaway dates at your convenience." In addition to the tickets and note, there are two thousand dollars cash for extra spending money.

Dillard's mouth becomes wide open. "Indigo, did you know this was for me?"

Dillard grabs me tight. With a quivering voice, Dillard whispers, "Thank you, Indigo."

"Don't thank me, Dillard. This wasn't my idea. I had no clue what Al had written or placed in the card. When Al knew about my 'Confront or Confess' masquerade party I was planning, he then asked that I deliver this to you since he wasn't attending."

Dillard stands rigid, his voice becomes intensely strong and states, "Al did me a favor. I'm happier not being in the dark. Now, this is how you make a proper apology! In this case, money has bought my acceptance of his apology. Before I leave Indigo, I want to give you a card to give to Al. All jokes aside, this was extremely kind of Al to do. I need this and appreciate his apology gesture. I know it's not from you, Indigo, but it's because of you he did this. Thank you, Indi."

"I got ya back, D! I love you and want to see you happy. And that's exactly what I'm seeing at this moment."

Dillard returns to his new friend. Before long, the two of them join others on the dance floor.

Every fifteen minutes, the microphone host pauses the music and extends an invitation to anyone who wants to take the microphone to *'Confront or Confess.'*

A few people are bold to take the stage. Most people are talking face-to-face, giving each other hugs; tears are shed at times. Notes are exchanged. Bullet surprises me from behind by grabbing my waist and kissing my neck.

Thrilled to see Bullet, "Bae, hey, you finally made it."

"Indi as soon as I landed, I showered, changed, and here I am. My excitement to share this day had me with jitters to see you."

"Well, baby, dismiss those jitters you're here with me now."

"As you wish, my lil' lady, jitters, are dismissed." Bullet kisses my lips then sticks by my side the majority of the night.

"Bullet later, I need to do my *'Confront or Confess'* to you too, Okay? But not now. I will before the night ends."

"Okay, whatever you want. Later then. I have a *'Confront or Confess'* for you too lil' lady. I want to go first, so whatever you have to say, keep it on hold until I'm done. But don't worry, mine is only written and short." Then he grins.

"Okay, deal."

I continue to commingle with the guest when Bayou takes my shoulders to turn me completely around to face the stage. I see Sky at the podium, wanting to *'Confront or Confess.'* Sky holds her face down while gripping the microphone.

The host instructs Sky, "Go ahead, young lady, the stage is yours."

Initially, Sky raises her head in mother's direction. She begins, "Mom I know I create stress at times. From today on, I will make a conscious effort to do better. Indigo, I have a confession that nothing ever happened with Bullet and me. Bullet was only ensuring I made it home safe. Bullet was a perfect gentleman. It appeared one way, so I went with it. Bullet asked that I tell you the truth, but I never did. This is my confession. I love my family, and sorry I'm the thorn to everybody's side."

Sky puts the microphone back in place, thereafter, walks off the stage. My mother, dad, brother, and myself congruently walk over to embrace Sky. The room claps for Sky's confession before the music starts to play again.

Pleasantly I whisper, "Thank you, Sky, for telling me the truth."

My mom is overjoyed. We are standing together, embracing each other, "Sky, you are not a thorn to our sides. That was very brave of you to take the stage for your sister. Sky I don't want you to change who you are for me. Sky, be Sky. I tell you things for self-evaluation. I want the best for you, all of you. I'm proud of all my kids. Each of you is different. Sky, our family wouldn't be complete without your personality, that goes for you too Bayou and Indigo. So don't ever think you need to change who you are to please me. Sky, thank you, but baby, we love you the way you are."

Bayou clears his throat, "From this day forward, let's make a conscious effort to stick together as a united family. No disappearing Indigo. No drama, Sky."

Dad breaks his silence, "Bayou your mom already told Sky she's fine."

Bayou looks at all of us then directs his statement to Sky. "Sky, you know you're drama. Dad trying not to hurt your feelings since you vulnerable right now, but we all know the truth."

Sky laughs. I laugh too.

Sky replies, "I know Bayou. That's why I took the stage. Mom, you being motherly not to hurt my feelings, but I know the changes I need to make. Bayou is right. This is my journey to do better, and I will. Indigo again, I'm sorry I was jealous. I will be a better sister. I promise."

Our family has one last embrace.

Afterward, Bayou pulls me to the side then hands me a *"Confront or Confess"* card. Bayou walks away as I begin to read. I open and see it's from Al.

"My Dearest Sunbeam,

Grab and seize your happiness. Sunbeam, let your array shine for everybody around to enjoy. Love endlessly. Freedom is yours. At this time, let's keep everything business so you can live your life without looking back for me. My confession to you; my butterfly, my Indigo, my Sunbeam, I will always love you and be here for you if you ever need me. Love Al"

Bullet walks up in the midst of me putting the card away. "Baby, who was that from?"

"It was from Al. He wrote a nice 'confession', basically telling me to share my light with the world. It was very kind."

Bullet blandly responds, "That's nice, baby."

The night is going great; Lex and Bam are getting along better. Lex's new male friend escorts her to the party. Edgewood is with some new chick, as usual. Drinks are continuously getting delivered. The later the evening, the more lively the room becomes. I am elated to see Dillard having a good time. More overjoyed, Arlo didn't press charges against him. I eye around the room and feel blessed. *"Confront or Confess"* is turning out to be a success.

I'm overjoyed, I survey the room, and my thoughts reproduce my delight in how some guest take the stage to *"Confront or Confess."* Others did it personally with one another via the secret folded card or with no hidden identity, straight up. Dillard suggests the *"Confront or Confess"* becomes a yearly event amongst friends and family. I concur. I am standing next to my mother when out the corner of my eye, I observe Bullet take the stage. I mysteriously smile at Bullet. Instantly the smile is returned my way. The room quiets to give attention to the speaker behind the microphone. However, Bullet points his hand up to signal for lighting. I glance around in amusement, next peep at my mother with a flabbergasted guise. My mother smirks, pointing her finger for me to focus in Bullet's direction. Bullet beckons for me to come to the center floor for his *"Confront or Confess"* session.

I don't hesitate to plant in place as requested. Bullet's session is entirely different from any other. He has lights dimmed, but the spotlight fixates on him and me while he is on stage. There is a photographer taking pictures and a jazz player on stage to play as he speaks simultaneously. A pin drop can be heard in the room. Everyone is engaged.

Bullet begins, "My *'Confront or Confess'* is for you Indigo. My confession is written the way we first met, a poem. Indigo, baby, this is for you. I hope you love what I'm about to say. This poem is called, I Realize.

I REALIZE

I just want to begin by letting you know that this is
    not a story
This is my true feelings and the insight of what I feel
    deep within my heart
We met at a poetry venue that I will never forget
We are very fortunate to have maintained a

relationship for many years

Over those years, our relationship happened to
    blossom
But I realize that there is one thing that I haven't
    accomplished with you
That is to put a ring on your finger and give you
    my name
The love I have for you is solid
I get scared at times that I won't be able to live up to
    your expectations
But then I realized that it comes down to what I
    expect from myself
and what I'm willing to sacrifice to become
    everything
we need moving forward. I search myself daily
And I began to see the change
I've made for myself to be a better man and be a
    better man for you
I love you
I welcome the chance to spend the rest of my life
    with you
and showing you every second of how much
I want and appreciate you"

BULLET IS STATING THE END OF HIS POEM AS HE WALKS UP TO ME with the jazz player in pursuit. My vision becomes tunneled, focusing exclusively on him. My ears mute any nearby sounds, excluding the sound of Bullet's poetic speech alongside the saxophone adjoining behind.

After completing the poem, Bullet gets on one knee, "Indigo Trinity Savoy, will you give me the honor of completing me and becoming my better half, my wife?"

. . .

BULLET DISPLAYS HIS HEART IN FRONT OF THE WHOLE VENUE. I feel like a princess. Standing proudly next to my soon to be spouse is enchanting. I don't hesitate to say my response, but I know I have things to reveal to Bullet as well before the night is out. His proposal just made my personal confession speech a bit harder to disclose to him. Torn inside, I begin to contemplate keeping my 'confession' a secret to avoid breaking his heart.

Shortly after the poem and feeling on cloud nine, one of the servers taps Bullet on the shoulder and hands him a secret folded envelope. Bullet takes the envelope and proceeds to open it.

Curiously I ask, "Honey, who is that from?"

Bullet frowns with confusion as he opens the envelope, "Bae, uhmm, I'm not sure. The guy with the tray gave it to me."

Bullet gives a cunning chuckle then states, "Are you trying to trick me lil' lady, and this is your *'Confront or Confess'* for me?"

Hesitantly I respond, "No, Bae."

Brushing me off, Bullet precedes, "Okay, Indi, whatever you say. I'm going to open this and see just what it is then." Bullet laughs.

Due to the lighting in the room, I can't see clearly what Bullet has in hand. Guests are approaching me with congratulations on Bullet's proposal. I start to talk to surrounding friends as they stand near with small chatter, not paying attention to Bullet. Bullet walks away from me. His focus is geared toward the newfound letter that was given to him. While I'm laughing and talking, Bullet pulls me away from the crowd clenching my arm firmly then brings me to a private corner.

In a fury, Bullet demands, "Indigo, who is Tracker?!"

The envelope and card dangle in Bullet's left hand as he is holding my upper arm with an aggressive squeeze with his right. Bullet then proceeds to hold up a small object in his hand.

I try to remain calm, "Bullet, what are you talking about?"

"This is what I'm talking about!" Bullet holds up the object and envelope.

Thereafter, Bullet throws the letter and object to the ground. Soon after, he pushes my arm away and walks out the building in a steaming rage.

Chapter 36

LETTER

*T*raumatized, realizing that Bullet now knows about
Tracker. Making matters worse, Bullet blatantly asks me
about Tracker immediately after reading the letter. Cottonmouth
and taken back, I melt in my guilt. Sidetracking my thought process,
I instantly start pondering, why did Tracker send Bullet a message?
Before making my next move, I pick up the *'Confront or Confess'* note
that Bullet tossed to the ground.

> Bullet, this is a true confession about things
>   concerning my beautiful Indigo. What I have to
>   say is simple and plain. Indigo and I fucked when
>   you were nowhere in sight. She longed for this
>   dick as much as I wanted her pussy. She belongs
>   with me, not you. If you don't believe me, this
>   video is proof of the night I gave her the ultimate
>   pleasure.
> I put down the real hard dick...
> Signed: Tracker

Along with the letter, I see a USB. Bullet never looks at whatever
is on the drive because he threw it down. But I can only imagine

what Tracker must have videoed the one night I called him to return to the house. I wanted that night to disappear from existence. It was a lonely night encounter that I regret. For goodness sake, Tracker works with me. I know my actions I took that night were a bad decision. I have been ignoring Tracker's continuous calls. He wants more from me, however, I merely can't give him what he wants. My sin confronts me with a confession I neglected to make in time. Instead, Tracker establishes a way to send his roaring letter to Bullet with a scorpion sting. If nothing else, Tracker ensured Bullet would be aware that I was with him, even if, it was only for one night.

My truth faces me front and center. I can't lie or hide this one night of lust. I gather myself then run outside to catch Bullet before he leaves.

Before catching up to Bullet, my chase is halted by a small crowd gathered around an outside commotion. I try to move in closer when I hear yelling.

"Put it down and calm down!"

It sounds like Bayou shouting. Immobilized in his steps, both my brother's arms are up. Alongside Bayou, stands Bullet.

Bullet imploring, "Man, it's not that serious! Just walk away and leave!"

The crowd thickens as I push my way through. Before getting to the front, I hear crying from a voice continuously saying, "NO! NO! NO! None of this is fair!"

The sound becomes muffled. Before realizing what is taking place, I have an eerie sensation. Losing sight of Bayou, I strain to hear Bullet's voice, but it's not there. Alternatively, I hear a brash thump to the ground, resulting in a tussle. In a flash within seconds, I hear a loud shot fired. Deafening shrilling screams echoes amid people scattering in all directions. Anaesthetized, everything is transposing in slow motion. I want to move faster, but my feet are lead. Visualization is clear on Bayou and Bullet. Hoping that my eyes are deceiving me, I observe Bullet face down with blood pouring from beneath him. Bayou's knee is on top of the perpetrator's face. Bellowing a piercing cry as I approach closer to the nightmare, I witness Arlo as the shooter.

Puddles of tears, unable to catch my breath, my whole body feels stupefied. Sirens begin to surround where I'm kneeling.

With a tight chest, lack of breath, and continuous sobs, "Bullet! Oh my—NOOO! BAYOU what happened?!"

My voice is cracking, and my tears are flowing like a flood. I become saturated in blood as I turn Bullet over, screaming for him to open his eyes. "Baby, please! Please just hang in there! Bullet baby, open your eyes!"

I can't see where he's shot. All I see is blood. Bullet is still breathing. His eyes open and stare at me with fear the entire time I have his neck cradled in my arms. I hold him close until the paramedics arrive and take over. Bullet's lifeless body is transported to the nearest trauma center. I stay beside him from when the paramedics pick him up until after the physician instructs me to wait outside in the waiting room.

A nurse hands me Bullet's belongings. Emergent surgery takes place to remove the bullet that is implanted in his back. Grieved to find out the gun wound was in his back; I plead with God that I didn't make his injury worse because I turned him over. Self-infliction of disgust overtakes me. I wasn't thinking. But it doesn't matter at this point; my only saving grace is prayer for life and recovery. Bullet is in surgery.

Soon Lex and Bam arrive at the hospital and run up to me, giving me a big hug.

"Sis, we are here for you. I'm sorry all this happened on your big night." Bam sympathize.

"Indigo, any word about Bullet? Is it serious? Will he die?" Lex's words are flowing top speed.

"LEX! Don't ask if he will die! NO, he will not die! Be sensitive!" Bam yells at Lex.

"Well, you know how I get nervous and-" Lex rebuts.

"Yes, we know, Lex, but this is a sensitive situation," Bam speaks in a reassuring low, calm demeanor.

Lex takes a deep breath to calm herself. "Indi, I'm sorry to come off-"

"Lex, stop, it's okay. I don't know anything. I'm just waiting for a word from the doctors." I respond.

Everything Lex and Bam are saying I can't register. They are talking, but all I remember is the last time Bullet and I spoke. I picture his anger and disappointment after reading that letter. I keep replaying two visuals of Bullet in my head. The last visual was the fear I saw in his eyes as I held him close to me, waiting for help.

Bam distracts my thought process, "Indi you okay?" Bam hugs me in tight from the side.

I hug Bam tight and wail out a cry. I am full of disappointment, guilt, fear, and shame. Both girls surround me. I am held by the two of them with no words spoken by either one of us. Lex rubs my back, and Bam holds me tight. I eventually calm down, wipe my tears, and inquire about the rest of the family. Bam answers most of the questions.

"Indigo, there's a lot to what happened tonight. Supposedly, Arlo went to Al's place right before coming to tonight's party. From what I heard, no one was home by Al's place. I think he wanted to harm Al. He then came to your event. He was trying to get in, but Bullet recognized him and was trying to stop him from going in. I think that's when your brother became involved. No one knew Arlo had a weapon until he pulled it out after some words were exchanged. Indigo, it's so much to this story I'm going to just narrow it down to a small short narrative. Anyway, Dillard and Bayou are at the police station for questioning, I guess. Your mom and dad said they were heading here. Edgewood went with Dillard, and as you can see, me and Lex are here now."

Weary, I respond, trying to keep my composure. "Bam, all this happened because of Arlo's altercation with Al and Dillard. I'm more than sure this is from a bitter heart. Bam, it's my fault. If I wouldn't have seen Arlo that day at the gym and-"

Bam speaks comforting, "Indi, stop it! It's no one's fault. Don't do this, Indigo. Arlo had a sick mind. None of us saw that coming. Indigo, now is not the time for you to play the self-blaming game."

Tears run down my stone face. I try to remain calm while praying for the best outcome for Bullet. My parents and sister eventually arrive for more comfort. The anxiety and stress have my head spinning. I remove myself for a moment from my family and friends; I go to a private room alone.

My mom comes in the room. "Indigo, are you okay, baby?"

"Yes, ma, I just want to be alone for a while."

"Do you want me to take the belongings you're holding and put it away?" My mom inquires with concern.

"No it's okay ma, I want to keep Bullet things next to me."

"Okay, Indi, if you need me, I'm right out here."

"Thank you, ma. I just need a minute, that's it."

I take that moment just to meditate. I sat and think about the first time Bullet and I met. It makes me smile. Bullet's phone then vibrates from his pocket. I go into reach for his phone when I see a piece of paper fall out of the pocket. The call is from an unknown caller, so I ignore it. The piece of paper has a title that intrigues my curiosity. I pull it out and begin to read it.

THE LETTER OF THE HEART

"I can honestly say that I never knew what it felt like or had ever experienced true love before. And it's not like she just walked into my life unexpectedly. But this was different; it was unlike anything we had shared. She opened up her heart and her soul to me. Something I had longed for, for so many years. Now it was in my grasp. I welcomed the early morning calls on her way to work. I looked forward to hearing her voice at lunchtime. And it was endless conversations all through the night until we were too tired to even talk. She made a point to give me all of her words of passion and inner feelings. Then there would come the times that we were able to be in each other's company. It only heightened what we would fantasize about on the phone. The warmth of her kisses made my body quiver. Then I would hold her in my arms, as she lay there close to me. I could feel her heartbeat when we were able to share that closeness that we longed to share with each other. It was the moments of pure ecstasy. Our bodies would meet to become one. I had the pleasure of exploring every inch of her body. The way her hands felt on my back as I sunk into her arms. Her signature is written across the galaxy that we have created between the two of us. I'm in the clouds and never want to come down. I look down to gaze into her eyes. 'There it is, I

can see it,' I tell her. She will ask, 'what is it that you see?' 'My future,' I will reply. Then to see that smile come across her face. I will lean in until my lips are locked tightly with hers. 'I need this the rest of my life,' she will say in a soft sensual voice. 'You have me for the rest of your life, my dear,' I will reply deeply. I know her so well that I'm almost certain she will begin to slowly move her body around in such a seductive way. Finally, when she rolls over on top of me. I will look and say, 'Indigo, thank you for being my wife'. "

- Bullet

Dear Reader,

Thank you for reading **PEACH BUTTER**. I hope you enjoyed this book. Stay tuned for more to come.

If you would like to know about any upcoming sequels and new releases, sign up for my newsletter at **CheryletteDoriane.com.**

You will only be contacted when I have a new book or content available.

*Connect on **Instagram** and **Facebook***
Instagram.com/Cherylette.d
Facebook.com/CheryletteDoriane

Enjoyed this book?
Your reviews are **GOLDEN!**

As a writer, reviews are valued as a precious stone. I would be sincerely grateful if you take the time to review this book on Amazon, which can be a simple like, one word, or a more detailed view. Help other fiction readers discover PEACH BUTTER.

Let's connect again in-between pages of my books.

Sincerely,
   -*Cherylette*

ABOUT THE AUTHOR

Cherylette Doriane is a writer, artist, and dancer from New Orleans, Louisiana. **PEACH BUTTER** traces the mysterious mask of love that takes place in Doriane's hometown. Her stories are inspired and birth from her romantic jazz city of love. Doriane is a transitioning nurse; when not caring for the sick, she writes fiction. She is a lover of romance, a collector of mask, and most importantly, a **SWEET ENTHUSIAST**.

Made in the USA
Las Vegas, NV
09 May 2021

22719428R00166